CW00558533

THORNWOOD ACADEMY: FOR DEAR LIFE
Thornwood Academy
Book 3

LJ SWALLOW

Chapter One

VIOLET

"I CAN SAFELY SAY that you've failed in your duties, Grayson. When assisting me with a murder investigation, I would expect you to avoid adding to the body count."

I suck a finger into my mouth to seal the cut made for the spell, an action that Leif appears particularly fascinated by, and survey my surroundings.

Grayson stands, arms wrapped around himself as he looks around, but doesn't respond. The blood rune spell that relocated us from the woods near the lodge hasn't affected him as badly as Rowan and Leif. The former kneels and stares at the Persian rug, face an odd shade between white and green, and the latter's face is covered in perspiration.

"Rowan. Please do not vomit on the rug. Eloise wouldn't be impressed," I inform him.

"I won't," he replies and swallows hard.

"He already puked his guts up when you were dead," says Leif, voice cracking on the last word.

"On the scale of 'things Eloise wouldn't be impressed with', I'd say vomit covered rugs ranks low," comments Rowan and rests his back against a low table's leg.

1

I'm already at the drawing room window, surveying the front of my parents' estate in Scotland. I'd chosen to 'arrive' in this particular room as it's infrequently used, and luckily that includes today. Our home's isolated—naturally—and woodlands form a barrier beyond the track leading towards the front of the building, and rugged mountains dominate the horizon.

The only car parked on the dirt to the side of the house belongs to Zeke—a small white Jeep that's often dwarfed by Eloise and Dorian's black SUV if they're home. Well, Eloise's—Dorian dislikes driving and other road users are fortunate that he rarely gets behind the wheel. The pair must be away today, which may be a good thing, considering the information I have for Dorian.

"Is this a good idea?" asks Grayson quietly, eyes darting around the room as if a portrait might come to life and attack or a mysterious Blackwood familiar may appear and assault him too.

Or my father might emerge from the walls and slit his throat.

Leif scoffs. "Good idea? Like the one you had when you killed the witch, Grayson?"

"I didn't think," he snaps, cutting Leif a hard look. "I saw Violet with a fucking fence post through her chest. Dead." Rowan visibly winces at the word. "If Rowan stood on that balcony, not me, he would've done the same!"

"I expect so, Grayson," I say. "But Leif is correct in pointing out how unwise you were."

"I thought you were dead!" His voice rises and so do my brows—and people wonder why I avoid emotions? Look at the mess *his* made of the situation.

In fact, look at the mess this has made of us all. New red stripes now adorn my black and white sweater, now ripped to reveal the wound still healing. I'm admittedly surprised and impressed by the size, although it's not a good look to return home with.

A shower would help. A change of clothes. Water from the lake can only remove so much from the guys—they're all wearing soaked clothes from where they attempted to remove as much of my blood as possible.

Leif drags a hand through his hair. "Are you sure your mental magic worked on Kai?"

"Yes. Memories messed with by both me and Rowan," I say. "He won't remember."

The guy was barely conscious when we placed him inside the boathouse, which made working on his mind easy. The magic the witch used on Kai wore off slightly, and he behaved as if in a drunken or drugged stupor, which gave us a perfect opportunity because we couldn't leave him at the lodge.

We needed transport. Before leaving the murder scene, Grayson checked the witch's pockets—no wallet, but he did find a car key. When we called Leif and Rowan to the lodge earlier, they'd passed a car along the track towards the road—a car that the dead witch's key opened.

Leif volunteered to drive Kai to the edge of town and the rest of us remained a short distance from the lodge and waited. Once Leif found somewhere suitable, he parked at an odd angle, half in a ditch. Then Leif moved Kai into the driver's seat and left an array of empty beer bottles around him.

Hopefully a passing driver discovered Kai and called authorities. Sawyer won't understand why and how his son appeared where he did, and in that state. What happens when Sawyer checks on his lodge? Will Sawyer report what he finds? Because there isn't much *to* find in the part of the house the witch died in.

"I'm worried about Maxwell," says Leif. "Authorities will find the body in the bedroom."

"Charred, yes," I say. "Identifying him may be difficult—that's if Sawyer reports this and doesn't go to witches for help."

"Let's hope the witches have a hold over Sawyer that'll interfere with his decision," says Rowan. "Kai told you Sawyer doesn't even like witches, so why's he associating with one?"

"Or more. He might not want to tell Maxwell's friends that one of them died," I reply. "And I'd like to know who Maxwell was."

Grayson's jaw tightens, and he looks away.

"I imagine Maxwell's someone with *other* powerful witch friends who're connected to the situation. Not the best person to murder," says Rowan.

"Why? Who would be the best person to murder?" I frown. "Maxwell's suspected involvement in the town killings places him as a reasonable person as far as I'm concerned. Not *sensible*, but deserving."

Leif mumbles something and sits on the black leather sofa. He's barely spoken since returning from his task of depositing Kai on the roadside, and I sense a barrier around his mind. Not one he's deliberately created, but as if Leif doesn't want to let the world in.

"You should've reanimated the bastard, Violet," says Grayson darkly. "That would've helped us."

"Grayson. You'd removed Maxwell's heart and relocated it to the lake bank. I can restart a heart, but don't have the surgical expertise to reconnect one." I wrinkle my nose. "And the organ looked rather damaged too. *And* his ribs were shattered. And—"

"Alright!" he interrupts. "Just saying, you're always so proud about how you're a necromancer and then do nothing when that magic's needed."

Rowan takes a sharp breath as I make a concerted effort to keep my hands by my side and not move them to around Grayson's neck. Luckily for Grayson, I'm weak after the death and used a lot of the remaining energy on the blood magic spell to move us from the woods and into my parents' house. Instead, I patiently reiterate that the dead subject needs all organs intact —in the right place—for the necromancy to work.

"What if the shifter remembers?" asks Leif gruffly. "He ran past me and Rowan into the trees. Saw us all."

"Well, he didn't die, so that's good," I say. "I mean, die *again*."

"The shifter that we've no clue who they are or what else they saw," says Rowan. "I hope he forgets what he's instructed to do."

"He won't die?" asks Leif cautiously. "Like, his master or whatever's dead, so he dies uh… properly?"

"He—or she—won't meet a permanent death unassisted, no." I chew on my lip. "As for memories? Possible but unlikely. What's the point in creating something to use for nefarious acts if said creature is *compos mentis*. A necromancer's revenant remains living in their old world and keeps their personality and memories, thus they're undetectable by most people."

"Which is how the Dominion used them to infiltrate shifter society before the Dominion and Confederacy stopped existing," says Rowan, "they planted thoughts and ideas to turn revenant shifters against the witches and vamps. The victims never knew they'd died and had become puppets."

"That's messed up," says Leif.

"And a legacy that colors our world still," says Rowan. "As we all know."

"We need to find who this shifter is, and soon. The injuries I inflicted will heal more easily on a shifter, but not as quickly as a normal supe's attack would."

"Grayson told us *he* attacked the shifter," says Rowan, and frowns.

"I did," he puts in and doesn't look at me. Why is Grayson telling them this when clearly I did?

Rowan looks between us in disbelief. "Sure."

"I have this," says Grayson in a swift distraction, and places a hand in his pocket. "From when I checked Maxwell's pockets before I left the room."

He holds up a black rectangular item. A phone? But nothing like one I've seen before.

"Why do you take things and never tell us, Grayson?" I ask and point at Leif's pendant. "That's the second time."

"You never asked."

I narrow my eyes.

"Is that a burner phone?" asks Leif and takes hold.

"What?" I shove at his arm. "Will that explode? A magical phone?"

Grayson almost cracks a smile. "No. A burner phone is a

basic one that you can destroy when you don't need it anymore. Used to hide who you are because the number is one of those pre-paid cards."

"I don't understand half of that, but do you mean this belonged to the dead witch?" I ask.

"Probably."

"But this isn't the phone we saw him using, Violet," says Grayson.

"Still, I reckon it's his." Rowan takes hold. "We should wait and see who tries to contact Maxwell. Maybe look at recent texts?"

"Why? How dumb was the witch? Surely he'd delete messages," says Grayson.

"He might receive a new message," Rowan replies. "Then we could find some info before others suspect that he's missing. I'm sure Maxwell would need to check-in with someone."

"Or maybe he used that phone to contact the shifter?" I ask. "But yes. Definitely. We keep this phone and wait. Use it if possible. Could I take a look?"

Rowan hands the heavy black phone over and I turn it over. "Where's the camera?"

"The phone's too basic."

"Hmm." I tuck the item into my deep sweater pocket. "I have many plans for this. Try your psychometry on the phone later. We keep this to ourselves."

"What? But Dorian—" begins Rowan.

Grayson's eyes go wide as he looks out the window. "Is anybody home?"

"I bloody hope not," says Leif. "*Especially* Dorian."

"Zeke's car's outside, but he might not be home. My father has a lot of energy and likes to explore."

"Does he run around shifted?" asks Rowan in shock. "What if somebody sees him?"

I gesture around. "We live on an estate in the Scottish wilderness. Who'd see?"

"But still, a tiger..." Leif shakes his head. "That's next level."

"My father's fondness for roaming the Highlands as an exotic animal isn't the issue here," I say.

"No. I'd say the *issue here* is why you're in his house with three blood-covered guys and what appears to be a massive, healing chest wound," says a familiar voice.

Zeke stands in the doorway leading to the hallway, his pupils still holding the edge of feline from shifting back, capped black t-shirt sleeves stretched across biceps, and revealing his faint but distinct silver and black striped arms.

I haven't seen Zeke since Dorian dumped me at Thornwood, and never spoke to him since, particularly annoyed with him as he refused to assist me in leaving, even when I impressed on him that Dorian made the decision to send me. Ethan's and Zeke's relationship with Dorian has an edge. Not of mistrust or dislike, but, as with myself, Dorian will never be 'normal' enough to behave in an acceptable way towards other people.

Others question whether the two guys should trust Dorian, but my family protected and killed for each other's safety. The trio center around Eloise and that created a strong bond between them all. Plus, they were stuck together on an island in exile for two years and they all survived. That suggests some modicum of fondness for each other.

The guys with me say nothing as Zeke keenly studies each one of them, the muscular shifter made more imposing by the physical traces of his latest shift.

"Why are you here, Violet? What the hell happened to you?" Zeke touches his broad chest and nods at mine.

"I died."

The words are barely out before Zeke has hold of me, touching my face, hand over my heart in a weirdly invasive but caring way. His Tigris healing saved Eloise's life once at Ravenhold academy, but that's not necessary for me. I disentangle myself but he holds my cheeks firm, half-squashing them.

"Violet," he says hoarsely. "How? Your heart is damaged. Who the fuck did this?"

"A fence post. And my heart is functioning again, as expected

7

for an immortal with self-reviving properties." Zeke stares at me as if I'm insane. "Not the best way to discover my immortality, but a temporary death *is* the only way we'd know for sure."

"Fence post? Did a crazy human student believe stabbing you through the heart would kill you?" His teeth bare, long canines visible and Grayson takes a small step backwards. "Name."

"Oh. This is Grayson, Leif, and Rowan. They're acquaintances I've made at the academy."

Another confused look from Zeke, who only glances at the guys. "No, the name of the person who stabbed you!"

"Nobody stabbed me. I fell." Huffing, I wave a hand. "I'm here because we had to leave the scene."

"Scene?" Suspicion replaces Zeke's confusion, his pupils dilating, and he steps into the room. Grayson edges further back and Rowan remains stock still, whereas Leif stares open-mouthed. "That suggests a crime, Violet."

Again, he studies each guy. How's Grayson coping with the blood on his clothes that he couldn't wash away? I'm not sure how I'd cope if the situation were reversed and I wore Grayson's blood. I'm keeping my distance from him, especially with the lingering tang of his blood from when the witch cut his arm.

"I need to shower and also to speak to Dorian and Eloise before I return to the academy. Things are rather complicated."

"You can explain to *me*," Zeke says tersely.

"Perhaps we should discuss this with all of us together? You know I hate repeating myself and I'm rather keen to remove these clothes." I pat Zeke's arm. "I promise I'll tell you everything."

"And your friends?" He steps further forward, scenting each guy. "They're scared shitless of me—what's their involvement?"

"They're all involved because they want to help me," I say. "This help is at personal risk to themselves."

"They protect you?" Zeke asks, unable to hide how incredulous he is. "What from?"

"Herself. Humans." Rowan breaks the silence, moving closer to me, and when he takes my hand, Zeke growls.

Good grief. For *that* response, I allow Rowan's hand to

remain around mine. "Why the pissed face, Zeke? Rowan has no ill intent towards me."

"I don't trust anybody's intentions, Violet. Not until I become *acquainted* too." He inclines his head at Grayson and Leif. "How acquainted *are* you with these guys?"

My lips thin. "I'm attempting to clear my name from murder accusations. I do not have time to experiment in sexual relationships. So, stop growling at them."

Zeke flicks a tongue against a canine but drops into silence, and I resist poking into his thoughts. Not that I need to, he's clearly unimpressed and suspicious. "Fine. I'm calling your mother and Dorian."

"Oh, shit," mutters Grayson.

If this is how Zeke responds, Dorian will be a problem.

Chapter Two

VIOLET

"VIOLET!"

Dorian's voice roars through the house and I blow air into my cheeks, continuing to towel dry my hair after showering and changing. I'm not sure where the guys are—Zeke begrudgingly agreed to find them spare shirts and told them to stay put. I hope he locked the door to stop Dorian storming into the drawing room.

I don't need my keen hearing to know Dorian's marching towards my room and brace myself. The door opens, handle slamming into the wall and, as suspected, his eyes are black with fury—literally.

"Hello, Dorian," I say evenly.

"What the fuck is happening?" he snarls. "Where are these guys that Zeke told me about?"

"Feeling fortunate that they're not looking at you in *this* state." I wave a hand at him. "They haven't harmed me in any way, so do not touch them."

But is Grayson safe? When I explained I'd take the four of us to my family's home using a spell, Grayson finally snapped out of his trance and suggested we leave him behind at the lodge. To be honest, I was tempted, still rather annoyed with Grayson's stupidity, but as the girl who half-killed a shifter, I can't really judge him.

"Zeke said you died." Dorian steps forward and hesitates before dragging me into his arms, something he hasn't done, nor been allowed to do, for years. Oddly, he smells like Eloise's sweet perfume. Evidently, they hug a lot. I clench my teeth.

"Why this overreaction?" I say, face squashed against his chest. "I'm alive."

"Overreaction?" His voice rises and I suck my lips together—I'm making this worse.

I breathe as he releases me, only to find myself wrapped in Eloise's arms instead. "Violet. Are you okay?"

Good grief.

I manage to extricate myself and step backwards, searching my dresser for a hairbrush. "I'm fine. My chest is a little sore, and I'm rather hungry."

"Chest? Why?" Dorian's eyes drop to my wound, now covered by a fresh black sweater. Has Zeke not told him anything?

"Violet, sweetheart," says Eloise gently. "What happened? Why are you here? Like your father said, Zeke told us you died." Her voice hitches. "But he didn't say anything else."

Hmm. Now *this* is the tricky part, especially considering the intensity that's still rolling from Dorian.

"I told Zeke we'd meet and talk together. I needed to shower."

"Violet..." she warns. "Don't be evasive."

"I'd rather discuss everything with my acquaintances present. We're all involved," I reply, pulling the brush through my hair.

"Are these the guys you mentioned last time we spoke?" she asks cautiously. I nod. "Including the vampire?"

"I honestly think this conversation is best held with all present." I give a tight smile and her eyes widen. She knows Grayson's here. "And I would like a guarantee for every guy's safety, Dorian."

He crosses his arms and pushes his tongue against his top teeth. "Did these boys contribute in any way to your death?"

"*My* death isn't the one that I'm worried about." I place the brush on my dresser. "Are my friends still downstairs?"

Friends?

Well, realistically this event has moved us out of the acquaintances category.

I'M happy to find that the guys remain physically intact and alone, although each now has a fresh, buttoned shirt, as Zeke promised. What have they spoken about while waiting, or have the three remained in their silent shock at the day's events?

When I walk into the room with Dorian and Eloise at my heels, Leif and Rowan immediately stand from their new position on the sofa. Grayson remains by the window. Is he considering climbing out if things become unpleasant?

Because there's no way he'll escape from Dorian discovering who he is today.

The only positive thing about Dorian's initial response is he doesn't ask for anybody's surname. He gives each of them a skeptical and disgruntled look, and even my scalp prickles when his eyes remain on Grayson a few moments longer than the others.

Eloise doesn't need surnames following our mother-daughter chat the other day, and her wide-eyed response to Grayson is followed by a horrified look to me. *Yes, Mother. The Petrescu.*

"Why is that kid wearing my shirt?" he says, face pissed as he jabs a finger at Grayson's black clothing.

"They needed clean clothes," I explain. "I asked Zeke to find some."

"I grabbed what was in the laundry," Zeke replies.

Silence.

"Did you expect the three to sit in here covered in my blood?" I ask and he snaps a look to me. "From when they *helped* me, Dorian."

Dorian glares as if Grayson took something precious from him, not a random clothing item. "You're lucky I'm in a reasonable mood or I'd make you remove that. Now."

"Good grief, Dorian," I say as Grayson mumbles an apology. "I thought you wanted to talk, not posture?"

Dorian demands we all sit while he stands opposite, Eloise touching his arm in an attempt to calm him. I do as he says, the four of us squashing together on the squeaking leather sofa.

Rowan's finding it difficult to stay away from me at all and his shoulder presses against mine, closer than Leif on the other side. Rowan asks if I'm okay and attempts to take my hand, but this time I only allow him to touch me for a few moments. Any signs of closeness to one of these guys could result in a worse response from Dorian than Zeke's earlier.

"Isn't Ethan joining us?" I ask.

"He's on his way, but may not be here until the morning," says Dorian in a clipped voice.

"Not 'collecting' him?" I ask and point at his healing palm from using his own blood spell for a speedy arrival.

"I am not leaving this house again until I one, know the full story and two, am certain you're safe." Dorian jerks his chin. "Explain what caused you to bring three strangers with you to my house. *Nobody* comes in here without *my* permission." I open my mouth. "Everything. Short and to the point."

As if I'm likely to embellish the story. Although where do I start and what non-essential facts should I leave out?

"I've—we've—discovered who one of the killers is and things are not straightforward, neither are their motives," I say.

"*One* of?" Eloise frowns.

"Rory killed Wesley, and we believe an unidentified shifter under a necromancer's control killed Rory. Today a witch asked another construct in his thrall to kill Kai. Hopefully this is the same shifter as killed Rory and that there aren't a large number of undead shifters roaming around." Eloise takes a sharp breath. "The necromancer involved was associated with Kai's father— we saw them together at his lakeside lodge. Sawyer has a few supernatural connections." I moisten my lips as I sense Grayson's tension. "Sawyer's attorney is a Petrescu."

Dorian's whole body stills, the calm I've often seen before his violent storms, but this time something deeper. Controlled, deadly hatred. "Petrescu?"

"The necromancer *was* associated?" interrupts Eloise and takes Dorian's hand in both of hers. "What stopped his association?"

"Hmm." I glance at the others. "The witch died."

"What the fuck?" asks Zeke from his position in the doorway. "Is that the scene you left?"

"Do you know this witch?" Dorian demands as he switches focus to Rowan, who shakes his head.

"We only know his name as Maxwell," I say.

Dorian's expression continues to grow thunderous. "What happened to the shifter? Please do *not* tell me that he died too. Or that the witch is connected to the town or academy."

"No, and I don't know," I reply.

"How can you be so calm, Violet?" whispers Leif.

"What use is hysterics?" I wrinkle my nose and give my parents a brief background on where we were and why, and an even briefer explanation about the witch's arrival and his subsequent demise.

I also downplay the fire the guys allowed to burn long enough to partially destroy Maxwell's body, held in check by Rowan, who then brought rain to end the blaze. Unfortunately, as the weather in town was fine today, that'll point a finger at an elemental witch creating the fire or storm—or both.

Dorian takes a deep breath and turns away, tipping his head to look at the dripping glass chandelier positioned above him. "Who killed the witch, Violet?" he asks without turning around. "You?"

"As I was temporarily dead at that point, no."

Eloise's mouth parts.

"I did." Dorian slowly turns, and his whole focus switches to Grayson, who spoke. "The witch used a spell to throw Violet over the balcony; I thought she'd died and lost my shit."

What?

"And the shifter you say is injured. Who caused *that*?" he continues.

"Again, me," says Grayson.

This is ludicrous. "No, I—"

"I'm sure you'd respond likewise if Eloise's or Violet's life was under threat, Dorian," he interrupts.

Grayson avoids my eyes, solely focused on my father. Why's he lying about the shifter? And why is he talking to Dorian in such a direct manner? If he's attempting to appeal to Dorian's empathetic side, Grayson's wasting his time.

"Stand up." Dorian walks slowly towards Grayson as he swiftly does as commanded. "Are you here to ask for my help in covering up a murder you committed?"

He and Grayson are a similar height and build, but Dorian could be a foot taller with his intimidating energy. Grayson doesn't look away, face betraying nothing—he's suffered at the hands of a threatening, powerful vamp before, but surely he understands Dorian is beyond anything he can imagine.

"No, we don't want a cover-up," I put in. "But as you know the facts, perhaps you could help us. News might travel your way. Such as if Kai remembers anything. If the shifter construct returned badly injured. Whether Sawyer reports the fire and if authorities look for the missing witch."

"If that Sawyer kid remembers anything..." Zeke says through clenched teeth.

Dorian's fixation on Grayson doesn't waver and I look to Eloise, silently asking her to move them apart before he asks the worst question. His name. "I'm unlikely to find out *any* of that without making inquiries."

Grayson winces and Dorian's eyes narrow before he spins back around. Swearing softly, Grayson rubs his temples and my stomach flips. *Dorian broke into Grayson's head.* Has he seen the truth?

"Someone is threatening my council and my daughter," he says curtly. "All supes are registered. We find this Maxwell guy's full name and who he's linked to. And we get this Petrescu lawyer to see me *stat*."

"I want to return to Thornwood this evening. As you've said yourself, my absence arouses suspicion," I say.

"I'm not happy about that," says Eloise.

"The boys can go. You can't," announces Dorian.

"Wrong. We stick together," I retort.

Eloise's mouth parts. "You're very different, Violet."

"These guys are my companions." I straighten. "I require their help."

"You don't need help, Violet," says Dorian, voice lowering. "I've taught you that."

"Rowan assists with my research, and Grayson helps me with…things, and Leif…" I pause and glance at Rowan, who arches a brow. "Has a good memory."

Rowan snorts out a laugh.

"I see nothing amusing here," snaps Dorian. "Your actions today could cause my council a lot of trouble."

"Violet's kind of right, though," says Zeke. "If somebody discovers the results of everything they've described, and the four are missing, it's hard to deny they're involved in the fire. And that could lead to Kai, maybe more."

"I'm concerned whether Rory's wake went ahead and whether there's an injured or deceased shifter," I add.

Dorian turns to Zeke. "I've little contact with shifters, as you know, but considering the possibility a witch—or witches—created a shifter construct, I'll need to involve my council more. You and Ethan will need to up your efforts to speak with that particularly awkward set of elders."

One thing about Dorian, if he *does* think before he acts, he thinks quickly and precisely. I pull out my phone to make notes, happy that the thing didn't suffer the same fate as my chest,

"I need to investigate Sawyer's activities and family history on both sides, his wife's too, and ascertain any other connections to supes. Then, I intend to conduct a thorough review of the academy, staff, and students, including your roommate, Violet," says Dorian.

I look up. "*Holly*? She's just a clueless human."

"With a lot of witch friends."

"Holly has a lot of friends, period. She's that type of exhausting person," I protest.

"Your missing potion?" says Eloise and arches a shaped brow.

"You think *Holly* took that?" I'd never once entertained the possibility. "She has no motive against me or you."

"I don't trust anybody," says Dorian. "And neither should you." He nods at Rowan. "A witch could want your magic, a vampire your blood, and a shifter..." Dorian tips his head. "Well, he'll have a reason."

"That's unfair," I say.

Dorian turns towards me. "If you're choosing to be a detective, Violet, tune out of your interfering emotions."

I choke. "I don't have interfering emotions."

"Your responses since you arrived in the house tell us otherwise," says Eloise.

I suck on my teeth and stab words into my screen as I type. They have no idea what they're talking about. *I* am the one in control here—of everything.

"Kai is the main problem currently," says Zeke. "And they burned down a house."

"It's a lodge, and *we* didn't set fire to the building. Granted, the place isn't an idyllic retreat anymore, but parts of the lodge remain." I look up. "The Sawyers might need to fix the fence, though."

"Violet," says Rowan in hushed shock. "Seriously?"

"Yes. Seriously. The lodge is salvageable. The Sawyers are fortunate you were nearby to put out the fire that *his* witch friend started, Rowan." Why are all three guys looking at me as if I'm making no sense? "What?"

"The fence comment," says Eloise. "Seems these boys have a lot to learn about you."

"Oh." I wrinkle my nose. "I didn't do too much damage to the fence."

This time Leif makes a strangled noise and the choking dark

aura around Dorian grows. "This is a complete fucking mess," Dorian says.

"But good that Violet came to us, right?" asks Eloise and smiles at me.

I smile back. Falsely. I'd hoped Dorian *wouldn't* be here and that we could swiftly shower and leave. I fully intended to tell Dorian about events and ask for help, but not like *this*. I wanted to speak to him alone and in better circumstances, *sans* blood and injury, once the guys processed events. And without Grayson present.

But at least my father's showing a modicum of rationality. Or did Eloise have 'a chat' with Dorian beforehand?

"And the dead witch." Dorian's face goes dark again. "If he's found in the lodge, that adds another problem. I'll need to retrieve his remains from the human authorities."

"Like father, like daughter," says Leif with a short laugh.

"Yes, I'm very much like my father, as you're aware," I say. "And occasionally my mother, now that I have this bond with Rowan."

"I mean the toe."

"Toe?" asks Eloise as Rowan hisses at Leif to shut up.

"Oh. Body parts for psychometry." I shake my head. "Not relevant in this case. Do continue, Dorian."

"You are a very odd group," says Eloise.

"They would need to be if they're Violet's friends," comments Zeke.

"We need to get back to the academy tonight because if somebody else finds a single piece of this puzzle, they'll use it to prove one thing—the Blackwood's guilt. I need to clear my name. As you said, Dorian, we find out who these witches are, and their connection to Sawyer and Maxwell. Look into Sawyer's and his wife's background. Infiltrate the shifters and discover who's connected to witches either by choice or not."

"Dorian," says Eloise softly. "You could make a couple of calls and ascertain if there're any police reports about Kai or a fire yet."

"Really? Why are you keen for me to leave the room?" he asks her.

"This is a charged situation, Dorian. Better for you to take time and respond in a logical manner rather than react without thinking. And there's a lot to think about."

Dorian turns to her. "Are you sure the reason isn't because there's a Petrescu in the room?"

Chapter Three

GRAYSON

MEETING DORIAN WOULD INTIMIDATE ANYBODY, even if the hybrid held no ill intent towards them. I've faced a lot, but I'm more worried about my safety now than ever in my life.

Minutes ago, Dorian wasn't subtle about shoving his way into my head and snatching images of me and Violet in the room at the lodge, but I'd hoped he hadn't picked up anything else about me.

As if.

I stood in a room while somebody practically threw his daughter over a balcony and impaled her to death. Sure, I wasn't close enough to stop what happened in a split-second and in a chaotic situation, but I was there. A *Petrescu* at the scene where his daughter died.

The moment plays over and over in my mind: could I've stopped her dying? Did I do enough? The fire had too much of a grip on my primal need to get the hell out, distracting me until I wasn't fully present in the room.

Violet died. She *died*, and it's partly my fault. When I thrust my hand through the witch's ribs and yanked out his heart, he wasn't the only one who'd filled me with fury. Some of the anger was towards myself, channeled into lashing out at the witch. I didn't kill him through fear he'd harm me. I ended the bastard because my Petrescu darkness gripped me in a bloody mist, and I took revenge in the most final way possible.

The girl with me now looks less like Violet, damp-haired and make-up free. Her eyes seem bigger and bluer, pale faced tinged by a natural pink, and my nausea rises again. How might this affect her? I take a shaky breath. Violet's more to me than the blood in her veins; she's captured me as readily as if she'd pinned me down in a headlock like the shifter earlier.

My gaze drops to her chest, the wound now covered in a fresh black sweater. The idea I'd lost her tore into my own heart. How can one girl walk into my life and change everything in a matter of weeks? And for me to *want* her to?

As with the moment I saw Violet's lifeless body, these seconds in front of Dorian drag into an age, the deathly silence choking the atmosphere when nobody responds to Dorian's announcement of what I am.

Now, Violet stands between me and Dorian while I brace myself for his reaction. Somewhere on the fringes of my awareness, words are exchanged over who stays in the room and who leaves.

Dorian remains and all but Violet leave.

Violet tugs on my hand to sit and Dorian leans against the closed door, his hands sliding into his pockets, an unnaturally casual stance. At least he doesn't kill Petrescus on sight. Small mercies.

"How very Petrescu of you to tear out a heart." Dorian glances at my hand, and although it's clean, I wipe my fingers against my jeans. "Who are your parents?" he asks coolly.

"Roman and Genevieve. I'm only distantly related to..." I trail off as the growing black now spiders across his irises. "Oskar."

"And the Sawyer's attorney?" he barks.

"Uncle," I say quietly. "Josef."

My mouth goes completely dry, and time pauses again when Dorian's glacial blue irises disappear into black holes. Shit. I stagger as he appears in front of me, fingers wrapped in the shirt Zeke handed me, and I'm yanked forward.

"What mind control are you using on my daughter?" His tone is savage, teeth sharper than moments ago.

"None," retorts Violet from beside me. "How weak do you think I am?"

I moisten my lips but stay quiet.

"You're a Petrescu. Your uncle associates with Christopher Sawyer. Christopher Sawyer associates with necromancers involved in murders. Murders designed to implicate Violet." His face moves closer. "Do you see my problem, *Grayson*?"

"Grayson's uncle hurts him, Dorian," says Violet calmly. "Josef killed him once. Grayson hates his uncle and isn't involved."

"Oh? So, Josef wouldn't be averse to killing Grayson *again* if he didn't perform whatever task given to him?" snarls Dorian.

"I'm willing to take the fall for everything," I say evenly. "If this all comes out, I'll deny Violet was with me and tell whoever that I attacked both the witch and shifter."

"Grayson, don't be ridiculous," says Violet.

Dorian finally drops his grip and I take a long breath as he steps back. "Why?"

"Why?" I ask.

"Why protect Violet? What do you want from her?" His eyes narrow. "Her hybrid blood? Looking for power, as all Petrescus do."

"Grayson isn't you," retorts Violet and Dorian jerks his head to look at her. "That was your original attraction to Eloise—her powerful blood. At least Grayson doesn't want to *kill* me."

"Doesn't he?" scoffs Dorian.

"I care about Violet and want to help her."

A muscle twitches in Dorian's cheek. "Care?" He scoffs. "If you so much as *touch* Violet, I'll end you."

And I one hundred percent believe him. Violet really *will* be the death of me.

"I'll thoroughly investigate your family, including you and your parents. They will be under constant surveillance and if there's even a *hint* that you're involved on *any* level, I will deal with you *personally*."

Hairs raise on my neck, and Violet steps forward to almost meet her father nose to nose—the man the supernatural world fears and who she's scared she'll become. "I understand that the Sawyer connection doesn't help, but you *were* once acquainted with Oskar Petrescu's grandson, and you accepted him," she says.

Dorian's stance changes as he cocks his head at Violet. "You *are* mind controlled. You would *never* stand up for somebody else in this way. Anybody. The Violet I know has no time for others."

"Ah, yes, well. Are you only averse to Grayson touching me or does that threat extend to Rowan too?" Violet looks him dead in the eye. "Or Leif?"

How often do they stand off like this—Violet Blackwood, the hybrids' hybrid. Is she actually *more* powerful than they are? Or is he just incredibly self-controlled around his daughter? Because I wouldn't risk punishment from this guy if he was my father.

"Ah. Yes. This imagined witch bond," Dorian says quietly. "Eloise told me."

"Of course, she did," mutters Violet. "And I assure you, the bond isn't imaginary."

"We'll see about that," says Dorian darkly. "I bet the witch craves your power too."

"Dorian. Pay attention—Grayson stopped me from killing *twice*. A human at a party and a shifter today. The reason he needed to? Rowan's magic—the bond—is changing me. *She's* with me now. The Violet we suppress."

"Aha! So, the Petrescu can control you!" says Dorian in triumph.

"No! Are you listening to me? Grayson *helps* me and he has never asked for or attempted to take anything." His eyes search hers. *Lies*. Violet knows I want the very thing her father's also convinced I crave. Her blood. But Dorian could never understand this craving comes from my desire for Violet, not the power she contains.

"And Leif? How did you move from not allowing others to

approach you to collecting three consorts, Violet? Badly chosen ones."

My muscles uncoil. Slightly.

"Good grief, is that what Eloise told you?" Violet rolls her eyes. "Leif's someone who also once helped me, and I'd like to return the favor. That's all. I'd like to introduce Leif to Ethan and Zeke. He's half-shifter and has issues I think they could help with."

Is she that blind to Leif? The guy always looks at her as if she's the sunshine to his life and not the gloomy black cloud that follows her around. No. Violet saw something inside Leif's mind that she didn't share, and she looked at him oddly afterwards. Leif kept a wary distance from her too, and whatever she saw, Violet must know Leif's feelings for her are more than 'friendly'.

The slackened tension tightens as Dorian blinks away Violet's answer and returns his steady, loathing gaze to me as he says, "You're naive, Violet. Perhaps we sheltered you too much."

"Or perhaps you should never have sent me to Thornwood?" she suggests. "Then none of this would've happened. I may be naive, but I'm not stupid enough to miss what's happening here. Someone intends to bring you down and will keep pushing until you play into their hands. I've given information, perhaps you could make some calls?"

Whoa. I can't believe the way this girl talks to her father.

"Well, you have your wish, Violet. You're leaving Thornwood and staying here until I've dealt with this."

"No."

Again, attention switches to her. "Excuse me?" he says in warning.

"You've said this yourself days ago—if I leave Thornwood, I'll look guilty. No. I'm solving these murders."

"Uh huh. And events like today help? Because you've managed the damn opposite and created a new victim."

Violet sucks on her teeth. "One dead witch means one less opponent to deal with, Dorian. Now, if you've calmed enough *not* to pull Grayson apart merely due to his ancestry, I'd like to join the others. Perhaps we could stay for dinner before heading back to the academy, as Eloise suggested?"

Conversation over as far as she's concerned, Violet steps past her father towards the door. I manage a single step before Dorian's palm slams hard into my chest to stop me following.

"I don't know how your uncle killed you, Grayson, but I can assure you the method I use would be slow, extreme, and agonizing." His charming smile graces me; the deception Dorian uses to cajole others. "Whatever rumors you've heard about me aren't true, Grayson. I am much worse than anybody knows." He pauses. "Well, worse than anybody who's *alive* knows."

"Understood," I say hoarsely. "I assure you I've no intention of hurting Violet."

"Well, then, you don't need to worry." He pats my cheek and I clench my teeth.

"Can I go?" I ask.

Dorian gives a curt nod. "Oh, and Grayson," he says as I walk by to leave, and I cautiously turn. "I wouldn't need to kill you. If what Violet says is true, and her darker side's emerging, my daughter would slaughter you first."

"I don't doubt that," I say. "I've met Violet's dark side."

Again, the captivating smile; Violet could learn how to blind and kill with that same charisma. "I don't think you have, Grayson. Not yet. Why do you think we taught Violet to close herself down?"

A shiver zips down my spine as I stare into eyes the exact color of Violet's. Dorian taught Violet *more* than to close herself down.

If Violet's response to me when I teased her in the woods came so swiftly after a minor annoyance, I really am dicing with death if I pursue Violet any further without knowing what she wants from me.

And figuring out Violet or what she wants is as impossible as persuading her father I'm Petrescu in name only.

Chapter Four

VIOLET

"WHAT THE HELL?" shrieks Holly.

I've never seen a human move this fast, the laptop almost flying from her knee as the girl in candy pink striped pajamas leaps from her bed. The bowl of chips beside Holly on the bed spill across the floor as she darts a look towards the door.

Rowan and Leif are sitting on our carpet beside me, Rowan head in hands, as with our last blood spell travel. Grayson immediately stands and gazes around the room. Leif blinks at his surroundings and remains still.

"Where did you come from?" she continues, at an unnecessarily high pitch.

"My parents." I stand and close my eyes, attempting to detect any unknown magical energy inside the room, but can only sense Rowan's.

"They live in Scotland," she replies.

"Yes."

Holly swallows hard as her eyes drop to my bleeding finger—then to where Rowan smeared some on the floorboards while pushing himself to sit. She covers her mouth with a palm, her wan skin turning whiter.

"Holly doesn't like blood," I announce. "We'd better stop bleeding."

I nod at Grayson, who can easily fix his—thankfully—as he puts a finger in his mouth. Irritatingly, the desire for his blood I've held my breath against isn't helped by mentioning bleeding.

"Oh." Leif grabs a white tissue from a box on my nightstand and wraps it around his wounded index finger. "Sorry."

I press my tongue against my own finger, sealing the wound, then take hold of Rowan's and lick my thumb before pressing the pad against his finger.

"You're very tactile, Violet," he says weakly.

"I want to prevent Holly from passing out." I drop his hand and wipe my thumb on my pants in case I'm tempted to taste the witch blood too. Who knows? Death might decrease the anti-bloodlust potion's effects.

"My blood phobia isn't the issue," Holly says in a wobbly voice. "I'm halfway through an episode of Married At First Sight and four people appear from nowhere in the middle of the bedroom floor!"

"As I said, we were in Scotland and wanted to return to the academy tonight, therefore our only option was the Blackwood travel method."

"Blood magic isn't permitted," she whispers. "Neither is guys in our room."

"I'm not keeping them here," I retort.

"Not even Rowan?" She gives a small smile.

Good grief. "We're all tired after a long day," I inform her and look at the guys. "Aren't we?"

Ever since we arrived at my family home, the guys lost their normal sense of speech and became rather subdued. My parents can be intimidating, but we were safer there than in the vicinity of a partially destroyed lodge containing a corpse. Besides, now Dorian knows I've become 'more amiable', which is what he wanted. Isn't it?

"You never told me you planned to go to Scotland," says Holly.

"I was pursuing leads in my investigation with the help of my acquaintances." I wrinkle my nose at Grayson. "*Mostly* they helped."

"In Scotland?" I consider Dorian's words. Should I be suspicious of Holly?

"My findings required a visit to Dorian. As you know, there's concern this may be aimed at him."

She seems to consider this for a moment, staring at me harder. "What happened? You look paler than usual, Violet."

"I'm not wearing make-up."

"I've told you before, all the black you wear washes out your skin. Even a tiny amount of color would help; if you want, I could—"

I huff. Fine. "I lost a lot of blood today."

Did Holly just edge backwards? "Are you alright?" Her attention switches to Grayson. "Did he take your blood?"

Grayson scoffs quietly.

"No. I died," I say casually and crouch to pull my trunk from beneath the bed.

"You *what?*" I cringe at her screech. "Violet!"

The runes on the trunk are intact, and with a careful inspection inside, I locate my anti-bloodlust potion still tucked beneath the spell book. "I died. But good fortune blessed me, and I am, in fact, immortal."

I snap the lid of the trunk shut and stand. Holly now sits on the edge of the bed, her paleness continuing to compete with the guys'.

"How did you die? What happened?" Her head jerks between each of us.

"I'd rather not discuss that." She gives me a thin-lipped glare. "Did you visit town tonight?" I ask her.

"Yes."

"Oh dear. I'm glad you're uninjured."

She frowns. "Why? Is the murderer loose again?"

"I believe so."

"*That's* who tried to kill you?"

Hmm. I blow air into my cheeks. What is their phrase? "It's complicated."

28

"I knew I should've stayed at Marci's!" Holly trembles as she gathers her belongings. "I can't share a room with you if you're next!"

"Next to what?"

"Next to die, Violet."

"Did you not listen? I'm immortal."

She chokes. "*I'm* not! What if the murderer gets us mixed up and kills me instead?"

"How on earth could that happen?"

"In the dark!"

Good grief, one mention of murder and the girl completely overreacts and loses all rationality. "We look nothing alike, Holly."

But is there another reason she wants to visit the witches? What if Dorian is correct and there's something suspicious about my human roommate? I should watch her more carefully.

"How can you casually stand in this room when you *died* today, Violet?" she asks hoarsely, turning from her packing.

"Because I'm not dead anymore?"

"This is too much." She hauls the bag onto her shoulder.

"Don't tell anybody," I say.

"About what? The death, your 'it's complicated' investigations, or that you've three guys in our room?"

"Two. Rowan will walk you over to Marci's."

"I wanted to talk to you, Violet," he says quietly and shoves a hand through his hair.

I point at my paper-covered wall and grab a black pen. "I have thinking to do."

"You died, Violet!" replies Holly, partly in disbelief.

"My brain is intact."

"She's mad," says Holly to my gathered friends. "If Rowan's 'accompanying' me, you need to look after her, Leif. The death messed with her mind."

"I'm as sane as I ever am," I reply. "I've merely had too much interaction with people today, and I would like to be left in peace."

"I can look after Violet too, Holly," retorts Grayson. "Or are you as prejudiced against me as everybody else is?"

Holly avoids his eyes—and a reply—before re-focusing on shoving items into her bag, including the academy uniform.

"I'd rather not spend time alone in your company," I inform Grayson, and his eyes go wide before he frowns and looks away. "You are very much aware why."

"Wow," he mutters.

Is that a smirk on Rowan's face? I approach him, moving into the aura that snaps together with mine when we're close, our bodies not touching but with the odd sensation we are. I tiptoe in order to reach his ear better.

"Watch where Holly goes," I whisper. "In case she sneaks away."

"I don't want to leave you alone," he murmurs back.

"Why?"

His hand brushes mine, the way he has several times today—cautious but subtle. "You *died*, Violet. We're bonded. Every part of me wants to stay and protect you."

"The protection part: ridiculous. The staying? No. You'd distract me," I say quietly.

"In a good or bad way?" he asks.

"Stop staring at my mouth. I'm not about to kiss you goodbye."

One of the guys chuckles and Rowan slices a look in their direction.

"I want to leave," says Holly. "And tomorrow I want an explanation."

I turn from Rowan. "Yes. I'd very much like to speak to you too, Holly. We should spend one of our girl's afternoons together." I try to smile in a way that suggests the idea thrills me even though I'd rather stick pins in my eyes.

Holly's energy spikes with greater shock at my suggestion than when four individuals materialized in her room. How else am I to dig into this girl's life and mind if I don't involve myself more? I'm rather cross that Dorian suggested my first ever female friend, the one who's teaching me to acclimate to the world outside my head, could be an enemy. The idea's ludicrous and I'll prove this.

"Goodbye," I say to Holly and the others, opening the door wide. I spot the wariness on Leif's and Grayson's faces as they hesitate. "I would like to rest and deal with the residual effects of my death. Please leave."

Holly mutters 'omigod' beneath her breath as she edges past Leif, who's in the doorway. He looks as if he's about to speak before shaking his head and following. Grayson shrugs and leaves, too. As the last one from the room, Rowan pauses. I startle as he takes my head in both hands and presses a hard kiss on my forehead.

"At least you look too shocked by that to kick my arse," he says, smirks, and turns to leave.

The door clicks closed behind the four, leaving me with an oddly empty sensation in my chest—one that grew hollower after Rowan's lips made sudden contact and then left me.

But I suppose an impaled heart would have post-injury after effects.

Chapter Five

ROWAN

THE SHEER EMOTION surrounding Violet's death swallowed reality because nothing like this would exist in my life before she entered the academy. Sure, seeing anybody with a fencepost through their chest would overwhelm them with shock and helplessness, but the response to Violet's lifeless body hit me beyond anything I could imagine.

My heart hurt too, not in a 'my girlfriend died' way, but literally felt as if Grayson had torn mine out, not the witch's. I couldn't breathe, legs collapsing as I screamed her name. For the eternity she remained dead, the same dizzying darkness claimed every part of me. Body. Mind. And right down to the soul we share, all made ragged as death tore away my bonded witch.

Grayson and Leif coped with their shock better than I did, and I mechanically performed the spell to extinguish the fire, a simple elemental spell I could almost do in my sleep. Leif took her body from the post without anybody asking, barely speaking, but face devoid of color and whole body rigid.

I don't know how he moved Violet because I turned away, vomiting, before composing myself and continuing to yell at the vamp. Grayson assured me over and over that Violet wasn't dead. At least not in the way a witch or human would be. He insisted that a hybrid like her couldn't be, but Grayson must've thought her death possible if he reacted the way he did.

The longer Violet didn't move or breathe—with no *heartbeat*—the thinner the thread between us became and the more my anguish grew.

Then Violet came back to us.

The monstrous wound from the fence post began to heal even before she started breathing again—something else Grayson pointed out as a sign her death was temporary. Within minutes, Violet barely noticed, only grumbling about the blood and how weak her muscles felt—blood I kept Grayson well away from. Fortunately for him, his own trauma kept him focused on the huge mistake and heart in his hand, more than the amount of Violet's blood soaking her.

Within minutes, Violet returned to normal.

Or her version of normal, anyway.

Violet's response stuns me. She's pissed about the post-death physical weakness, but as soon as she gathered herself, Violet returned to her 'business as usual' persona. Through the bond, I felt that Violet's almost *happy* she died; pleased that there's no longer doubt about her immortality.

Yeah, well, I'm far from pleased. I'm still bloody terrified something else will happen. What if there's a delayed response to her death and Violet needs help?

If Violet thinks I'm leaving her alone tonight, she's wrong.

After leaving Holly at Marci's, not stopping to talk, I shower and change. What will Holly tell Marci? Because she made a few pointed comments to me about the blood on my jeans. Without a clean shirt from Zeke, I wouldn't have managed to dismiss the blood as 'nothing much'.

I shudder. Today wasn't the best circumstances to meet Violet's fathers, and I'm happy if I don't see Dorian again anytime soon, and even happier that I'm not Grayson.

And now? I knock on Violet's door, readying myself to fight against her if she tells me to leave.

"If you're here to kill me, I've had a trying day and I'm not in the mood. Come back tomorrow," she calls from inside the room.

I smile wryly and call back, "Do you really think shouting that would stop someone from walking in and killing you?"

The door opens and a fresh-faced Violet appears, dressed in black sweatpants and a familiar black and white striped sweater. How many does she own? She looks me up and down, then scratches her cheek. "Did something happen?"

"Um. Yeah. The girl I'm bonded to died and I'm freaking out," I reply. "Can I come in?"

Violet pauses before pulling the door open further and silently allowing me into the room.

"I thought something else must be wrong if you came back," she says.

"I thought you were headed to bed?" I ask and point at the papers strewn across.

"Why? Is that your intention? To climb into bed with me?" I open my mouth to respond, but she continues. "I wanted to make some notes while everything's fresh in my mind. Although my head is rather fuzzy. Things aren't connecting properly."

"That would be the death and blood loss," I say lightly and close the door. "Violet, you should sleep."

Her lips purse and she points at the burner phone. "Nobody called yet. I'm waiting."

"That's good. One less thing to deal with tonight." I walk to her bed and begin gathering the papers, then place them in a pile on her desk.

"Why did you return?" she asks, surprisingly not interrupting my action.

"I have something for you." I dive a hand into my pocket and pull out a bar of chocolate. Violet stares. "You've hardly eaten. I'd take you on one of our fun dinner dates, but guess you're not in the mood. And it's late."

She lifts her eyes to mine. "Why? Are you worried I might attack a student to replenish my blood?"

"No. I'm worried about *you*. Yeah, a chocolate bar isn't exactly a lot, but that's all I have."

Taking the purple-wrapped bar, she sits on the edge of the bed. "Right."

"You don't *have* to eat the chocolate. It's just a gesture, Violet." I stand over her, not daring to sit on the bed, vaguely irritated that she doesn't appreciate my thoughtfulness.

Well, my chocolate bar was an excuse to see her again, too, I guess.

Silently, Violet unwraps the bar and breaks a piece off, the confused look on her face not leaving as she eats. "Thank you for your gesture."

I'm still never sure whether Violet's thanks are because 'it's expected' or if the thanks come from *her*. "You're welcome."

"Welcome where?" She snaps off another piece.

"It's a response. Like 'don't worry about it'."

"Worry? About what?" She sighs and rubs her head. "My brain isn't working correctly, and I do *not* like that."

I smirk. "When does your brain ever work correctly, Violet?"

Not replying, Violet stands again and places the half-eaten chocolate bar beside the papers on her desk. "I'm not craving blood, by the way."

"Good to hear."

She turns. "Do you think Dorian's correct and that Holly might be involved?"

"I *think* that you should rest, Violet." As I cross to stand by her, everything ordinary we've returned to evaporates, and the day's events suddenly slam into me, shoving away chocolate bars and casual conversation.

"I honestly thought I'd lost you," I say hoarsely, and tuck Violet's hair behind an ear, again desperate to connect. Violet allowed me closer since the lodge, a handhold or touch here and there, but I'm not expecting more.

Violet appears non-plussed by events, surely this has affected her in some way? "How do you feel? Honestly." My fingertips linger on her cheek, and she makes no attempt to move them, or move away.

"Dying is an odd experience. I don't often dream, but the

void in my mind seemed greater." She blinks. "And only felt like seconds."

"No, Violet. You joke about your death. Dismiss what happened. Even you parents made it clear this is a big deal." I lace my fingers through hers, gauging the right moment to hug her.

"Well, yes, not an everyday occurrence." She smiles, but I catch a dip in her energy, Violet's heart skipping out of rhythm just once. "Don't worry, Rowan. I've no plans to repeat undeath soon. And I'll be extra careful around witches."

"Because you're fallible?"

She frowns. "No, because we can't afford to lose any more witnesses or suspects. I'm perfectly aware that you'd also kill someone if you believed I'd died and they're responsible."

"Don't say that," I breathe out. "I can't go back there in my mind."

Violet pulls her fingers from mine and my sinking spirits rise again when she gently rests the tips on my cheek. "You've said yourself; my mind works differently. I'm alright."

"I don't believe you," I whisper. "Even if you're not scared of death and pain, you're frightened because you weren't in control as a hybrid, or this Violet."

Violet's breath hitches slightly, and her clear eyes grow wider. "I hate when things aren't in my control, yes. That's why I want to be alone. With myself. My thoughts. All your responses disturb me."

"Why? Why aren't you disturbed, *anyway?*"

"I don't know," she whispers. "Perhaps because the girl who died wasn't this Violet but me in a different state."

"The hybrid one you hide from?" She nods. Sighing, I stroke my thumb across her eyebrow. "Nobody can control everything in their lives, Violet. That's impossible. You can hide from yourself, but not me."

The mask-like expression she's kept attached since she returned to me slips, and I'm again with the girl who opened up that night. Here's the bonded witch, not the Violet Blackwood who clashed with Rowan Willowbrook, or the one laser-focused on her investigations in order to keep all other thoughts at bay.

"Do you know what frightens me more than any rogue fenceposts?" she whispers. "Or that we can bring out each other's power, create an unstoppable strength if we focused? You affect me. Mentally. I'm weaker around you."

"Violet," I say softly and take her face in my hands. "Why does that frighten you? Because you want to allow me into that space between you and the world? The one I've snuck across now?"

"No. Because in weak moments like this, I want you here. With me."

My chest goes tight. Violet's again another step from the girl who practically shoved me through the door with Holly and the others and didn't want me to walk back in.

Today, Dorian accused Violet of allowing her emotions to weaken her. If that's what he taught Violet, it's wrong. *He* has emotions. Connections. Bonds. Love. Hell, hatred is an emotion, and he has that in spades.

I've seen kids under pressure to meet parental expectations as they project themselves onto their son or daughter. How much of that's happening here? Or is she merely a daughter who loves her father and wants to follow his lead?

Violet's brain is wired differently, but she's still a person. A supernatural oddity, but a person.

Without thinking, my lips meet hers. This time when I kiss Violet, I struggle to hold back, hugging her hard to stop the emotions from breaking free. She responds hesitantly again, but this time her mouth stays on mine for a little longer even though her fingers remain curled around my upper arms as if she might push me away.

Violet's sweetness is another step away from the acerbic girl who'd once throw me across the room for even looking at her the wrong way. I taste the chocolate on her lips, inhale the subtle fruit scent in her hair, and I'm half-blinded by the ache to move beyond this tender moment. To show Violet everything she means to me because I'm still unsure she understands my feelings are more than from a bond.

"I can't lose you," I whisper, as her head tucks so naturally beneath my chin and I stroke her hair. "And I'm sorry I make you feel out of control."

Violet's hands move from my arms to circle my waist as her warm breath brushes my neck. I could push into her mind, see Violet's thoughts in this moment, because I'm catching hints that her mental barriers weakened too.

But I won't invade her mind, and as Violet holds onto me, not moving, she's communicating more than she could imagine. This girl who's a world away from everybody is allowing me into hers.

Finally, she looks up at me, still silent, those glacial eyes unreadable.

"I'm staying," I say firmly. "Even if I have to sit on the floor all night." Holly didn't react well when she heard I'd slept in her bed, which kind of annoyed me like she's some little girl bothered by boy germs.

"The phone. The witch's," she says eventually.

"What about it?"

Violet moves away to take the phone from a desk drawer, the loss of her from my arms weirdly as big a hit in the chest as when I held her by the lodge. "Can you confirm who this belonged to using a spell?"

Subject change. "Now? I'm pretty tired, Violet."

"I'll help with the magic energy," she suggests and holds out the phone.

With a wry smile, I shake my head. "Back to business, huh?"

"I don't understand."

"Alright. But I'm not leaving," I repeat.

She rubs her lips together and nods at the phone, so I sit on the floor beside Violet's bed and motion her to join me. She places herself down, back against the side of her bed, and holds out a hand.

The magic passing from Violet is much weaker than last time we worked together, and even with my own, I can't find much at all from the phone's past. Still, I relish her soft hand in mine, the thrill that comes from her energy meeting mine that's a different level to the physical desire earlier—a part of us already joined by fate that courses through my soul and my life.

"There's a charm on the phone," I say, eyes still closed. "Which shouldn't be a surprise. I guess we'll use the old-fashioned human techniques and wait for somebody to call or send a message."

Violet doesn't respond with either a frustrated retort or a—less likely—word of understanding. As I loosen my grip on her fingers, Violet's hand slides from mine, and I open my eyes. Her head lolls forward, dark hair falling over her face. Panic strikes, and I kneel to take both Violet's hands. She mumbles something, still breathing thank god, and shifts to rest her head on the bed.

I suppress the laugh that tries to bubble from me, at how annoyed Violet would be to lose control to exhaustion and fall asleep mid-spell. Although vulnerable, I'm betting the hybrid would spring into action if she felt threatened and I hope to hell that hybrid sleeps too, as I gather Violet from the floor.

I'm tempted to sit on the bed and hold her, but that's too big a reminder of the girl who bled out in my arms earlier. Instead, I lay Violet down and pull a soft fleece blanket to cover her.

Violet's face softens with sleep, and I run the back of my fingers across her cheek before placing a kiss on her forehead. Half a bar of chocolate remains, partially unwrapped on her desk, which I take and sit back on the floor beside Violet's bed.

Silently, I eat the chocolate chunk by chunk, again listening to the breaths of the girl who crashed into my world and flipped everything on its head. Violet Blackwood, a force of nature beyond anything I could create. She's right. If I'd stood in that room and not Grayson, that witch would've died at my hands—but not instantly. I would've taken my time to kill him.

Chapter Six

VIOLET

I DON'T REMEMBER FALLING asleep or Rowan leaving, but find a note on my desk beside the phone and an empty chocolate wrapper, telling me he's left. Well, *obviously*. How long did he stay?

I'm troubled by the thought I've no memory of him leaving the room but manage to cycle through all other events of the day and don't believe anything's missing. If I were still suspicious of Rowan, I would question whether he'd added a spell to the chocolate that sent me to sleep. After all, the guy did attempt to steal from me the first time he entered my room.

But I'm far from suspicious of Rowan nowadays, as the bond that infuriates me also offers a strange comfort I never expected nor wanted. Like the hugging. Kissing. Each time we do, there's a resonance that takes hold and interferes with my belief that kiss and touch are merely to elicit a physical response from somebody. That there's something soothing, a quietly unspoken admission that stepping across emotional boundaries is as significant as the desire.

But I've more pressing matters than to pontificate on such growing desire for Rowan.

Dying, for one.

How do I feel about the event? I've never considered that I'm *not* immortal, but there was always the chance. Life's more secure with immortality, although I'd prefer to avoid the side-effects of pain and weakness. I suppose I can't have everything.

How far does the immortality go? Removing the heart and burning the body is the only way to ensure a final death for an immortal vampire. My heart can be removed, but fire never burns me—how would anybody rid the world of me permanently?

Another annoying side-effect is I'm mentally tired, my head stuffed with cotton wool and unable to piece together everything. *That* is not normal and extremely irritating. This morning, the only messages are on my normal phone, Grayson and Leif checking in on me.

None on the burner phone. No calls either. Did the witch operate alone? That would be most unhelpful.

Concerned about Holly's role in this, I can't reattach papers with our latest discoveries on my makeshift murder wall where she could see, and so pull out a notebook. Alongside a carefully written timeline, I note the new names in the unclear mix. I also add a list of tasks for Rowan which I tear out and tuck into my nearby skirt pocket, ready for a more ordinary academy day.

Holly hasn't returned, and I repeatedly glance at her side of the room, casting an eye over the entrance to her closet that's stuffed with clothes and various teen paraphernalia. Somewhere to investigate?

I glance at the door to our room. Holly was adamant she didn't want to remain in an upcoming murder location; she won't return soon. I saw her uniform shoved into the bag that Holly took, therefore she intends to go to class.

Can I justify my invasion because there's a threat to mine and others' lives? I'd upset Holly if she knew I rummaged through her belongings, but not as much as if she discovered that I suspected her. Surely Holly wouldn't notice if I checked inside her closet, since she doesn't keep the space tidy? Decision made, I brace myself to deal with the disorderly mess.

Holly's closet is deeper than I expected, the recess a jungle of hanging dresses and tops, some half or completely off the hangers and now mingling with the mismatched shoes strewn amongst discarded outfits. Towards the back, more shoes are resting on a small set of white drawers, and I pull one open.

Scarves in an array of color and prints.

Another drawer contains enough make-up to paint the faces of the whole of Darwin House, and also a plethora of earrings and necklaces.

I'm practically suffocated by the closet. If my choice of black clothes was caused by an allergy to color, I'd be mid-seizure by now. And honestly, the jumbled mess sets my teeth on edge. How can anybody live such an unorganized life?

"I'm sure Holly would lend you clothes if you asked," says a male voice. "Although you'd need to promise not to lose them this time."

Half-startled, I turn to where Grayson stands at the entrance to the closet, his lithe figure blocking the way. He isn't in uniform, but a cleaner version of the black jeans and T-shirt combo that he favors.

"Where did you come from?" I ask.

"I *did* knock. You never replied, and I worried."

"Well, here I am, unharmed. You can leave now." I step forward to exit the closet, but he doesn't move. "Grayson."

"We need to talk, Violet." He looks down at me, and the exasperating mix of his presence and blood fill the air, dizzying me.

"Yes. Later."

I eye a couple of large bottles of perfume on the small drawers. Holly inadvertently disguises her human smell with fragrances, but I doubt soaking myself or spraying him in her choking, artificial scents would help against Grayson's effect.

"Funny. I never expected to find you playing dress up with Holly's clothes." He smirks at me and reaches over to take a dress from behind. His scent intensifies and I shuffle backwards. "Holly's right. Black is boring. Now, floral would be good. Or this, perhaps? You'd look like the sunshine you love so much."

He holds out an offensively bright item, a worse option than even the hot pink jacket I borrowed. I snatch and then shove the voluminous, gauzy dress back onto the rail.

"Very amusing, Grayson. Please leave. I'm busy."

He slides hands into his pockets. "No."

"Fine." I turn my back and push through the scarves in the drawer, attempting to detune from him and back to my search for anything resembling a magical item.

I've no need to turn to detect his stronger blood scent as he moves into the closet, the strength not aided by the stuffy, narrow space between the rails.

"We need to talk about what happened yesterday afternoon," he says. "Before we meet the others again."

"I'm busy," I repeat.

He's closer still, and hairs on my neck lift. "I killed someone, Violet."

Holding a gauzy leopard print scarf, I pivot to face him. "*This* is information that I'm aware of."

"And I saw *you*. The Dorian part of you."

"You've seen her before. At Kai's party."

"Not like this, Violet. The attack on that shifter was something else..." He shakes his head. "I swear if the witch hadn't cut me, you would've killed the Ursa."

"I have little recollection of events."

"Isn't that the problem?"

I twirl the scarf around my hand. "Do you have a clear recollection of tearing the witch's heart from his chest?"

His jaw sets harder. "Yeah."

"Isn't *that* the problem?"

"I don't understand."

"I was in a state where my hybrid-self emerged for self-protection. You made a conscious decision to relieve the witch of his heart. You *chose* to kill, Grayson."

Grayson laughs at me and inches closer, eyes glittering as he looks down. "Something overrode my thinking, Violet. I'm hemia and a killer. Petrescu. One who's more dangerous than most because I calculate before I strike. This time? I didn't calculate but reacted to seeing you impaled, and to the witch bastard laughing at me."

His blood runs faster, closer to the skin, and I hold the scarf against my nose, inhaling Holly's perfume. "You panicked because the witch might kill you next?"

"No."

"Lost control and acted on emotion?" I ask, voice muffled. "Now do you see why I avoid engaging with mine?"

"Are you serious?" he whispers.

I'm growing increasingly claustrophobic amongst the hanging clothes, now on the verge of pressing myself into them to escape Grayson's presence. What if the same's happening to him as me, but he can't fight the temptation? If Grayson yields to that and I spill his blood when I retaliate, the situation will end very badly for me, him, and the condition of Holly's clothes.

"Can you leave?" I pause. "Please."

"I wanted to kill the bastard who created the whole situation," he says hoarsely. "Literally, my mind honed in on the quickest way to do that."

"Grayson. What is this need to always *talk* about things?" And the more he does, the more his body reacts to the memory of my death, Grayson's blood coursing faster until the scarf can't block his scent anymore. I back up further and hide my head behind a sweater.

"Violet. What *are* you doing?" he asks. "This is important."

"Not important enough to corner me in a closet and discuss things that could wait until later." I inhale the spring-fresh detergent on the sweater. "If you don't leave, this situation could end badly."

Grayson yanks the hanger to one side, pulling the fluffy white clothing from my hands. "I've never killed without thinking. And I've never reacted to anybody in the way I do to you, Violet. I killed a man because of you."

I straighten. "Excuse me, *what*? I never asked you to, nor did I use mind control since I was no longer in the room—or breathing. Good grief, Grayson."

"Your blood," he says, voice low and thick. "Every time I'm

close, I want your blood so much I can't think straight. But that's not what took over, Violet."

"You're not making sense," I say equally hoarsely and edge to the left, cotton dresses dragging over my head as I attempt to make my way to the exit.

"I held you. When you died, Violet, I held you while Leif calmed down a hysterical Rowan." His voice cracks. "There was a lot of blood. Your blood. But you know what there *wasn't*? My usual obsession with tasting you."

I pause, terrified that I'll say or do the wrong thing. Evidently Dorian's wrong—not all Petrescus are ruthless killers who've no conscience.

"I care about you a *lot*, Violet. When I held you, I felt as if someone punched a hole in my chest and let out all the air. I couldn't breathe anymore."

I moisten my lips. "I believe that's called a panic attack, Grayson."

Grayson swears and forces apart hangers either side of my head, his eyes darker hemia than their usual emerald. "Violet!"

"If you're about to sink your teeth into even the smallest vein, beware, because I am really *not* in a mood to accommodate unwanted advances."

"How?" He half-shouts and drags both hands through his hair. "How are you like this? Yesterday was a fucking big deal. I'm trying to tell you what you mean to me and you're telling me I had a panic attack!"

His breathing grows faster and shallower, but I hold off suggesting he's having another one.

"Grayson. You and me in close proximity in this way feels rather familiar. I'm focusing very, very hard on not..." I hold a palm to my forehead. "Move away. Please."

"'Very, very hard on' not doing what? Shoving me against the wall and trying to take my blood again?" he asks in a harsh voice.

"Don't," I warn. Has he not considered yesterday's blood loss could've exacerbated the possibility?

His shoulders drop, and he rubs a palm across his eyes. I grab the opportunity to duck beneath the clothes, but my feet get tangled in several pairs of boot laces. I trip forward, snatching at a nearby coat to right myself again, but fail. Grayson catches me and pulls me up beneath the arms.

I'm close. Too close. His blood flows fast and near to the surface, and immediately, my hands are between us, palms against his chest, where his heart thunders against them. Grayson's arms suddenly surround me, trapping my own uncomfortably between us and bringing my face far too close to his jugular.

"Grayson," I say stiffly. "You have three seconds to let me go before I impale you with a coat hanger."

Too late. *She's* already here—the Violet who craves Grayson's blood, not his affection, and who'd accept his touch as the opportunity to move my mouth closer to that. So, when he pulls away and looks down at me in the way Rowan does, I panic for different reasons, moistening my lips as I look at his.

If I kissed Grayson, I could bite and taste the blood my heart wants to beat through me.

The fool *completely* ignores my threat, instead attempting to take my hand. "I don't care if you bite," he says quietly.

"I assure you, you would," I say and pull my hand back, focusing away from him to the floor. "Wait. I need to do something." I drop to my knees.

Grayson goes utterly still and silent as I shove aside a shoebox placed on the floorboards, revealing the whole of a mark I'd spotted partially hidden beneath.

Runes.

What?

Chapter Seven

VIOLET

THEY'RE TEMPORARY RUNES, chalked in blue, and now my pulse runs fast for other reasons. Why are runes hidden in Holly's closet?

I open the lid to the cardboard box and peep inside. Long, white leather boots take up most of the space, but there's a small black velvet pouch tucked into a corner, barely larger than a ring box, tied by a red ribbon. The item twirls in front of my eyes as I hold it up by that ribbon.

Spellbag.

All secretly placed here by a witch with ill intent? No. Despite the mess in this closet, Holly would know about the runes. "Grayson." I tug at the leg of his jeans, and he looks down, the same startled look on his face. "Look at this."

As he crouches, I tip the contents of the bag into my palm— rose quartz, black onyx, and moldavite.

"Is this yours or Holly's?" he asks

"Not mine." I squeeze the stones in my hand as I move everything aside to look at the small circle more closely. "And these runes. They're used to focus energy."

"Whoa. Holly isn't a witch. Is she?"

I scratch my nose. "No. I'd sense if she is, even if only a little. Do humans join covens at Thornwood?"

"No. Well, not that I'm aware of. I'm not popular with witches, am I? Maybe ask Rowan?" I side glance Grayson as he remains beside me. "What will you do?"

"I can't take anything," I say as I hide the stones and bag beneath the ostentatious boots. "Do you have your phone?"

With a nod, he reaches into a pocket, and I stand again to take a photo of the runic circle. I've a lot to investigate—what else might be hidden in this space? Holly's love of strong perfume could serve a greater purpose than attracting a mate. Are the scents she uses designed to mask even *my* ability to pick up on magic energy?

"Good grief," I mutter to myself. I've trusted someone who's at the center of everything happening to me.

I startle as the door to the room opens, my pulse speeding as I stand and shuffle as far back into the dark space as I can. Grayson stands in alarm too, and I grab his jacket sleeve, tugging him after me.

"Holly," he whispers, and I nod as I scent her too. "I bloody hope she isn't here for a change of clothes."

"Holly never misses lessons," I whisper. "She won't change from her uniform until this evening. That's why I thought I'd investigate her closet now. Forgot her books maybe?"

"Yeah, but still."

My chest goes tight as I sense her approaching, and Grayson squashes himself against the wall in the darkest corner. Ordinarily, I'd protest at him pulling me closer, but Holly steps into the entrance to the closet and we need to take up as little space as possible.

Thank the stars she doesn't have supernatural senses.

"I have a green one," she says, and clothes hangers slide metal against metal.

"She's with someone?" I mouth at Grayson.

"Witch," he mouths back.

I tense further. How far back into this closet is the 'green one'? "Good grief," I mutter to myself again, and press harder to Grayson's chest. "How on earth do I explain this?"

He places a finger to his lips, and I seal mine together.

Twice Grayson's held himself against me like this. Once when he stopped me screaming in the woods and again when I was half-crazed for his blood at Kai's party. The first time caused no physical reaction, besides the shock at the taste of his blood. At the party, I experienced an odd mix of desires for the blood *and* kissing him.

This time, the airless space becomes a vacuum that sucks me further into him. I swallow and vainly focus on the newcomers.

I've never encountered whoever's with Holly in the room, otherwise I might recognize their aura—but definitely witch.

"Or did I wear that yesterday?" Holly asks herself. If she did, the girl would take some time to find the item as there's usually a discarded clothing pile surrounding her bed. "Check the drawers at the back."

No. Oh, no. *No.* I meet Grayson's eyes. Even Violet Blackwood's crazy reasoning couldn't explain why I'm in the corner of Holly's closet with Grayson Petrescu. Clothes move and Grayson shifts again, pulling us beneath the coats opposite the drawers, this time squished further together.

His heartbeat thrums abnormally loud in my ears, and I can almost taste the blood again. I hate the knowing look sparking in his eyes—that I'd struggle to walk away from him even if the way was clear.

I hold my breath. Right now, my focus is on explaining *why* I'm here if Holly encounters us.

"Oh. No. Is this the color you needed?" asks Holly.

"Sure. That one's good," says a female voice, no longer close by.

Holly leaves the closet. I'm aware of nothing else, purely focused on where the girls are and hoping that no other colors are required. Only when the room door closes do I untense.

Who was the witch with her? Marci, or any one of Holly's many witch friends.

As I snatch the chance to move away, Grayson's hand catches

mine again. "Sometimes it's hard to pull back from the edge," he says hoarsely.

I lift my eyes to his.

This guy's definitely looking at me the way Rowan does, and not in his 'I want your blood' way. I clear my throat. "Edge of what?"

"Trying to kiss you." His fingers tighten. "Problem is, if I fall over that edge, I'll hurt myself. Or rather you or your father will. Shit, he was worse than I imagined."

I'm still chest to chest with Grayson and encompassed by the thought of how he'd taste if I kissed him as much as another taste of his blood. Desperately, I keep my mind on the runes and magical items.

Because I swear, he's about to nudge himself off that ledge.

"Do I need to suspect Holly now?" I ask flatly.

A new sensation replaces the one that's been with me all the time with Grayson. A twisting in my stomach at the disbelief. Somebody *fooled* Violet Blackwood?

"Wasn't she on your suspect list?" he asks, neither of us moving away.

"No."

"That's not logical for a detective."

I scowl. "Neither is killing someone, Grayson."

He scoffs. "At least I wasn't fooled by a human."

"Excuse me," I growl. "Why would I suspect the girl who's *nice* to me?"

"Are you serious? That's enough for you to discount her as a suspect? Your human roommate and your things disappearing? She's probably connected."

Any yearning for his mouth or blood melts away. "Don't speak about Holly like that. She's a friend."

"*I'm* a friend, but you suspected me for a long time," he retorts. Grayson's breathing now speeds to match mine. "The great Violet Blackwood, with all her superior intelligence, has been fooled by a mere human because the girl was *nice*?"

The mocking edge to his tone sets my hackles rising. "We have no evidence against Holly."

"What the hell is that, then?" He gestures behind me.

"Not *enough* evidence," I correct. "And your presence in this closet could've created a huge problem."

I make to step back and yet again, his hand takes mine. "Yeah. Not sure how you'd explain why you're making out with me in your roommate's closet."

The words are finally spoken, and I'm aware how easily I've allowed the blood attraction to wind around us both. He's touching me and every place our skin meets Grayson's blood pulses against mine. For once, I'm happy he's taller and that he'd need to dip his head to bring his mouth any closer.

"I don't think you should help me with the investigation anymore," I say softly.

"Why?"

"Because you get in the way and do unhelpful things like separating suspects from their hearts." I clear my throat.

And distract me.

"Am I a suspect again?"

"No. But it's safer for us both if you stay away." I manage to disentangle myself from the strange Violet that *wants* to entangle with the guy. "Specifically, by leaving this closet."

"Before you kiss or attack me?"

I gawk at him. "No. Before Holly returns for a different colored scarf." He watches how my hand shakes when I brush the front of my shirt. "And this airlessness won't help with this next panic attack you appear to be heading towards."

Grayson closes his eyes and bites his bottom lip hard. No. Is he about to draw blood to tempt me? "Like I said, I'm close to the edge sometimes." He places both hands on my shoulders and maneuvers me away from him, sucking in a huge breath. Then he pushes through Holly's dresses towards the room. "If you don't investigate Holly now, you're an idiot, Violet Blackwood."

"I will investigate her," I retort.

He pauses and looks back. "And if you push me away and refuse my help, you're an even bigger idiot."

"Are you threatening me?" I ask coldly. "All because I won't *kiss* you?"

"You think this is all about kissing, Violet?"

"Kissing and nakedness and, in our case, blood too, yes." I tighten my mouth. "That's what you want."

He stares but with a harder, definitely 'don't want to kiss you', look. "You really believe that? Don't you think I could go elsewhere for kissing, nakedness, and blood?"

I huff. "I don't understand anything about guys apart from what Holly tells me and the shows she watches. So, I'm perfectly aware what happens when a guy and a girl become pressed together in tight spaces."

"And what is that, Violet?"

"Kissing and touching."

"Yet we didn't. That's reserved for Rowan, right?" He arches a brow.

"No."

"You're blind to a lot, Violet, and not only the 'friend' who's hiding things from you." He lifts his head. "I hope you haven't discussed your investigations with Holly."

Pissed, I march out of the closet to face him. "Well, I won't tell her you killed someone."

"Killed because the witch *hurt* you, Violet," he says through clenched teeth. "I'm not repeating myself. I'll stay away if you want, but I guarantee you won't stay away from me."

I watch Grayson walk away, telling myself the heat coursing through my body comes from anger and not how his scent still covers me despite not touching, or how I can almost taste him on my tongue.

At how I almost *was* one of those stupid girls in Holly's TV shows making out in the closet with the boy.

Ugh. Well. I know where *that* leads.

I glance back to the hidden runes and that knot inside my stomach tightens. Has Holly betrayed me? But how can she 'betray' someone who was never really a friend? I'm merely Violet Blackwood, the rude roommate who's fooled by Holly's niceness as easily as if a witch had used a spell on me.

One thing I am sure about—Holly's scared of my father. If I find out she's part of this, I'll deliver Holly to him myself.

Which means I need to do everything I can to prove that Holly isn't involved in the murders.

Chapter Eight

ROWAN

I RESPECTED Violet's wishes last night and left, even though every ounce of me wanted to stay in her room. Does Violet honestly not care what danger she's in and realize that staying alone might be a bad idea? Fine, she's immortal, but she *can* be incapacitated. Did a tiny part of me worry how Violet's hybrid might react if she woke up confused by someone sitting in the dark beside her? Yeah, probably. That's definitely the entire reason I didn't climb onto the bed and hug her to me.

The way to keep breaking through the solid rock around Violet is slowly chipping into the wall; hitting against her barriers won't do anything. Violet wants me to stay away? I'll stay away until there's time to talk about us.

Violet's never sociable but is more subdued than usual today. She's late to class—odd that she comes at all—and sits at the back of the room. Not with Holly. Or me, or Grayson. Alone. And not that she pays attention to what's taught in Physics class for humans and Transmutation class for us. Only high-performing elemental witches successfully change the matter from solid to liquid or air, most other witches practice moving objects a short distance. Violet created ice from water and back again into various shapes, an air of boredom hovering around her. Understandable as that's simple magic for us. Me? I decided to be a smartass and created a tiny topaz from playing with the rock the professor handed out.

Physics seems a pretty pointless class for vamps, unless they've modern-thinking parents who want their kids to pass human subjects. Or vamps who've heard about human college life and fancy trying the lifestyle.

Leif's absent, also weird, as he normally *does* attend everything. I checked on him earlier and he messaged back saying he's tired today and decided to skip class. At least he's safe, but there's something not quite right with him.

Did Dorian speak to Violet again and he told her to keep away from us? I'm expecting Dorian to visit today as a follow up on yesterday, a prospect that scares me. Although not as much as it would frighten Grayson, I'll bet.

If Dorian doesn't get to us first, I expect Sawyer will. Or the police. I swallow hard. No reports of anything yet when I checked online, but once people investigate the half-burned lodge, they'll easily see signs of elemental magic. And if Kai remembers a single thing…

Morning lessons over, I meet Violet in the library where she's standing between two bookshelves, dragging out book after book, her consternation growing as she flicks through the pages before dropping them onto the nearby table.

"What's wrong?" I ask as I dump my bag and approach her.

"My roommate hides magical items in her closet," she replies. "I'm looking for a book that can identify the effect of the stones contained in the spellbag she possesses."

Whoa. "*Holly?*"

"How many other roommates do I have?" She grabs another thick black leather book.

"Have you considered the bag might not be Holly's and that a witch planted it?" I suggest.

"And a runic circle chalked on the floor? The girl changes her clothes often. She wouldn't miss that. What if Holly's part of a coven?"

Violet still doesn't look at me.

"Oh."

"And there was a girl and a scarf." She waves a hand. "A blue one. And Grayson."

"With a girl and a scarf?" I shake my head. "What exactly happened? How do you know all this?"

Finally, she pauses and turns to me. I recognize the sour look from our early interactions, but this one isn't aimed at me. "Grayson ignored my request to stay away," she growls.

"Last night, after I left?"

"No. This morning." Her brow tugs deeper. "The spellbag contained rose quartz, black onyx, and moldavite." She looks at me expectantly.

"Moldavite's a rare stone for Holly to get her hands on, and if *I* don't immediately know what the combination does, she won't know either. Violet, Holly can't be involved with witchcraft. Humans don't join covens—their energy weakens the magic between coven members and interferes with spells." I bite my lip. But this is odd.

"Yes. But Holly could still be *working* with witches. Like the wonderful Marci."

"Marci?" I scoff. "I doubt that. She's a little... *superior* around humans."

"You're not listening!" she says in exasperation. "Dorian could be right. Holly might be a spy. Helped by witches."

Violet slams the spell book on the desk and the sound echoes. "Violet." Cautiously, I touch her arm and she looks ahead, jaw set tight. "We knew there's a possibility Holly's involved. Let's do everything we can to prove the theory wrong. Stay calm."

"I'm frustrated! I don't want yet *more* things confusing my investigation!" she retorts.

"No, you don't want Holly to be an enemy," I say quietly. "That's what's bothering you."

The bond. Violet must be aware that I'm picking up on her struggle against accepting a betrayal. Gently, I take another book from her hands and place it on the desk. "Leave this with me. I'll find out more about the spellbag."

"I don't like when things change that shouldn't," she whispers and allows me to take her hands. "Holly isn't who I thought. Why did that have to happen?"

"Maybe. Maybe not." Willing to deal with the consequences, I press my lips to the center of Violet's forehead.

She stares back at me but says nothing.

Minor victory?

"Have you seen Leif this morning?" I ask. Violet shakes her head. "Odd. He told me he couldn't be bothered with class but I thought he might meet us."

"But he's still at the academy?" she asks sharply. "Nobody took him?"

"Not earlier, but why don't you check on him later?" I suggest.

"Perhaps I will." Her lips purse. "He seemed rather disturbed by events."

"He wasn't the only one." I sigh. "But good that you care."

Interestingly, Violet doesn't respond to that.

"Do you have the burner phone?" I ask.

"Oh. Yes. That's irritated me too." She delves into her skirt pocket. "Look."

I tense. There's a message on the screen.

> What happened?

Thank the stars Violet never replied.

"What a vague and useless clue," she says.

"When did you get this message?"

"On my way here."

"Okay. Can I look?" Violet hands me the phone.

I type and send a message:

> Still dealing with it. Meet soon to explain.

"What are you doing?" she asks.

"Um. Replying?"

A reply pings through.

I'm in town tomorrow. Why the delay?

I'm on it. Meet where?

Usual place. 8

I huff. "Great."

Violet purses her lips and studies the screen. "If this is Maxwell's phone, the person sending messages doesn't know he's dead. That's helpful."

"See." I smile and rub her arm. "Not all bad news."

Her mouth tightens. "I understand you're attempting to comfort me, but you sound rather condescending. The bad news is we've no idea where 'usual' is, Rowan. We have until that meeting to figure out where, or the person will know Maxwell's dead."

"Well, you know what's interesting?" I ask.

"Is that one of your rhetorical questions or am I to answer?"

I smile. "There's no report of a fire."

"What?" Violet's miserable face brightens—a little.

"I've checked local news sites. Sawyer never reported the fire. Nobody attended one since I extinguished it. Interesting, huh?"

"And Kai?"

"Nothing public."

"Maybe Sawyer's too scared to say anything? But scared of who?" Violet scratches her nose. "More moving parts." She points at the book. "Tell me what you find, and I'll investigate Holly."

"And what about the witch?" I ask.

"We hope Dorian finds something."

"*And* hope he doesn't discover you never gave him the phone."

Violet smiles sweetly. "Dorian has a long-standing reputation: he operates by his own rules and only selectively shares information. I *am* his daughter."

"Violet..."

"Again, he'll trample over everything and scare the

58

perpetrator—or perpetrators—and make my investigation harder." She straightens her blazer sleeves. "Holly first."

"Promise me one thing, Violet."

"Promises aren't my forte, but go ahead."

"Don't tell Dorian I knew about the phone."

Violet's pause before answering flips my stomach. Surely not too big a promise? "I have everything in hand, Rowan."

If only.

"Alright."

Violet continues to study my face, and I'm unnerved by the intensity in her eyes. Not as unnerved as I am when she leans closer until her face almost touches mine, her hair fresh with a familiar fragrance.

"I'm glad that hasn't changed," she says and pulls away.

"What?" I ask, one tiny step away from tugging her plump, pouty lip with my teeth and kissing her. Properly.

"I don't have a new desperate desire for your blood since I died. Fortunately. One barely controllable urge around Grayson is enough to deal with."

"Right." Her lips still close. Temptation staying.

"Therefore, my attraction to you must be for different reasons."

Her *what?* My reverie breaks. Any sensible guy would take advantage of the moment, but any sensible guy around Violet knows not to. I delve into my head for a response, but my thoughts and voice are missing.

"I'm going to find Holly." Violet hesitates and drops her gaze from my eyes to my mouth and back again so quickly I might've missed it. "You look different when you comb your hair. Goodbye."

I've still not regained the power of speech as she wanders away.

Any sensible guy with a *normal* girlfriend would've pressed her to those bookshelves and kissed her, and so much more.

But there's nothing normal about Violet. And if she heard me refer to her as 'my girlfriend', who knows what the outcome would be.

I guess it's just me, my memories, and the patience of every human saint—and more research to work my way further into this girl's heart. Violet expects me to do all our research. Maybe I should start trading my discoveries for kisses? I chuckle at the concept and unfasten my bag.

Chapter Nine

VIOLET

THE EASIEST WAY TO catch someone who doesn't suspect that *you* suspect *them?* Act normally. Or rather, act abnormally in my case. Or normally? I'm unsure. Everything grows more confusing.

I regret asking Holly for our 'girl's afternoon' as she insists our activities should expand outside these four walls. She claims that once I've practiced socialization with her, I may even enjoy doing so with others. *Other teens, willingly, outside of lessons?* If Holly seriously believes this, she has no understanding of me whatsoever. More evidence that this friendship is all a ruse.

But, paradoxically, to spend time with Holly, I must take part in social occasions she enjoys. The fire Fridays no longer exist following Wesley's unfortunate passing, and the majority of Holly's activities seem centered around the academy now. In particular, her witch boyfriend.

Despite my reticence, it would help to spend time with her off-campus and dig into what's happening with the humans in town. Perhaps Holly can help, although I worry her association with me on the night of Kai's party precludes her from joining that social scene.

My other concern—I've yet to discover the outcome of the day of the wake, both for the shifters and Sawyers. And especially Kai.

But first, I need to discover Holly's involvement. I refuse to believe a human fooled me, despite evidence that suggests otherwise.

Holly arrives back at the room late afternoon, carrying several paper bags adorned with store logos, and I watch with half-interest as she unpacks yet more items of clothing. No wonder she requires such a large space for her closet. Holly sings to herself as she lays a short green dress onto her rainbow bedspread and produces a multi-colored necklace and earrings that she arranges to create an outfit.

"Another party to attend?" I ask, with both hope and dread.

"A date."

"With Pursuit?"

She pulls a disparaging face. "His name is Chase, Violet."

"Uh huh." I feign disinterest and write in my notebook.

"Do you go on dates?" she asks.

The pencil almost snaps in my hand. "Dates?"

"With your guys."

"We sometimes go for dinner while investigating, I suppose," I reply and return to my doodling. *Once. With Rowan. Under duress.*

"I mean, do you ever go to the movies, bowling… I don't know, like, ordinary things."

This time, I turn to look at my auburn-haired, shiny-eyed 'friend'. She sits on her desk chair too and watches expectantly.

Interesting. Is Holly instructed to keep tabs on my whereabouts? Perhaps ensure that I'm in the right location and ready for a murderous incident to occur?

"Ordinary things?" I purse my lips.

"Oh, okay. Graveyard picnics." She chuckles. "Long walks in the woods."

Hmm. "Why would you suggest that I like the woods, Holly?"

"Uh. Because there're popular walking trails with romantic spots to sit."

"And the occasional murder site," I remind her.

"Oh. I guess. Any closer with your investigations?" Holly gestures at the now bare wall. "Do you have an answer and that's why you took down the notes?"

"My father wanted to read them," I say casually. "He's pissed. Told me he doesn't care what or who's involved, human or supe, but that he'll make an example of them."

Is she paler at that comment? Hard to tell under the amount of foundation and contouring she again attempted to teach me.

"I wouldn't like to think what an 'example' made of by Dorian Blackwood involves." She shudders, then slants her head. "Why are you looking at me in that way, Violet? Have I upset you?"

"You know this is how I look most of the time."

"Ah, yes. Violet Blackwood, World's Greatest RBF."

More teenage code. A human accolade I've no interest in receiving since she's amused and not solemn.

Holly busies herself swapping more earrings and necklaces with each other on the bed, before wandering into her closet, re-emerging with a scarf. A leopard print one. Is there significance to these scarves?

"Are you wearing that dress to your date?" I ask her.

"This is for a dinner with Chase later in the week. I'm wearing boring jeans tonight, but I can still find a cute top." Again, she ambles into her closet, re-emerging with an armful of multi-colored sweaters, several pairs of 'boring jeans', along with a pair of black ankle boots tucked beneath her chin.

I perk up. *Tonight.* "Can I come on your date, Holly?"

The boots drop to the floor. "Um. You don't want to be the third wheel, Violet."

"The what now?"

"Although… do you bowl?"

"On wheels?" I rub my forehead. "Explain."

"Bowling." I look at her blankly. "Throwing balls." I shake my head. "A competition. See who can knock down the most pins."

"Knock down *what?*"

With a chuckle, Holly produces her phone and opens the internet browser. By the time Holly's given me a full explanation of what bowling entails and how the 'sport' is a favored teen pursuit—including educational videos and enthusiasm about her own expertise—I'm a little more aware but still fail to see the attraction.

"Do the town's kids attend here?" I ask and point at the bowling establishment highlighted on her phone. She nods.

Teams. With balls. There's a rugby team at the academy, and I've briefly witnessed that bizarre activity. I've no idea what the game entails apart from too much rather rough touching and a fair amount of shouting. Bowling balls appear different, though. "And when the teams play, do people get injured since the balls are heavy?"

She splutters a laugh. "Alright. You can come with me and Chase—if you bring one of your guys."

"As a fourth wheel?"

"And a fifth and sixth if you want all three with you?" she says, still amused by something.

Hmm. She wants the four of us together. Or only two of us? "When?"

"We're meeting at seven." She pauses. "So… they *are* all your guys!"

"They're not possessions. We're a team. I'm the leader."

She snorts. "Of course you are. That would work well for bowling, although I've only ever seen Leif at a bowling night."

"And what wheel does he play?" I ask.

"Violet. There aren't any wheels."

"You are utterly confusing," I mutter. "I'll select one of the guys to accompany me and join you."

"Maybe not Grayson," she puts in sharply.

"Why?" Is he due to meet his uncle tonight and Holly must ensure he does?

"Vamps have an unfair advantage—superior physical skills," she explains.

"Then so will I."

Holly bites her lip and looks me up and down. "You've never bowled before? I doubt you'll have an advantage."

Challenge accepted, Holly. Including the one to catch you out and reveal who you are.

Chapter Ten

ROWAN

> I need you

I'VE BARELY READ Violet's message before I have my blazer in hand, ready to leave the room.

> What's wrong

> Where are you?

I swing an arm through a sleeve as I reply,

> Meet me in the library again

Crap. As I rush across campus, I scout the front of the building for familiar cars—police, Dorian, Sawyer... None.

Huh?

The hallways are empty, as is the library. The only time anybody comes to the place at a weekend is when cramming their brains full of information that they've no chance will stick before exam week. In fact, the library's empty most days apart from those.

I slow down as I enter, side-eying the young, female librarian, who's facing the other way before half-sprinting up the stairs to our corner. Violet's studying something on her phone, the cute crease on her brows. I'm about to hug Violet before she spots me, and those defensive arms go across her chest.

"Are you alright?" I say.

"You're pink and breathing funny," she says. "A number of things cause this. Which one?"

"I ran here."

"Ran?" She looks me up and down as if I told her I flew.

"Your message?"

"Yes?"

"That you need me. I panicked!" I say.

"Oh." Her eyes go wide. "I meant I need you tonight. This evening. To come somewhere with me."

"Then this isn't an emergency?" I pull out a chair to sit, catching my breath. "Violet, be more specific next time."

"Very well. Tell me. What items might exist in a bowling alley that could kill?" she asks.

"Depends on how gruesome you want the murder, I suppose," I reply, completely confused. "There're the heavy balls. The machinery. Shoelaces for strangling someone with. Why?"

"Can you do it?"

My voice drops to a hushed whisper. "Do what, Violet? *Murder* someone?"

"Good grief, Rowan. That would not be at all helpful. Can you throw balls at...whatever they're called?"

"Yeah. Why?"

"Will you take me?"

"Bowling?"

"Please keep up, Rowan."

I laugh loudly enough that she looks taken aback, then I look down at the cute, diminutive ball of danger. "Are you asking me on a date, Violet Blackwood?"

"No. I'm asking you to accompany me somewhere for an evening."

"Otherwise known as a date." I bite my lip, enjoying the

frustration I triggered in her. "I would *love* to go on a date with you."

She bares her teeth at me. "I don't go on dates."

"Like you don't kiss people?" She shows me more teeth. "Is that supposed to scare me away?"

"Holly is going on a date with Chase and has invited me and…" She pulls a face. "One of my guys. But not Grayson."

"Not Leif?" She looks at me, unblinking. "I'm your first choice?"

"You are my *choice* because you're a witch and if I need help you can use subtle magic. And I mean, *subtle*, Rowan. No indoor earthquakes."

"Okay. Back up." I run a hand through my hair. "What are we doing?"

"I believe this is an opportunity to watch Holly."

"You still think she's up to something?"

"Yes. I checked her closet again this afternoon and someone removed the magical items. Holly is definitely a suspect. She's friendly with a few witches and there're a few on this dance committee. Including her best friend."

"Marci?" She nods. "Again, I doubt that, but Marci *is* powerful. The other witches on the committee aren't focused on their studies at all; they can barely make a simple potion. Their parents would be pissed if they knew they're wasting time on human traditions and not studying."

"Human traditions? You're not attending the Spring Ball?" she asks.

"Why? Are you? Is this an invite? I'll need to get back to you because I may have other offers."

"I highly doubt that, Rowan."

I snort. "I'll ignore the insult and accept your offer."

Violet's cheeks go pink. *Pink.* "I am *not* going to the Spring Ball." Whoa. Okay. The snarled vehemence thrown at me means the color isn't embarrassment. "Stop pushing your luck, Rowan."

I shrug. "Tonight. Bowling. It's a date." Another glare. "I'm still confused. What do you intend to do tonight?"

Violet blows air into her cheeks. "I want to watch Holly, but she knows that when the four of us are together we're up to something. Therefore, we go somewhere as two. You can be my date if that's what you insist on calling the evening. I want to watch everybody Holly speaks to outside of the academy, especially humans connected to the Sawyers."

"Maybe Kai will be there tonight too?"

"Oh, how joyous that will be, considering how his party ended."

"And the little incident where we almost burned down his father's lakeside lodge with him inside?"

"I didn't set fire to the lodge, the witch did."

"The dead witch." I scratch a cheek. "This is all a distraction that we don't need."

"Dead witches?"

"Bowling. Holly." Violet shakes her head and mutters something. I lean across the desk towards her, hands clasped together. "Any updates from Dorian?"

"I spoke to him earlier. No recent complaints about supernatural behavior," she says. "And still no mention of anybody hospitalized—shifter or Kai. I believe our mental magic has worked on an uninjured Kai, but why hasn't Sawyer reported anything?"

"I don't think we'll understand anything about Sawyer until we figure out who Maxwell was and their connection. *And* who's pulling the strings." I consider my next words. "And if there's Petrescu involvement."

"Hmm." She switches focus to her phone. "Grayson."

"Is Grayson bothering you?" I carefully consider my words. "Do you suspect him again?"

"No, but he's a touch unstable." Violet concentrates on typing.

"Yeah. A vamp with control issues who occasionally pulls out witches' hearts," I say quietly.

She looks up. "No. Grayson's suffering from panic attacks."

"Panic attacks?"

"And yes, he's killing suspects. Grayson is honestly not helpful to me." My jaw drops. "What?"

"Do you know how awful that sounded, Violet?"

She sets down the phone. "You like and trust him now?"

"As much as anybody. Grayson cares about you and not just your blood. That's obvious." I sigh at her unreadable expression. "The vamp's waiting for the day you offer to open a vein for him, but when you bled to death in front of him, his first instinct wasn't to go for your blood but to help. I swear if I hadn't stopped Grayson, *he* would've opened his own vein."

Her eyes go wide. "What?"

"To give you his blood to help. I don't know how that works with hybrids. Leif stopped him—two of you bleeding out everywhere wouldn't be great."

"No. Grayson forcing blood down my throat while I'm temporarily dead would've achieved nothing." Did Violet just moisten her lips?

"What I'm saying is, cut Grayson some slack. Like you did me."

"That was the bond, Rowan. Not me."

"Uh huh."

Violet's thoughts wander, her eyes focusing on a spot nearby, her mind definitely elsewhere. She's in calculation mode. In the past, I would've taken this as the end of the conversation and walked away, but I've now known Violet long enough to wait.

Her intense eyes return to me. "How many people will I need to communicate with at a bowling alley? More or less than at a party?"

"Don't worry. I doubt many people will want to communicate with you, Violet."

"Right. Plan. You come with me to—"

"—on a date." I smirk, and she gives me a perfect Violet scowl.

"To *the bowling alley*. I will avoid speaking to people and watch instead. You can talk."

I scoff. "Aren't you forgetting we trashed the house at a party we went to? Even if I *was* a talkative person, I doubt many people would talk to me."

Again, the faraway look. "Maybe I *should* ask Leif." I open my mouth to protest. "Actually. You make a very good point, Rowan. Leif wasn't involved that night. More people like him than like you, anyway."

Wow. Just *wow*. Violet nods and tucks her phone away. "You don't want me to go with you?" I ask.

"You sound irritated."

"Mmm hmm." Did I really just talk myself out of a date with Violet?

"Now you *definitely* sound irritated." She tips her head back to look up at me as I stand. "You didn't actually *want* to go bowling, did you?"

This girl. Again, I'm pissed at her dismissive, heartless actions, but I say nothing. Violet still isn't aware how her behavior can be hurtful—or is Violet aware and just doesn't give a shit about me still? I could be the one cutting *her* too much slack.

"Do you understand what you just did, Violet?" I ask in a clipped tone.

"I don't understand."

And she doesn't. Genuinely. "Violet, you can't snap your fingers and expect me to come running, then shove me aside when you *then* decide I'm not useful."

For a long moment, Violet stares at me, taking longer than she once would to form her response. "You want to go bowling?"

"No, I stupidly thought you wanted to spend time with me."

Another longer than average pause. "I don't *not* want to spend time with you. I'm merely identifying the most useful person for this evening."

"Jesus, Violet." I blow air into my cheeks and step closer, holding my thumb and forefinger a centimeter apart. "I am *this* close to not helping you again until you change your bloody attitude to me."

"Is this because you want to go bowling?" she repeats.

"No!"

"You are extremely confusing at times, Rowan." Violet pushes her tongue against a canine. "If I've upset you, we could go bowling tomorrow?"

71

"This isn't about the *bowling*..." I trail off. "Forget it. Maybe Leif might leave his room if you ask him to go with you."

"Right." She pauses. "Besides, you'd distract me."

"Oh? Meaning?"

"Take that as you wish."

Hands behind my back, I lean forward, close enough to inhale the ocean-scented soap she uses. How would Violet smell to me if I was a vampire—especially if I was Grayson? I've barely touched her skin or hardly tasted that sweetness, and if the smell of Violet's blood tempts him in the same way, Grayson's more controlled than I imagine I would be as a vamp.

"I suppose I'll spend the evening practicing my new magic then," I whisper.

"Psychometry, I hope," she says, not moving. "If you even *try* to touch the shadows, I'll drain your magic energy until you can barely conjure anything simple for a week."

"You can drain my energy any time, Violet." I pull back and smile.

"Good grief, Rowan. That's extremely unhelpful." She holds my gaze, a glimmer of something in her eyes that recognizes what I'm saying.

We've never spoken about the kissing, and considering everything that happened between then and now, kisses seem low on the list of 'life-changing events for Violet'.

She doesn't move as I hold my mouth close enough to hers that they almost touch. "I hope you find a dress you like," I whisper.

Why won't you just put your lips on mine, so I know what the hell is happening here?

For one hopeful heartbeat, I think she will, but Violet pulls her head back. "A dress for bowling? Holly's wearing jeans."

My mouth pulls up at one side, and irritation flares across Violet's face and into her aura at my next words. "For when we go to the Spring Ball, Violet."

Chapter Eleven

LEIF

VIOLET STANDS in the entrance to the bowling alley, her sullen face and black clothes a massive contrast to the name above her in pink neon lights. Sounds of pins knocked over echo from one direction ahead, and to our side there's an arcade filled with brighter lights and mingled music and voices, some kids crowded around and shouting at the more popular games.

I'm unsure which of the two locations Violet's viewing with the greater dread.

"What's that *awful* smell?" she asks.

"Shoes."

"Excuse me?"

"You need to wear special bowling shoes. The alley hires them with the games. They have an... odor."

Horror strikes her face. "Shoes other people have worn? No. That will not happen."

She looks around, her face one of a girl brought to a funeral and not for an evening out to somewhere that involves fun. Actually, maybe that's what she would prefer. What *did* Violet do in her spare time before Thornwood? "And what is in *there*?" Violet jabs a finger at the arcade.

"Arcade games. I'll win something for you later—I'm pretty good at the claw machine. Not many people are." I grin.

"Claw machine? I'm almost curious, but no. Only if Holly visits the machines. Where is she?"

Not waiting for an answer, Violet marches through to the area spanned by bowling lanes, a place I've spent some good evenings inside over the years—winning usually. The thud of the balls and the monitors flashing with names and scores announced by a disembodied voice cause a surge of memories, but Violet halts as if I've brought her into a circle of Hell.

"Good grief."

"Come on." I forget myself and reach out to take Violet's hand but completely miss since she's already striding over to Holly, who's chosen a lane close to the entrance.

Holly's open-armed enthusiasm at her friend's arrival isn't matched by stiff-shouldered Violet, who backs away. I half-expect Violet to back out of the place altogether. She continues to stare at everybody and everything with calculating suspicion, especially Holly's companions.

Apart from Chase, there's another human/witch couple— Marci and Jon. Jon jerks his chin in greeting, and I nod. Violet stares at Marci for what would ordinarily be an unacceptable amount of time, but typical for Violet.

Everybody knows Marci. There's always something superior in her manner, not uncommon for the more skilled witches, but she's an undeniable charm used on all students that somehow commands respect without being unapproachable.

Quite the opposite to Violet.

Although I'm surprised she's dating a human. The slender guy isn't a popular kid but never seems short of girls, although not often witches. Maybe because he matches Marci's level of attractiveness, something else that no doubt keeps her popular. Glossy brown hair and soft features, often covered in a smile.

Again, quite the opposite to Violet.

Marci and Violet don't greet each other.

Violet claims she doesn't know her shoe size and therefore

can't change footwear, and I cajole her into handing over a boot. Then I leave to collect the shoes that Violet informs me she's no intention of wearing.

Once that task is completed, I return to a still-standing Violet, who now watches those around impassively. She sits beside Holly and takes the burgundy shoes from me.

Honestly, you'd think I'd given her a shoe full of dog crap the way she behaves when lacing them up.

"Vamps don't usually join teams," says Chase.

"I'm not a 'vamp'," she retorts, not looking away from her observation of Jon, who's bowling close by.

"Is Rowan not with you tonight?" asks Marci as I lower myself onto the shiny bench beside Violet.

"Why?" she asks too sharply.

"Because he's your boyfriend. Right?" Marci's refusal to break Violet's hard stare doesn't bode well.

"No."

Marci's eyes flick to me. "Then Leif is? You're dating a human? Huh."

Violet sucks on her teeth. Man, if only that were true. Ignoring Marci's comment, Violet stands to inspect the balls, and I'm drawn to staring at her ass in the tight black jeans she chose to wear. The girl's still oblivious to my thoughts about her, even after the awkward memories she saw in my mind.

Doesn't help that Chase winks at me in a knowing way. He leans across. "What's she like?"

"Violet?"

"Duh. Yeah. You and her?"

I sigh. "We're friends."

"Correct," announces Violet and turns around, a black ball in her small hands. "Leif doesn't know what I'm *like* as he hasn't touched or seen me in the way he imagines he'd like to."

"Yeah?" Chase straightens. "And how's that?"

"Naked."

Oh, no. "Violet," I interrupt. "That's a sixteen pound ball. It'll be too heavy for you."

"Don't be ridiculous," she says and lifts it above her head with both hands.

Wow. Okay. I completely forget how non-delicate this slender girl is.

Chase continues to snicker at us. "Must be awkward being 'friends' with a mind reader, Leif."

Violet steps forward, ball between her hands as if she held a soccer ball not the heaviest one possible to choose from. She flicks her tongue against her teeth. "At least Leif actually has a mind to read. Yours is rather empty, Chase." She pauses and her eyes widen slightly. "Actually, I *can* see something." Violet places hands either side of the ball and holds it above his shoes. "You plan to use magic on Holly so that she'll remove her clothes." The ball slips slightly in Violet's hands, and Chase attempts to move his feet.

He swears when they won't budge.

"I hope nothing happens to injure your feet and end the evening before the fun even begins," she says, deadpan.

"Bullshit," Chase replies, but his eyes dart between the ball and his feet. "I wouldn't do that to Holly."

"That's why I'm here," says Marci quietly. "Chase has a reputation."

"What the fuck?" he snaps.

"You're here to protect Holly?" asks Violet evenly, switching her attention. I don't miss Chase's relieved look as the magic breaks and he jumps to his feet.

"Partially. We're close friends, Violet. I look out for her."

The two regard each other again. Uncomfortable atmospheres between Violet and others are common, but there's something odd here, especially when Marci gives her a sweet smile and stands to take her turn bowling.

Did Violet detect the pointedness of Marci's comment?

Holly flops onto the squeaky red bench, her mouth-turned down. I glance up at the screen. "Ouch. You only hit three."

"I'd like some fries," she says to Chase, ignoring me.

Chase leans across the space and plants a kiss on Holly's

mouth, who watches him as he leaves to order, her eyes filled with delight.

Violet continues to stare at the back of Marci's head. "You shouldn't be friends with these people, Holly," she announces and drops the ball with a thud into the row of returned ones.

"Why?" asks Holly.

"I don't like them," she says simply. Jon scoffs, and she throws him a look. "The witches, not you. I've seen you around the academy. You're innocuous."

"In what?"

Violet's eyes close, and she shakes her head. "Insipid."

Jon looks to me for help. "She means harmless," I offer.

"No, I don't. I mean that he's innocuous and insipid." Violet makes a soft, derisive sound and looks away.

"You don't tell me who I can and can't be friends with," retorts Holly. "At least I'm safe with Marci when not sharing a room with Dorian's psychopathic daughter."

Violet's lips thin and she glances at Marci now standing behind Holly, who gives another saccharin smile.

"Sorry, Violet. I didn't mean that. I don't know why I said those things."

"I do," says Violet, pointedly looking at Marci.

Oh, hell. We're here five minutes and the evening's already descending into Violet-level animosity.

"Holly feels threatened by you, Violet," says Marci as she returns.

"Is this true, Holly?" Violet replies.

"I think you're up, Violet," I say and point at the screen that's awaiting her score.

"Up what?" she asks.

"Her own ass," mutters Jon, and Marci joins him in laughing.

I slice them a look, then stand between Violet and the people trying to antagonize her. "Your turn to bowl, Violet. Do you want me to show you how?"

"How to throw a ball at some wooden sticks?" She scoffs. "No."

"Try and hit some," says Marci. "That's the aim."

"I've studied those around me. I'm perfectly capable," she says and stomps off.

"What the hell are you doing with that weirdo, Leif?" asks Jon. "Does she use spells on you too?"

"Huh?"

Marci points at Holly. "Violet's using magic on Holly."

"Uh. She isn't," I say. "Is she Holly?"

"Violet needs to pretend she can make friends. Fit in," Marci continues. "A cover for the real reason she's here."

"You think Violet's the one killing people?" I ask in disbelief.

"Why else do you think I've Holly staying with me some nights?" asks Marci. "Holly's scared she'll die."

The explosion from a strike in our lane draws my attention and Violet turns, face pretty sour for someone who knocked down all pins on her first ever bowl. Although, I'm surprised her strength didn't knock the ball through the back of the alley's pin return.

"Shush," Holly hisses at Marci.

"Shush what?" Marci asks.

"Don't start an argument with Violet," says Holly. "Please."

"I heard all that." Violet stands completely still, and her look moves slowly from Holly, to Marci, and to Jon. Then to Chase as he approaches with a wicker basket of fries smothered in ketchup.

"Show me this arcade thing, Leif," Violet says coolly.

"I haven't *upset* you, have I?" asks Marci.

What the hell is happening here? Violet pulls on her lip and remains silent long enough that I exchange an uncomfortable look with Jon. She doesn't speak until Marci breaks their mutual challenge by looking away.

"No, Marci," she says softly. "People rarely upset me. Particularly witches who manipulate people weaker than themselves."

She turns to me, kicking off the poorly tied bowling shoes as she does, and grabs her boots. "Arcade, Leif."

As Violet turns away, Marci speaks again. "Say hi to Rowan for me, Violet. I miss our chats."

Violet doesn't pause or react, nor does she say goodbye to Holly.

She rarely mingles at school, but here Violet's in a world of teenagers along with her newly emerging emotions. What happens if the new Violet loses her temper with bitchy girls?

Chapter Twelve

VIOLET

INTERESTING.

Leif can't decide if he wants to eat or not, so we pause close to the food serving area, where the odor of greasy food and popcorn engulfs the atmosphere. As he debates what delicacy to choose, I pull out my phone and make notes of my recent exchanges, and all the names of people present this evening that I recognize. Irritatingly, my exchanges with Holly and Marci bring me closer to admitting Holly tricked me with her niceness.

Holly's under the influence of a witch who evidently dislikes me, if not worse.

Rowan informed me that Marci's powerful. Did she ask Holly to steal my potion? Involve Holly in witchcraft? I press my lips together. This is the tip of an iceberg smack bang in the middle of the academy—who decided Holly and I should room together?

"Are you okay, Violet?" asks Leif, looking over his shoulder at me. "Marci was pretty bitchy."

"Bitchy?"

"Rude and unpleasant."

"Like I am?" I place my phone in a pocket.

"You're different."

"Apparently so."

"Half the time you don't mean to be rude, you just come across that way."

"I've had this conversation an irritating number of times. I speak my mind. Sometimes that's rude and I don't care." I look around the teen scene presented to me. "Humans are odd in the way they categorize people. Tonight, I feel as if I'm in one of Holly's shows."

"Yeah, those aren't reality, Violet."

"But some are called 'reality TV'." I frown. Now I'm confused. Again.

"The producers pick people as certain personalities and just show what fits that type. Like, if a girl is 'the bitchy one', the show only uses footage to create a bitchy character. They won't show when she's nice. Clever editing to entertain."

"How curious and pointless." I purse my lips. "Still. I'm learning a lot from the shows, reality or not."

"Such as?"

Marci. I'm vaguely amused by her attempts to upset me. As if mind games from someone as inferior as that girl would bother me.

"They aid me in identifying the social hierarchy. Where do you fit, Leif?" He shrugs. "Well, people *like* you, and you're nice, but not too popular. Slightly on the edge. Around the middle level of popularity, maybe?"

He chuckles at me. "And what would I be if I was a character in one of the shows? The 'nice guy who likes the oblivious girl'?"

Oblivious? "I'm aware what you think of me, Leif. I find it odd that all three of you have romantic and sexual feelings about me."

"Uh." His eyes go wide, and he rubs the back of his neck. "Well, I do think you're cute. I mean pretty." He stumbles over his words. "Strange. But I like you because you're so... Violet. Sorry if I make you uncomfortable. Friends is fine too. Or acquaintances."

"Still, an odd response to me. I'm neither a romantic or

sexual person. Although my mother does need three men in her life to satisfy her needs so perhaps that will change." Leif chokes on his own saliva and his eyes water as he stares at me. "Did you want to ask something? I can tell by your weird look."

"Uh. This is a weird conversation."

Hmm. I watch a couple pass, the tall human guy walking with a confident gait, arm around his diminutive girlfriend's shoulders, hugging her close as if someone might snatch her away. "I'd rather speak about this issue than ignore such things."

"Right." Leif blows air into his cheeks and taps on the counter.

"Am I making *you* uncomfortable?" He shakes his head. "That's a lie."

"Is it okay if we don't talk about this? I don't know what to say."

"I expect one day I'll change my mind. As I said, my mother's a very..." I pull a face. "Physically affectionate person. For now, I have more pressing concerns than considering sexual activity with you or any of the other guys. As do all of you."

"Tonight has been interesting," he says swiftly, changing the subject.

"Yes. Very much so. I have new leads." Subject put to rest? Good. With a smile, I gesture around. "Do you know much about Marci? Or the human guy, Jon? Is he your friend too?"

But Rowan. For a reason I can't fathom, that comment niggled. Marci and he are or were friends? More?

"I know the guy, but not well. I've never spoken to Marci until tonight." He rubs his forehead. "We didn't finish bowling, Violet. Is that because Marci made you pissed?"

"Is there an accolade for the winner?" I shake my head. "No. Therefore, futile. I've ascertained what I need about Holly, ensured she remains clothed tonight, and there's nobody else relevant present. Now I want to visit this arcade to note who else is attending in case there's a death."

He grins, showing dimples. Why did I never notice Leif has dimples? "Any particular reason you brought *me*? Are you and Rowan fighting again?"

"I require you to speak to people. Humans from town. You're the only one of us they'll speak to, I imagine."

"Oh. Okay. Well. Not if they know I'm with you."

"As I said, people seem to like you." I wave a hand. "I saw them greet you when you retrieved those awful shoes. Talk to someone—find out if Kai is alright. Unless Kai's in the arcade, he isn't here. Dale's around. They seemed close at the ill-fated party. Talk to him."

He blinks at me. "You definitely want to check out the arcade? Cool. I wanted to win you something."

"Win me something?" I continue to study passersby. Seems the place becomes more popular as the evening grows later. "In what capacity?"

"Have you never visited an arcade?"

"Do you never catch up to the 'Violet spent her childhood away from the world'?"

"Good. I like being the first to show you new things. Your reactions are priceless. Come with me."

I point at the long-haired young woman dispensing fizzy drinks into the bowling alley's branded cups from a machine. "I'd like a soda."

A short distance away, a guy in bowling shoes leans on the counter talking to her. She's disinterested in his attentions, her smile falser than the ones I use.

Leif snorts in amusement. "Because Dale is over there and I can conveniently speak to him?"

"Yes." I point at one of several red plastic seats arranged around a circular table that's covered in empty burger wrappers. "I'll wait here for information."

How odd—Leif has the same tendency to mutter beneath his breath as Rowan does when we're together and does so as he walks away.

Tonight's teenage activity bore more fruit than that ridiculous party. Holly's unexpected companion means this evening could be a more useful one than I thought. I *knew* there had to be a connection inside the academy, and Marci's link to Holly makes perfect sense. Now to figure the connection between Marci, any professors in the academy, and who her family is.

I'm close to the entry into the arcade's ear-splitting noise and eye-watering illuminations, and I wince every time glass doors slide open and close. Some kids walk from the bowling lanes towards this attached area, others straight through the door after completing their night of pointless fun.

Holly's amused when I call things 'pointless fun' and tells me 'isn't fun the point?' as if having fun is a necessary aspect of life. Then we held a conversation about what 'fun' means to me. I told Holly I'd get back to her with an answer. My murder investigations *were* fun, as was the solitude and focus on magic permitted at home, but both are constrained by a different reality now.

Leif returns with an oversized cup of soda and a straw which he sets on the table. "Arcade?"

I suck the straw and pull a face at the artificial sweet orange fizziness, ignoring what's happened a few times now—food isn't particularly pleasant tasting any longer.

Why? Dorian and Eloise don't sustain themselves with blood —I share meals with them on occasion. I'm unfortunately aware that they enjoy each other's blood, and that Eloise isn't averse to sampling my other fathers'. Is that enough? And does she do this for a physical thrill or to satiate a thirst?

I stare at Leif's pulse point, subtly inhaling his freshly showered scent.

Not the same appeal as Grayson's.

Or Rowan's, but I'm increasingly avoiding thoughts about a possibility arising from our bond—I haven't admitted to him I lied and that his blood *is* more appealing. But isn't that inevitable for a vampire and witch, even a hybrid? Especially if Rowan became more attractive to me since the bond snapped into place?

And I kissed Rowan, which was strangely pleasant, although disconcerting. Again, perhaps encouraged by the bond? His affection and care come from more than what the bond prompted in him, as does our attachment, since I'm drawn to Rowan in unexpected ways.

Fortunately, I'd no desire to bite when we kissed—as I promised—but the two desires will entangle should they grow. Therefore, I must take care. I highly doubt Rowan would appreciate the move from hesitant lip touching to raging hybrid.

Or maybe he would.

"Violet?" asks Leif. "Did you hear me?"

"Excuse me. No."

"I spoke to Dale. Kai's fine. Apparently, he's under curfew for stealing a car that he crashed and was arrested for DUI."

"Oh, really?" I lower my voice. "The ruse worked?"

"Yes. Has Sawyer hauled you and Grayson in front of him again yet?" asks Leif. "Didn't he say you had twenty-four hours?"

"Oddly, no. Not yet. Perhaps Dorian intervened." I hand him the drink, which he takes. "And that tastes disgusting."

"I love how you're such a gracious and grateful person, Violet."

"How? I'm not."

"Exactly." He sips through the straw. "You're funny. It's endearing."

I straighten. *Not this agai*n. "Perhaps ask Grayson what makes me *un*-endearing."

"Yeah. He told us. You're also scary."

"Thank you."

"We haven't spoken about what happened when you..." He wrinkles his nose. "Died."

"I presumed you didn't want to, which helped because I don't enjoy people's focus on the event."

He sits and grips the cup. "I never spoke to you when you uh…came back because everything felt surreal, and I got caught up in fixing what happened. Autopilot. But since then, I can't get images out of my head. I was the one who..." Leif swallows.

"Removed me from the fence post?"

He's pale now, rubbing his forehead. "Yeah. Rowan had already lost his shit—a thousand times worse than the night the shifters attacked you."

I nod. "Understandably."

"At first, I thought Rowan would run into the building, but luckily Grayson came out. I felt useless, sick, had no idea what the fuck to do, and then the shadows came."

"What?" I ask sharply and sit upright.

"Shadows came from Rowan." Leif shakes his head. "I've never seen that magic from him—like when he sparks magic into lightning energy but more engulfing. Black. Even if I hadn't been sitting on the ground with you, I doubt I could've touched and calmed Rowan. He wasn't... *him*."

"Good grief," I mutter. Rowan conveniently missed telling me *this*. "Did he use the magic in any way?"

"No. Grayson yelled at him to calm his shit, that the witch was dead—too bloody loudly—and that you weren't." Leif swallows hard again. "Then Rowan took you from me and just sat with you in his arms, totally still and silent."

"But the shadows left?"

"Yeah, what was that? A bond thing?"

I sigh. "A Blackwood thing. I've warned him against using them." Leif scoffs and I frown. "Why is that amusing? Shadows are *not* amusing, Leif."

"Rowan wasn't in any state to decide at the time. You... your death triggered them."

"This is not good news," I say. "Rowan isn't strong enough for, and nor should he encourage that magic. I shall have words with him."

Leif smiles wryly. "And what would happen if someone 'had words' with you about your abilities, Violet?"

"I'd ignore them."

"Rowan's the same and he will ignore you. Whatever Rowan thinks and feels about you, the guy will never allow anybody to tell him what to do."

"Rowan normally does what I tell him."

"Are you serious?" Leif's mouth parts. "You think he'll run around after you and always do what you say?"

"He usually does, although sometimes after an argument. And if he doesn't, I do whatever I intended but without him."

"Exactly. Rowan agrees because he wants to keep you out of trouble. Violet, you can't treat people in that way. We're happy to help you, but aren't your servants."

"I said no such thing," I retort. Is this what bothered Rowan earlier?

He watches me for a few moments, rubbing his mouth. "You haven't even asked me how I feel about that time at the lodge."

"I presumed you'd tell me if you wanted to. You mostly kept away from me since we returned to the academy." I sigh. "And you just *did* tell me."

Leif leans across the table. "I was fucking traumatized, Violet. I keep seeing your blood on my hands. Remembering how it smelled."

I wish I could empathize, to understand what trauma means, but I'm also happy that I don't. Yet something skitters through me. If I become closer to these guys, will I react badly if they're hurt? Would something inside this new Violet not cope and I'd respond as either Grayson or Rowan did?

Leif's trauma remains with him, palpable in this moment, and I'm sorry that he had to be part of *that* moment.

I *can't* empathize, but I *do* feel concern for what I've inadvertently pulled Leif into by forging a link. "I'm sorry, Leif."

Each time I use those words, I understand them more—sometimes they're the only ones people are capable of using in a situation.

Chapter Thirteen

VIOLET

I ALLOW Leif to decide if he wants to continue to talk, and I'm thankful when our conversation ends by him slapping both hands on the table and standing.

"Arcade, right?" he asks.

I stand too and, in a strangely brave gesture, Leif grabs my hand, then tugs me after him. We approach the glass entry to the cacophony of sound and blinding light. Perhaps I should ask to leave, but I don't need to as Leif halts and swears before we cross the threshold.

"What?" I ask.

His hold on my hand remains, and I'm acutely aware how small mine seems. In fact, how slight I am compared to this guy. Then I'm suddenly struck that Leif agreed to come with me tonight when he's reluctant to leave campus. I slant my head to look at the side of his face where his heavy brow is pulled lower, the pupils in his amber eyes dilated, before following his line of vision.

Shifters. Ah. I thought I could smell something strong over the odor of the awful shoes.

"Show me the dazzling delights," I say, this time me tugging *his* hand and walking forward.

I step into a metallic maze walled with mirrors that double the size of the area and the number of lights, disorientating me further. *So much shiny silver.* I squint around, then lead Leif to the opposite end of the arcade, away from the shifters who haven't spotted us. They're crowded around two car steering wheels attached to one large machine, filling the air with their noisy presence.

"You're holding my hand, Violet," Leif says once he pulls himself back to normality.

"I've held your hand before." I attempt to extricate my fingers, but he tightens his. "I suggest you let go now unless you want me to take another look into your mind."

The speed with which he releases my hand surprises me.

"I don't want to stay here long," he says.

"The shifters?"

Leif nods. "Yes. Partly because I don't want an incident between you and them."

"Oh, Rowan isn't here. I'd say we're safe from seismic events, and I doubt I'll lose control again."

"Right. The bond thing."

I purse my lips. "Yes. The bond thing."

"Y'know, I would've happily smacked the shifters threatening you that night I stepped in," he says.

"Happily? How odd."

Leif looks down at me, which only annoyingly taller people can manage. "I might not have spells or flesh-ripping teeth, but I'd fight any bastard who hurt you."

"Thank you, Leif, but that won't be necessary." I flick my fingers in their direction. "I'm more than capable of dealing with these people."

"Violet. That's why I'm offering. Grayson explained what you're 'dealing with people' looked like. If you're trying to keep out of trouble, best you let me deal with the situation."

"And let *you* get into trouble when you've shifter elders waiting to snatch you?"

His throat bobs. "Just saying. If I see you tearing into someone's flesh, I'd intervene."

I study him. Joke or not? "If I'm tearing into someone's flesh, intervening would not be a sensible idea. The hybrid Violet is unlikely to differentiate whose flesh, if there're too many limbs in the mix."

Leif breaks into a smile. "I was joking."

"I was not." I massage my neck. "Looking up at you is uncomfortable. Consider my curiosity piqued and show me this claw machine. Do you need to fight the claw?"

"I suppose."

"Is that not dangerous?"

He laughs. "Only dangerous to my wallet."

"The machine steals from you? Is that the game?"

"Oh, Violet," he chuckles. "And yes, I suppose it does steal."

How bizarre. I refocus on the shifters while Leif ponders some of the contraptions around me.

Which shifters are these? Not Viggo. If he was here, I would've definitely heard him before I set eyes on his delightful self. There're three, but I only recognize one—an assailant from the park the other night.

Reaching out with my hearing rather than into their minds, I pick up the shifters' conversation. Dull. Something about cars. They swap places in the fake leather seats, where loud revving noises and an accompanying irritating male voice emanate from the machine the steering wheels are attached to.

I turn to Leif, who's midway through an explanation about how something works that I'm not listening to. "How many shifters do you know?"

"More than I'd like. Why?"

"Do you know *that* one who barely has any hair?" I indicate the burly guy who needs to buy clothes in a larger size—and who has wounds healing along his bicep and the side of his face.

"No. Like I say, I keep away from shifters."

"Do you have your pendant? The one Grayson took from Logan?"

"Yes, I haven't taken it off. No way would I leave campus unless wearing the pendant. Why?"

The shifter Rowan attacked stares at me in a rather aggressive way; now I've no choice but to approach him. "Wait here, Leif," I say.

"Violet. What if—"

But I don't catch the end of the sentence, already approaching the shifter from the park. He takes a look behind me. "Where's your witch groupie tonight?"

"Practicing spells for the next time he meets you." He's chewing gum, a habit I find absolutely disgusting. The sound alone is like nails scraping on a chalkboard. I drop a look to his ankles. "Did Rowan burn you during your unwarranted attack on us?"

"Nah. I'm not scared of you."

"Yet you ran?"

"I *left*."

"At speed, therefore you ran." He ignores me. "Who are your friends?"

"Piss off," he says.

"How charming. Where's Viggo tonight?"

The shifter looks down his long nose at me. "With his girls."

"Girl*s*?" I pull a face. "And don't you have *girls*?"

"None of your fucking business, bitch."

"Now, that's rather rude," I say lightly, all the time stalling the conversation to edge closer to the slashed guy.

"Get the hint and piss off. You killed one of us. Tried to set fire to me. Make the most of your freedom with your *boys*." He jerks his chin at Leif. "And tell him to watch his back."

"Such unnecessary aggression." I nod at the guy pretending to drive a car around a pixelated screen, as a masculine voice from inside the machine shouts encouragement. The tense adrenaline runs from him—humans and shifters alike are easily entertained with inanity. "How did Rory's wake go?" I ask.

Another shifter snaps his head around. "Are you fucking serious?"

"Always. Deadly. Why?" The pair glance at each other and

the suede-headed guy grips the steering wheel tighter. "Am I to know something which I do not?"

The one I'm speaking to moves closer, trapping me between himself and the side of the seat. The smell of mint and testosterone wafts over me.

"Rory's wake never happened," he growls.

"Why?"

He glances at his other friend who's standing, arms crossed. "You know why."

"I'm not in the habit of asking questions if I already know the answer." He glowers. "Why? Do *you* need to be told something a number of times before you understand?"

"Watch it," he snarls.

"Please do enlighten me *why* Rory's wake never happened." My mind trips over a few theories: *Another witch? The injured shifter? So many options.* "Did something cause a postponement?"

The shifter's attempt at a menacing glare intensifies. He's evidently *not* planning to answer my question, so I casually slide into his mind.

Then reel.

Because there wasn't a body anymore.

No Rory to bury.

The guy at the wheel smacks the machine hard and swears as the moving seat judders to a halt and I hold in my shock, about to dig inside his mind for more when the seated guy stands and knocks into me.

I stumble and he sneers, believing the force of his movement unsteadied me, but that isn't why. This shifter whose injuries still show on his arm?

He's the one I attacked.

Maxwell's construct.

I'm between two of them now and not intimidated, but my mind continues to spin. I slice a look at a watchful Leif and shake my head. *Stay away.*

"Do not attempt to threaten me again," I say icily. "You're aware of my capabilities and that I don't hold back."

"Yeah? And cause trouble for yourself? You wouldn't touch us," says Park Shifter.

"Wrong. I can't help myself." I tap my lips. "My magic seems to automatically target assholes."

"Watch your mouth, little girl."

With a last disdainful look, I turn to the reanimated shifter behind and study his eyes closely. They're the typical shifter amber that Leif has too, with no sign of vacancy in them. Well, no more than usual for these guys. "Are you Ursa?"

"Yeah."

"Were you a friend of Rory's?"

"Yeah."

"And a friend of Viggo's?"

"Yeah."

"Are you able to use words with more than one syllable?" I mean, I know constructs don't have much of a mind of their own, but honestly...

But honestly? This is *not* good.

Chapter Fourteen

VIOLET

I'VE NEVER MET a necromancer's construct. Not a human one, anyway, and the shifter genuinely *doesn't* know. If he did, he'd never take part in his ordinary life, and these guys would sense his behavior change. They're shifters—despite these particular individuals' bone-headed personalities, the race is keenly tuned to each other physically. Do constructs not *smell* different?

I need his name. Somebody needs to know what's happened. Dorian. Apart from anything else, and considering Rory's fate, the shifter's second life will be in danger. I've a small sense of relief that the scowling guy hasn't recollected our last encounter.

"Who inflicted your injuries?" I ask. "Recent ones since they haven't healed yet. I do hope you didn't attack humans."

He narrows his eyes as he looks behind me, every muscle in his overly large body tensing. Scars from freshly healed scratches show at the edge of his T-shirt collar, touching his neck.

How close did I come to seriously injuring or killing him?

"Violet. Come on." Leif. Now by my side.

"He can't remember who hurt him," says Park Shifter and has the audacity to jab me in the chest. "Just like he can't remember the night Rory died when some murderous asshole killed him. Is she the one you saw hanging around, Oz? Recognize the bitch now you see her? Was the other witch around?"

Oz peers at me. "Something's familiar about her, yeah."

"I'm well known in this locality."

"Violet," repeats Leif and uses handholding as a distraction.

Park Shifter sneers at his action. "Aww. Sweet. What does the witch think? He gonna kill *this* shifter for touching you?"

I pull my hand away, unable to drop my focus on Oz, desperately pushing into his mind and getting nowhere, because there's nothing but a void swallowing my magic.

"Nah. She's screwing one of each," says the third guy. "Shifter, witch, vamp. Probably all at once."

"I'm not a shifter," says Leif coolly.

"And neither are we intimate," I add.

Oz knocks into me again, a deliberately hard nudge from his shoulder which doesn't move me at all. His mouth opens and I wait for whatever not-smart comment comes next. Instead, he staggers forward, and I take a step back before he can collide me. The shifter makes a gargled sound and drops to his knees, grasping the machine's chair to steady himself.

"Dude, what's wrong?" asks Park Shifter. "You said everything's okay now."

Both Oz's hands cover his head, and he responds with an inhuman, high-pitched whining.

Everything? Every *what*?

"What's wrong with him?" asks Leif

The whining builds, competing with the jangling cacophony of music from the arcade.

"Told you he'd taken shit again, Garrick," mutters the other guy. "Oz, get up."

But the shifter now convulses in the small space between the machines, and I watch in horrified fascination as pink foam spills from his mouth, his limbs jerking.

"Violet!" urges Leif, and pulls me backwards.

"He doesn't usually do *that*," snarls Garrick, and lunges at me. "What did you do to him?"

I deftly side-step. "Me? Nothing. I haven't touched him."

Apart from the other night when I tried to rip his skin off.

The third shifter wipes broad hands down his face and crouches. "Oz! What the fuck have you taken?"

"You indulge in drug taking?" I ask them.

"I'm calling an ambulance," says Leif in panic as others approach, a small crowd gathering in the claustrophobic space.

"What did you do?" shouts Garrick. "Oz never reacted this badly before."

"You just intimated Oz is suffering from a reaction to illicit substances," I retort. "I did not supply him with such."

"And that makes his fucking ears bleed does it?" snarls his friend beside him.

What?

Blood leaks from Oz's ears and the foam spittle turns deeper pink as the shifter gasps and gargles, the mess streaking the gray tiles beneath his head.

"You're killing him! Stop!" shouts Garrick.

"I'm not doing anything," I say calmly.

But cold trickles through my blood, a new uncomfortable and annoying response to the world, the same as when Grayson had the witch's heart in his hand.

Panic.

Is Oz's current condition what happens to a construct when their witch dies?

"Get him out. No ambulance. No human's touching him. They'd use the excuse to finish the job. Or that bitch's dad would interfere, so she gets away with this." The third shifter speaks quickly, holding Oz beneath the arms, then lifting him.

Oz can't stand—makes no attempt to—head lolled forward as the pair struggle to stop their friend crashing to the tiles again.

I look around to where Leif stands nearby on the phone, fingers gripping his hair as he speaks. A male uniformed staff member joins the throng, and he commands me to step back.

But I need to watch.

To understand.

The burly shifters half-drag Oz away and they hulk over and

argue with the slender girl who served Leif the drink earlier. By now, some from the bowling lanes crowd the exit from the arcade, and as the shifters rather charmingly shout at everybody to fuck off, they pull Oz across the floor, his boots squeaking as they do.

Many visiting this place of teen frivolity are from the academy, and others are from the fateful party. Accusing looks are thrown my way and whispered rumors begin again. While others stare, unmoving, I follow. I *must* see every second of this scenario.

Two paramedics in distinctive green clothing appear and I'm convinced a fist fight will break out between the shifters and medics as they extricate the still convulsing Oz from his friends. Both shifters pursue the medics to the ambulance, and I sneak outside the building onto the sidewalk, hiding as best I can amongst the onlookers.

The pair of shifters enter the rear of the ambulance with one of the medics and Oz, and the vehicle dashes away into the evening, lights flashing as brightly as the arcade's. As I stand and watch, Leif emerges and winds an arm around my shoulders.

I huff and pull myself from Leif's attempt to hold me.

"What did you do this time?" a surprisingly brave human guy asks me.

I regard the humans gathered on the sidewalk too, where a girl in a thin shirt beside me rubs her cold arms.

"Nothing. If I were the murderer, I'd hardly commit a crime in a public place."

"You made a mistake with Wes, didn't you?" Marci stands nearby, arms folded across her chest. "Why are you killing shifters?"

"You evidently have poor eyesight. Oz is unwell but not deceased."

"Yet," she says flatly and steps towards me.

We're a similar height, but Marci's not as slim as I am— muscular shoulders and torso, and I imagine a good swimmer with her physique. What's her surname? I must ask Rowan when I 'say hi' for her.

"If you're concerned I'm killing shifters, then there's no reason for Holly to stay away from me, since she's human," I say calmly. "But I am not, and I'm becoming tired of these attempts to implicate me."

Was Oz's state a response to Maxwell's death or another attempt to frame me? Rowan never mentioned that food or drinks could be poisoned in a bowling alley murder scenario.

Holly stands nearby watching, Chase behind with his arms around her waist. Has Marci convinced Holly I'm somehow involved or has Holly watched me ever since day one?

Marci's eyes flick to Leif and then back to me before she stares at his chest and laughs softly. "You're going to need that, Leif."

The pendant.

Marci turns back to Holly and speaks quietly. Holly's gaze meets mine, and the fizzy soda in my stomach suddenly burns when she turns away.

I remain totally still, challenging anybody else to speak to me until every one of them moves away. Then I turn and walk back into the building.

There could be clues. Remnants of magic or poison if used.

Leif hurries after me. "You okay?"

"Why wouldn't I be?" I ask, wandering back to the arcade. Yet another male staff member, older and grumbling, already arrived to mop up the mess Oz made on the floor, a yellow sign beside him warning of a slippery surface.

"Uh. Are you okay after more accusations?" he asks in disbelief.

"I've had a most enlightening evening, and the fun isn't over yet."

Leif's look is one that's become familiar amongst the guys—somewhere between confusion and concern.

"I'll call Rowan and ask him to join us," I say.

"Join us in what?"

I gesture at the arcade. "I'm not running from the scene of my so-called crime. I shall call Rowan, ask him to meet us, and then we can visit the hospital."

"The *what*?" Leif's eyes go extra wide.

"Tomorrow, we should investigate Marci, her position at the school, and parentage." I take hold of the pendant that's warm from resting against his skin. My fingers brush his chest as I do. If I did ever need Leif's help, he certainly matches my father Ethan for his stone-like solidity—although his skin is surprisingly soft, and he doesn't have scales like Ethan's. "Marci knows what this means. Yet she isn't wearing one and neither were any of her male friends tonight."

Leif blinks in the direction Marci walked. "This is mad."

"Show me one of these machines you're eager to play with," I tell Leif as I pull out my phone to text Rowan.

"I can't believe we're staying here," he mutters.

"Then should I ask Rowan to meet us at the hospital instead?"

He stiffens. "That's a bad idea. Rowan won't agree."

I tap the screen.

I need you

The message wings its way to Rowan, and I pause. Hmm. I alarmed Rowan the last time I used those words. He requested that I'm more specific in the future.

Dutifully, I add and send:

A shifter I met might be dead

There. Clearer information. Less for Rowan to panic about.

My phone immediately rings, and I answer.

"What the fuck, Violet?"

Yet *still* Rowan panics. Will Leif? I pivot to look up at him. "I forgot to mention—Oz is the Ursa shifter I almost killed." He looks at me as if I've slapped him, and I grin. "I think we're onto something."

Chapter Fifteen

VIOLET

A CIRCULAR WOODEN bench surrounds a solitary maple tree, one of several saplings at intervals along the sidewalk outside the hospital. I sit with Leif on the edge, as I run through events in my head, making connections, looking for gaps.

The skies clouded since I stood outside to watch the ambulance leave with Oz, adding an apt chill to the air. Holly grumbled the other day about how the weather isn't very spring-like recently. Another odd human trait—the need to discuss local meteorological conditions.

In the time we remained in the arcade, Leif indulged in his love of clawed machines—which aren't as fascinating or sinister as I imagined—while I snooped around for hints of magic. Although hampered by the array of scents in the bowling alley and attached café, I'm confident there's no sign of magic use. This included a subtle scout around the area Marci occupied. Nothing. If somebody within the arcade poisoned the shifter, he or she either left or was one amongst a large number playing on the machines at the time I entered.

I deduce that the effect on Oz resulted from his broken link to Maxwell. If witches intend to retrieve or kill him before anybody discover what he is, risking that discovery by creating something public makes no sense.

Unless they intended him to die in my vicinity?

Always a possibility.

I conducted a calmer phone conversation with Rowan that became less calm when I told him about Rory's missing body. At least Leif dropped into the silence that *he* favors when I communicated the unpleasant revelations to him.

Holly was still at the bowling alley when I left for the hospital with Leif. Oddly, many humans and witches returned to their evening frivolity after the interruption. Perhaps if Oz had actually died they might've paused for thought?

"Witches are slow," I grumble.

"Rowan doesn't have a car and can't walk as fast as me or you, Violet," Leif reminds me.

"We honestly need to improve our resources should our investigations become a regular task," I comment.

"Excuse me?"

"Well, you don't think these murders are the only thing that will ever need solving, do you, Leif?" I shake my head and he scowls at my despairing look. "You don't *need* to stay involved."

"As if," he mutters.

"Honestly, I never realized the world held such mystery and challenge, otherwise I might've *asked* to come to Thornwood." I can't deny the small thrill that zings through each time I discover an answer or solve a problem. Who knew this activity could enliven me? Be *fun*.

A long bus with a huge female face advertising lipstick plastered to the side pulls up to the nearby stop, and I stand expectantly as the doors hiss open.

Rowan leaps down the steps and marches over, and I wait for an awkward hug, but Rowan doesn't appear to be in a hugging mood. This face and aura generally mean he's irritated with me.

"Why weren't you more specific?" he demands. "How 'almost dead' is the shifter? *Who* is the shifter?"

"Oz, and I haven't inquired yet. We're waiting for you,

Rowan. I thought *that* decision would cause a better mood than this."

Rowan peers at the bench and grabs something. "What the hell is this?" He holds the white plush toy—presumably a dog of some description—by the ear. "Something for my psychometry? Why would a shifter carry a toy?"

"Leif gave me that," I say. "From a pointless exercise that involved a metal claw and a lot of money."

"I succeeded on the third try," Leif replies coolly. "Some people never win anything."

Rowan's burst of laughter drifts through the empty space. "You won a *toy dog* for Violet?"

"I was aiming for a different item," he retorts. "But at least I won *something*."

The joy on Leif's face when he achieved his bizarre task seemed disproportionate to *what* he won, and I had no idea how to respond. At first, I thought he must be attracted to plush toys, as Holly is, but he denied this and seemed rather annoyed. I then suggested he could gift the toy to Holly, since she may wish to add to her plush animal collection. That seemed to annoy him more.

Then he stared at me for a very long time until another theory settled in my mind.

Leif retrieved the item for *me*.

Good grief. *A toy dog?* I hastily added my gratitude but requested he carry the monstrosity.

"Perhaps you could explain, further Rowan," I say. "I'm also confused by his choice. Why would Leif not select an item *he'd* like?"

"Are you completely clueless?" Rowan asks me.

"Pardon?"

"Forget it," mumbles Leif.

"No. Violet needs to hear these things," says Rowan firmly. "Leif won that for you because he's a guy who likes you. You were on a date."

I stare at Rowan. Then I look at Leif. And back to Rowan. A lot of responses enter my head, and my new and improved ability to hold my tongue needs utilizing. Why on earth would a guy give a girl this fluffy dog as a token of affection?

I'm unsure what's the most difficult in my life currently. Navigating the sea of murder charges or riding the choppy waters of relationships. *All* relationships, not only the romantic ones circling me.

The pair look at me expectantly.

"Leif's gift is thoughtful, but I prefer body parts."

Rowan's smile drops a moment, and he exchanges a glance with Leif. One thing I'm learning to enjoy is the ability to say things that a) shut people up and b) keep them guessing because 'it's Violet speaking'. They want me to learn self-awareness and consider other's feelings? That, I'm working on.

"Ha ha, Violet," says Rowan. Cautiously.

Pursing my lips, I take the fluffy toy from Rowan and tuck the thing under my arm.

"You need to give the dog a name," says Rowan with a sly smile.

"That is the most ridiculous thing anybody has ever said to me. Why would I name an inanimate object?"

"Just leave it, Rowan," mutters Leif.

"I said, I appreciate the gesture. Now, can we move our focus away from toys?" I say. "I'm concerned whether Oz died a second time because if he has, that will be extremely inconvenient."

Chapter Sixteen

VIOLET

THE HOSPITAL DOORS open to a large reception area, where the white cleanliness bounces from wall to ceiling, and I wince at the glaring spotlights above. A vague, unpleasant smell of human sickness and disinfectant fills my nostrils.

A long desk complete with a tall Perspex screen greets us. The woman sitting behind does not. Honestly, she should be sleeping, not working, because the young woman's brown eyes are circled black, and not from kohl. I approach, and I momentarily consider she might be hemia, due to her severely scraped back brown hair and pale face. But the possibility a human hospital would employ a blood-feeding vamp are below zero.

"I need to visit the emergency room," I say and show my teeth in a smile.

"What's wrong with you?" she asks and looks me up and down.

"I'm not sure. There are many theories."

The woman sighs and taps her keyboard. "Why are you here?"

"To visit a friend. In ER. He collapsed and foamed at the

mouth. Blood also leaked from his ears. An ambulance collected him from the arcade; therefore, he must be here. Oz. Take me to him."

"Violet," whispers Rowan. "Let me." He attempts to make his way between me and the screen.

The woman looks up. "Are any of you immediate family? No? Then, no."

Ugh. I do not have time for that many nos. Fixing my eyes on the woman's unimpressed ones, I wind her thoughts around my mental fingers—ones filled with rather rude opinions about me "You should let—" A slicing white pain slashes my own mind and I clutch my temples. "Rowan!"

"Mind control is illegal," comes his voice beside my ear.

"And in this case, necessary," I growl.

The woman beckons at someone behind us. "Come forward," she tells them.

I'm forced to move to one side as a sweaty-faced young human man shoves a wheelchair almost over my feet, which contains a woman with a contorting face who's holding her overlarge stomach, face also perspiring.

"Not here!" she yells at the pale man, whose hands shake on the handles.

Then the curly-haired woman makes such an appalling noise that I hastily back away. "I never touched her!" I protest.

Rowan snorts a laugh and I protest again as he pulls me aside to allow the man to speak to the woman behind the screen. I stride over to Leif, who waits close to the exit on the off chance Oz makes a miraculous recovery and leaves via this route.

"Why didn't you go through into the ER?" he asks.

"Violet," answers Rowan, with an entirely too weary tone for a guy who's spent so little time in my company tonight.

I suck on my teeth and again step aside as the doors to the hospital open. A guy limps by, a blood-stained, makeshift bandage wrapped around his leg, and he joins the strange fray ahead of us.

The large woman continues to yell at the man about his level of stupidity and that once this is over she intends to do unpleasant things to him. I'm not known for my gratitude, but this man accompanied her to the hospital when needed, and therefore deserves thanks and not threats.

"That woman radiates excruciating pain. She'll definitely enter the ER. We could sneak in after her?" I suggest.

"Violet. She's having a baby, and the father brought her to the wrong part of the hospital," says Rowan.

I recoil. "Oh. Ugh. I've seen that on a show. She won't lie down and produce the thing here, will she? That will make an unpleasant amount of mess, and more than a mop would be needed."

"Violet," urges Rowan. "Why do you have to be so *loud?*"

The horrific pain radiates from the woman despite her dropping back into silence. "That is another reason I'm not interested in a sexual relationship with you, Rowan," I announce and point. "Look at the result."

Leif snorts as Rowan drags me closer and through the exit. "Again, loud voice, Violet."

The doors swish closed behind us and the breeze ruffles Rowan's hair.

"Sounds like you need a chat with your mother about certain things," says Leif with a throaty chuckle.

I narrow my eyes. "Do you still heal quickly, Leif?"

His laughter instantly stops. "Alright, I'm sorry for teasing."

"No. Can I bite you?"

"Huh?"

"I guess she really hated the dog," says Rowan.

"Good grief!" I shake my head, still unpleasantly aware of the woman, and man with the injured leg. Was I unwise to walk into a hospital environment? Not due to the blood, but this *bloody awful* new ability to sense people's feelings.

"Can I bite you?" I repeat. "The nurse might let everybody through if one of us is injured or in great pain."

"Are you insane?" whispers Rowan.

I slant my head. "Have we not discussed the issues with society's definitions of insanity?"

"Yeah but asking to bite a guy so that he's injured enough for us to enter the emergency room fits the 'psycho' definition."

I ignore him. "Yes or no, Leif?" Is he stepping backwards?

"Leif would very much like your mouth on him but probably not your teeth," says Rowan.

A yell that would wake the proverbial dead manages to force through the doors and into the night, and I spin around in alarm. Several uniformed hospital staff appear and all focus switches to the unfortunate woman and her semi-hysterical partner. The woman behind the desk is now on the phone, while the other man has collapsed on the floor and his leg bleeds onto the shiny tiles.

And people say that my society is macabre?

"I'd rather have another fence post through my chest than experience *that*," I comment as I stride past the woman to hit the large red button on the left of the doors to the ER.

"Your child would probably eat its way out," comments Rowan.

I halt and blink at his bizarrely rude theory. "And you say *I'm* insane? *I* didn't enter the world that way."

Or at least I don't think I did.

"You might regret that comment," Leif whispers to Rowan as he passes us. "You heard what Violet said about a sexual relationship. Never happening if you say things like that to her."

Rowan glares at the back of his head. "She should've bitten you."

"Good grief!" I say at the volume Rowan recently found inappropriate. Although my exclamation isn't in response to their conversation, but the scene of misery ahead of me.

Row after row of gray plastic chairs fill the emergency room, and there's a similar smaller reception desk nearby. At the opposite end of the room, another set of double doors lead somewhere else. A woman in a green uniform emerges from behind those doors and towards the reception desk.

Some injuries aren't visible, but blood seeps from some humans' skin or soaks their clothes. "Has anybody seen Grayson tonight?" I ask.

"Headed off campus for one of his meetings?" suggests Rowan. "We should stop him from going to his uncle anymore. What if something happens?"

"Something *will* happen—to Josef and not to him," I say. "I'll guarantee that."

"I'll check on Grayson once we're done here," says Leif.

Despite the amount of human misery, nobody's writhing on the floor, although there *is* some yelling and children crying at an eardrum-piercing pitch. I wander to the desk, teeth on edge. I thought shopping malls were bad, but this misery-filled purgatory is a whole new level of human Hell.

I approach a desk manned by a guy with a nurse's lanyard and the same weary look as his colleague. "What happens to the half-dead individuals who arrive via ambulance?" I ask.

"Take a seat," he says curtly.

"They take a *seat?*" I turn and scan the room again. "Which seat?"

"No, miss. *You* take a seat."

"But I'm looking for a half-dead person," I continue. "A shifter. Have you seen him?"

The nurse ducks his head to take a clearer look through the screen at my companions. "Is she with you?"

"Yes, *she* is. It's extremely important that I find this person," I continue. "I believe his life might be in danger."

Tired brown eyes turn my way. "Well, if he's half-dead, yes, he would be in danger, but will be receiving treatment. Sit down."

The man pushes hair from his face and looks at a computer screen, so I take a calming breath.

He flicks another look at me when I don't move. "Are you a vampire?"

"How's that relevant?"

"There's a policy against allowing the blood-sucking ones into this hospital. I'll call security if you don't leave."

"I'm half-vampire, but I don't like blood."

"Half?" He peers again. "How does that work?"

"I am also a necromancer so could offer my services if you'd like to keep your hospital death rate low."

"A necromancer?" He arches a brow. "Oh, really?"

"Yes. And these companions are the result of my excellent work," I continue, indicating Leif and Rowan. "Can I visit the half-dead person now?" The nurse's lips thin until I can barely see them. "Please?"

He swears beneath his breath, then tips his head as if paying attention to someone else. Glancing at me, the nurse then nods, before gesturing to his right, towards empty seats. Leif takes my shoulders and guides me away.

"You indicated to the nurse that I'm mentally unwell," I retort. Rowan stands over me, so I'm forced to sit. "Which one of you did that?"

"Remember how acting like a normal person can help with your investigations, Violet?" Leif says. "Because this behavior really *isn't* normal or helpful."

"I was merely playing for time. Talk of necromancy tends to distract people and could've given you an opportunity to find Oz." I huff. Do they never appreciate my skills? "Rowan won't let me use mind-control so we *need* to do something."

"It's likely Oz's through there in triage." Rowan points to the second set of doors. "We need to figure out how to get inside or at least discover if they took Oz to a ward. Or ICU, possibly."

"Well, a bit of mind control would help with that," I say pointedly.

"Right. So. A shifter collapsing and convulsing half to death in front of Violet Blackwood who then arrives at the hospital and uses mind control to find him, and *then* he possibly dies. Good scenario?" Rowan shakes his head. "Even your presence inside the hospital isn't a great idea. We shouldn't be here."

"I'd do what I want, whether you agree or not."

"Sweet Violet, don't you think I've learned that by now? At least when I'm with you, I can minimize the damage."

I ignore his saccharin name for me. "He'd better not die," I mutter. "Die *again*, I mean."

"You think he might?" whispers Leif, who sits in the bolted down seat beside me.

"If I'm unlucky, yes."

"Hmm." Leif's lips purse. "You mean if *he's* unlucky?"

"Oz isn't blessed with good fortune as it is, Leif," I say pointedly. "A permanent death is an unpleasant prospect, but which would you prefer? Death or undeath?"

"I hope I never bloody find out."

"But what do we *do*?" I ask. "Apart from attempt to get through there." I point at the doors the female nurse has returned through. "Are you *sure* I can't use mind control?"

Rowan looks at me as if I'm stupid, so I bare my teeth at him.

"Snarling doesn't help with the 'act like a normal person' idea, Violet," he says.

"Be quiet. I need to think."

"Anybody want something from the vending machine?" asks Leif and points to one in the opposite corner. I've seen these around the academy, usually empty. I've also frequently seen Leif using them.

"Um. We're busy?" I say.

He shrugs and stands. "I'm not staying here to listen to the Violet and Rowan Show. I'll get a soda; tell me what you decide to do."

Leif wanders away, through the rows of suffering. Humans must lead extremely inconvenient lives. The burden from physical damage or disease would be enough to deal with, but the *waiting*. Humans are always waiting for something.

Slumping back, I drag my phone from a pocket and run through my notes. A woman in green pants and top to match the guy behind the desk holds her lanyard up to a pad on the left of the door I'm itching to walk through.

"We need a lanyard," I say and nudge Rowan. "Or can your computer-magic-whatever help, like at the police station?"

"No, I can't locate the hospital computer mainframe and disable everything," he says.

"Why not?"

"Do you even understand what I said?"

"No, but that's not uncommon." His lips press together. "Why can't you?"

"Because it's impossible." He studies me for a moment. "How was bowling?"

"Brief."

"Did you have fun?"

I frown. Why the sudden interest and cold edge to his aura? "Define fun."

Rowan looks at me. "Did anything make you smile? Elicit small feelings of happiness?"

"Are you being sarcastic? I can never tell when your face doesn't move."

"At least you didn't leave empty-handed."

"Agreed. The evening was fruitful, despite not speaking to many local humans. Kai is under curfew and hopefully safer. We now know who the bear shifter is, and if he's still unalive, that will be an added bonus."

Rowan nods at the dog's ear protruding from my pocket. "I meant that."

"Oh. Right. Well, I observed Holly's interactions with Marci, and I have new suspicions. We need to discuss Marci tomorrow. What do you know about her?" Rowan shrugs. "She said something odd, Rowan. Marci told me she 'missed your chats', which implies that you and she were once in a relationship."

There're a lot of silences tonight.

"Yeah. Kind of," he says eventually and digs hands into his pockets, stretching out his legs.

"Oh." That twinge in my chest again, like the time he walked out of the room the night I died. I place a hand over my heart—hasn't my body healed fully?

"Does that bother you?" he asks cautiously. "Mine and Marci's relationship ended a long time ago."

"Not at all. In fact, your past dalliance could prove useful. You'll know plenty about Marci." I lower my voice, even though the nearest human, a young guy with a glazed look, sits several seats away. "She's now on my suspect list."

"Why?"

"Because she doesn't like me."

Rowan chuckles. "That puts a *lot* of people on your list, Violet."

"Only the ones I disagree with."

"You argued? Crap." Rowan straightens. "Where is Marci?"

"We didn't *argue*. Marci finds me disagreeable and informed me of such. Besides, she isn't a shifter. Nobody will kill her." I look over my shoulder to where Leif stands in front of the vending machine. Is the decision what to eat *that* important?

"I admire your confidence, Violet."

"Thank you."

A man in a crisp, charcoal gray suit approaches the desk, closely followed by another. Witch energy hits me and I study them closer. The sharp cut of their suits accentuates slim, athletic physiques. One has a dark wave of black hair, slicked back neatly and not a strand out of place, adding a touch of suave sophistication to his appearance. The other shares a well-groomed appearance but more artfully styled hair. Quite the contrast to the scruffy humans and their ailments and injuries.

They strike a perfect display of authority that would easily persuade the nurse they're here for a legitimate reason.

Especially as one shows the nurse an ID card or similar, and I nudge Rowan. "Look."

The nurse finds the men worth conversing with and I watch, pissed when *they're* not dismissed to a waiting seat.

Why are they here? Witches have their own, private medical facilities—which doesn't assist the 'them and us' conflict with humans. Like the shifters, humans wouldn't know that Oz isn't fully alive any longer, or that his brain's practically dead. As far as I know, shifters deal with minor medical issues themselves, and only use human hospitals if the shifter suffers life-threatening injuries.

Such as convulsions and abnormal bleeding on the floor in a bowling alley.

The witches shouldn't be here and are clearly not ill or injured. From the supe council? They're official looking in their suits and with the cards they're showing the nurse. Rowan swears and slumps down in his chair, yanking up his blue jacket hood to obscure his face. I merely straighten and watch.

As one witch speaks, the other turns and takes a casual look around, hands idly in his trouser pockets. His gaze rests on me for a few seconds, but his expression remains unchanged. I search for my phone.

As I hold it on my lap and subtly take a photo, Rowan slaps my hand. The witch makes to walk over, but he's interrupted by the second one who points at the double-doors to my current dream destination.

Rowan almost falls from his seat as someone hits him in the back. I twist around in mine in case said person attempts to assault me too and look straight at Leif's own broad back.

"Get out," he growls, not turning. "I know them."

"But I was about to get through—" I point at the doors even though I hadn't quite decided *how* I was about to get through. *Point*-lessly since Leif isn't facing me.

"The witches have seen us. We need to leave." Rowan stands, looking between Leif and the door.

"Who are—" he begins, but Leif's already almost out the other door in long strides.

Chapter Seventeen

VIOLET

I'M TORN between asking Rowan to follow Leif while I follow the witches or go with him to our friend.

I leave with Rowan

Leif isn't in the now-empty hospital entrance, and when we make our way outside, he also isn't on or near the bench by the bus stop. Or anywhere on the smoothly paved approach to the hospital building.

"Where is he?" Rowan asks.

I walk to the edge of the sidewalk and look in both directions, focusing all my senses. "This way."

Leif's scent takes us along the side of the ER and to a tree-lined path that leads towards another part of the hospital grounds.

"The trunks aren't large enough to hide behind, Leif," I inform him, approaching the muscular guy's position semi-hidden behind a maple tree. Low bushes also run along the dark pathway, and I push my way through.

"I'm not hiding; I don't want the witches to see me."

"Isn't that the same thing?" I ask.

"How do you know the witches?" asks Rowan.

Leif's silent, and his aura thickens. "Memories."

"From the night Rory died?" I ask and glance behind me. Nobody. "The witches were there?"

"One of them definitely," he says stiffly.

Chewing on my lip, I locate my phone and the picture. "Him?"

Leif nods curtly.

"Did *you* recognize either witch?" I ask Rowan.

"No. And he won't like that you have his picture."

"I took the photo *subtly*, Rowan."

"Unlikely, Violet." I open my mouth to protest. "He'll know who you are," Rowan continues. "What if the witches look for you?"

"They're here for Oz." I slide the phone back into my pocket. "Isn't that obvious?"

"To do what?" asks Leif, voice rising in pitch. "*Kill* him?"

There're a number of possibilities here and none will end well for Oz. Not that things are going brilliantly for him right now. "How many exits from the hospital?"

"Loads." Rowan huffs.

"I don't think we'll get through into the triage area, Violet." Leif pauses. "The main entrance and the place ambulances arrive are worth watching. You go. I'd rather stay out of sight."

"And what if the witches take you too?" I say. "No."

"If the witches are here for Oz, I doubt they'll hang around," replies Rowan.

"They might finish him inside the hospital," says Leif. "Make it look like *that's* how he died."

"No. The witches want his body. Him," I say.

Rowan wanders back along the pathway and stands in the shadows, to the left of where streetlights illuminate the way. I march after him. "Why did you walk away?"

He glances back at Leif. "I'm worried about him."

"Leif's remembered something. That's positive," I say.

"Mmm." Rowan looks forward to the hospital entrance again. "Maybe."

"I'll send the photo to Dorian. They were officials—or

pretending to be. They're linked to Maxwell in some way." I straighten. "This is exciting. We're getting closer."

Rowan's eyes glint in the dark as he looks back at me. "Helpful yes, but exciting isn't the word."

I tap my lips. "They won't walk out the front. Too obvious. Where's this ambulance place? Or somewhere with less surveillance?"

"You sure about that?" asks Leif, who approaches us. "Reckon they *expected* us to look elsewhere."

Three men walk across the pavers leading towards the sidewalk. The two witches and Oz. Walking without support.

"What the hell?" mutters Rowan.

A dark sedan pulls up close to the bus stop, and I scramble to get my phone from a pocket, ready to dart out and take more pictures. They already know I'm here and I *want* the witches to know that I'm onto them. But the three move too fast and by the time I'm ready, the car sped off around the corner, before I have a chance to read the license plate.

"They might be powerful enough to pull off what they did to get Oz out of the hospital," comments Rowan, "but at least they needed to use actual transport."

"Rather than blood magic?" I clench my jaw and glare at the place the car stopped momentarily. "Only witches with Blackwood blood mixed in their ancestry can use blood magic, and even then only basic."

The founding witch families' magic determine every witch's personal specialty—their skills match which family's bloodline is strongest inside them. The school of magic that they're linked to is noted on a database, as the close supervision of all supernaturals is key to our accords with humans. Each witch is tested around their twelfth birthday to ascertain this. If not, their parents are prosecuted.

But there're always exceptions and the number must be growing if Dorian had no idea who Maxwell is. Where are these witches hiding? Are vamps involved too?

"They might know blood magic but keep that hidden," says Rowan. "Plus, they're aware we've seen them."

"I don't understand the shifter connection to the witches," says Leif. "And Sawyer. Do you think he's aware what's happening?"

"Maybe?" I say. "But he's worried about Kai's safety. If Sawyer was involved in the murders, he'd know not to worry because the man wouldn't ask someone to kill his own son."

"No, that was his witch buddy's idea," says Rowan. "Kai's a definite target. And still no police reports about anything but Kai's DUI. What has Sawyer involved himself in that he needs to cover up?"

"And Grayson's uncle?" I ask.

He shrugs.

"The most important thing is Oz's life," says Leif. "What if the witches kill him?"

I exchange a glance with Rowan. "They can't kill him, Leif. He's already dead."

Leif's whole body tightens, and he stares ahead. "Yeah."

"You alright?" asks Rowan. "You're pretty freaked out by the witches."

"Did you remember anything else the witches did that night?" I ask. "Should I make a note before you forget again? Which one touched you? What else did they do?"

Leif doesn't move or look back at me, and Rowan doesn't respond either.

"*Now* what have I said?" I ask. There wasn't one negative thing in that question. Leif's new memories helpful to both me *and* him.

Nearby, more humans head towards the hospital, their voices cutting through the silence I've created.

"At least I can use blood runes," I say. "We can return to the academy quicker and look over tonight's findings."

More silence. Surely they don't want to catch the *bus*.

Leif finally turns to me. "I'll walk back to the academy. See you tomorrow."

And he's gone, figure moving swiftly to cross the sidewalk.

"What's he doing? Isn't Leif worried about shifters?" I ask. "Didn't he hide until a few days ago?"

Rowan turns his eyes to mine. "Maybe Leif remembered something he didn't *want* to, Violet, and doesn't appreciate your interrogation."

"Oh."

"Let me guess. You hadn't considered that possibility."

"And now he wants to be alone?" I rub my nose. "Should we follow him? I don't want anything unpleasant to happen to Leif."

"Why? Because he's useful and also not immortal?"

Last time I voiced concern for Leif's welfare, I barely understood why I'd said the wrong thing, but this time I'm aware. "No. Because he's a nice guy," I say, and show Rowan the toy dog. "Even if he doesn't understand me at all."

"Leif understands you more than you think, Violet. We all do." He gestures around him. "Choose somewhere to paint your blood runes that won't freak out passing humans. I'll fetch Leif back here and we can leave. Together."

Chapter Eighteen

VIOLET

HOLLY POSSIBLY RETURNED to the academy and our room—
if she isn't staying with Marci—so I aim the blood runes spell at
the woods near the edge of campus. I don't want to land in the
middle of our room again if Holly's there because I don't want
questions.

Dorian removed the block on my using blood runes within
the academy, but I no longer care that I'm using magic banned
in the school. Besides, trouble with faculty about illicit magic is
the least of my current worries.

The two guys sit on the ground, as dazed as they were last
time, and hold a quiet conversation. I stand close by, kicking at
the dirt while I wait. The trees stand guard around us, and
Rowan pulls himself up, a hand on a trunk silhouetted against
the gloomy night.

"What do we do now?" I ask him.

Both his brows raise. "*You're* asking *me*?"

"Oz. How do we find him?"

"I doubt we could tonight, Violet. We've no idea where to
start. Tomorrow, we'll figure this out."

I grit my teeth. He's correct.

"You need to tell Dorian before we do anything else," he adds. "And don't look like that, you can't do everything alone. Dorian can look into the witches, and we'll explore Marci and Holly's involvement. Look into every professor's background."

"Oh. Yes. We can. I could start tonight. Can you get me a full list?"

"Violet. Can this wait until tomorrow? There're more important issues." Rowan inclines his head to Leif on the ground. "Can you talk to Leif?" he asks quietly.

"What? Now? Here?" Why hasn't he moved? "Oh. The memories issue." Rowan nods. "Very well. Get me the list in the morning."

Rowan moves a strand of hair from my face, watching how his cool fingers touch my skin, mouth tipping at one corner. "Good grief," he says. "Is that a sliver of empathy?"

"Leif helps me, I'd like to help him."

"Uh huh."

"You can stop touching my hair now."

Rowan shakes his head and steps back. "You're hard work, Violet Blackwood." I scowl when he pokes my nose. "Although I am looking forward to the Spring Ball."

"You're going to the Spring Ball?" asks Leif as he looks up.

"No."

"Yes."

Rowan and I respond at the same time, then Rowan smirks his smirk and wanders away.

"List!" I shout after him.

"Dorian!" he calls back.

I shift to look down at Leif, who's in the same position as the day we spoke alone, knees against his chest. "There's no point in me asking you to the dance, then?" he says, annoyingly amused.

"No. Because I'm not going. I've repeatedly told Holly such and I'm not backing down." I kneel on the damp grass in front of Leif. "What's the matter? Is there something in your memories you want to discuss?"

Leif falls into silence yet again, and I hear his heart rate speed as the faint breeze carries through the trees. He shivers. "Am *I* one?" he whispers eventually, eyes to the ground.

"One what? I wish people wouldn't be so obtuse."

He looks up. "A necromancer's... 'thing'. What if I am and don't know? Oz doesn't and Rory didn't."

"No, Leif. You are not."

"How do you *know*?" he presses.

"Because I could see your mind and memories. A very splintered version, but your mind is your own. If you were reanimated, your mind would be a void."

"But what if the witches used magic to change that?"

Leif's panic surrounds him—in his wavering voice and his eyes, wide and shining in the dark. How long has Leif convinced himself of this?

"Leif." I reach out to him, surprising myself as much as Leif when I rest fingers on his warm hand. "I promise that you are very much alive and under nobody's influence."

His fingers grip mine, as if holding onto me could transmit the truth. "And the mind-control? What if that's happening? You once thought Rowan controlled me. Why was that?"

"Because I suspected Rowan was capable of underhanded things. Nothing you did or didn't do prompted me to think he controlled you." I allow Leif to keep a hold of my hand. "*Have* you remembered something?"

"Only that witch's face—the one from the hospital—and clearer images of my surroundings. There were *three*. One could've been Maxwell. What if they're all necromancers? There could be others out there who they killed and—"

"Highly probable. I'm glad you're not a shifter, otherwise they might've killed you too that night." Leif chokes a small sound. "Because I suspect they're only using necromancy on shifters, since they're already partially disconnected from society."

And easier to attack magically.

Leif's silence returns before he eventually says, "I hadn't considered that."

I'm distracted by his hand around mine, another reminder

how Leif really *is* closer to shifter than human size, but don't pull away.

The more I'm around people, the more their incessant need to touch begins to make sense. They're doing what I've spent a lifetime avoiding—connecting. Leif's hand hold isn't the odd and slightly proprietary type from earlier, but a need for reassurance. The idea I could reassure anybody remains laughable to me, but as I might say or do the wrong thing should Leif's distress grow, I prefer his hand on mine.

But I don't like that he's distressed.

"Are you looking for more memories?" he asks hesitantly.

"Not currently. Why?" I squeeze his fingers and he winces. "I am attempting to remove some of your anxiety."

"Like, with magic?"

"With touch, like normal people do." He takes my other hand, and my eyes go wide. "I don't need to hold both of them, Leif."

"Can you look into my mind again, Violet?" he asks, and his worry clouds us again.

"Perhaps not tonight. You were—are—distressed after seeing the witches, and I don't want to make matters worse."

"Two days ago, you would've jumped at the chance and not cared," he says quietly.

Leif's half-correct. Partially, I want to answer him with an enthusiastic 'yes' and get inside his head tonight in case the memories fade. But if Leif's emotional state descends any further, I don't have the skills or capacity to comfort him. All I'm capable of right now is stepping away from my single-minded and self-centered tendencies.

"I would very much like to look inside your mind, Leif, but even touching the edges would be pointless. You're too upset. Your worries interfere with memories." I bite my lip. "Tomorrow?"

"You reckon I'm okay?" he presses.

"Witches have altered your mind, so even though you're not under anybody's influence, you are not okay." This time, his grip tightens. "But you're unharmed and alive," I suggest. "That's a positive outcome."

Unsure whether his quiet is the end of our exchange or not, I untangle my hands from his and stand. Leif stands too and picks up the toy that fell from my pocket when we arrived. "There's blood covering the dog now. From the spell."

I take the object and examine the streaks. "Then the gift is more suitable for me in this state."

Leif cracks a smile. "I'll never know when you're serious or joking."

"I rarely joke, Leif. Rowan indicated that I'm ungrateful for your efforts. I should thank you for expending energy and money to win this prize for me." He shrugs. "And I should also thank you for joining me tonight."

"I enjoyed the time," he says. "Up until Oz almost died, and I saw the witches."

"Those are some of the reasons *I* enjoyed the time." I hold the dog by its long ear. "Don't scowl at me, Leif. We have valuable information, and I would not have that unless you'd accompanied me. So, I am grateful."

He chuckles. "Quite a back-handed compliment, Violet."

"And we achieved this without the need to bite you. Isn't that a positive?"

"Do you ever feel like biting me?"

"No. I have a potion for that."

"Then I can hug you?" I tense. "I won't do anything else. A kind of thanks for helping settle my mind and like I want to show you I care, Violet."

"And would such contact remove some of your distress?"

"Yes, Violet," he says. "I've wanted to hug you since you… the incident at the lodge. At your parents. Tonight, many, many times. I want you to feel safe, even though you don't need that from me."

I nod at him and cautiously he wraps his muscular arms around me, barely at first until I'm submerged in his hug, cheek against his racing heart. I briefly squeeze him too, although unable to get my arms all the way around his waist.

Did Eloise's half of me prompt my agreement? The part of me whispering that this guy's emotions and thoughts are causing him distress and he's a friend who needs comfort? Or is this my old need to ensure he doesn't break apart before we find everything in his mind?

Rowan's comment the other day echoes.

Because he's a nice guy.

A guy who's helping me despite my rude and dismissive treatment, and at risk to himself. If a hug helps atone for any past actions that I'm unaware upset him, that's easier than attempting to explain myself.

Plus, apologies choke me more than his tight hold.

And hugging Leif isn't entirely unpleasant.

Chapter Nineteen

VIOLET

I WAIT until morning to communicate with Dorian. He receives the photo of the witch and listens—patiently, for once—to my explanation of events. The witches know how strained Dorian's council's relationship is with shifters, despite Ethan and Zeke's attempts to bring unity between the elders and other races. Thus, the witches know that the lack of co-operation between the two will aid them in hiding their activities.

The shifter elders would never open their doors and arms, let alone hand over information about their people.

How do we discover what happened to Rory, and whether Oz met the same fate last night? If Dorian can't identify these witches or find his way into the elders' good books, we're at a dead end.

The only people likely to gain clues as to the pair's whereabouts—and bodily state—are me and the guys. The shifters speak to us. Granted, this is usually to communicate their displeasure and dislike of me, and in offensive terms, but they get close enough for me to sneak into their minds.

At least Oz's medical emergency took place publicly in a

human location and he was taken to a hospital. That requires human authority involvement.

Dorian informs me he's attending the academy today and may spend a couple of days staying locally, which I'm unsure is a good or bad thing. Dorian forcing his presence front and center could distract others from my investigations, but he could also cause trouble I don't need.

Late morning, I'm called to a meeting, and eager to discuss anything Dorian found.

I haven't seen Grayson since our rendezvous in Holly's closet, and I'm surprised that he's the only one of us present when I arrive at the waiting room. He's in uniform today, a look I still find odd on the guys. Grayson watches me warily as I enter the waiting room, before lounging back into a *faux* casual position on the sofa.

"Good morning," I say and sit on the armchair opposite.

However hard I deny Grayson's effects, I can't avoid them. Part of the problem in the closet wasn't the desire for his blood, but because whenever I see him, memories of the party always intrude. Specifically, how I almost kissed him. Has Rowan's attention now opened up possibilities that touching and kissing could be acceptable and even desirable in some cases?

Because since the teenage movie moment in the closet, I'm acutely aware how the mutual attraction sparked. I'm in denial when telling Grayson and myself that only his blood interests me.

All extremely confusing.

"Gazing into my eyes again, Violet?" he asks.

"They are a striking and unusual color, therefore attract my attention."

"Every time?"

I smooth the skirt of my uniform. "Where are Rowan and Leif? I would've thought Dorian might wish to speak to them about events too."

"About the rabid shifter?" He arches a brow. "The whole academy knows. What happened?"

I lower my voice and give Grayson a staccato report of last

night's events and when I ask where he was, Grayson merely shrugs and tells me 'nowhere of interest'.

"We're not waiting here to see Dorian, by the way." He folds arms across his chest and sinks further into the sofa.

"The headteachers?" I ask.

He scoffs. "Sawyer. Remember, we had a deadline?"

"Ah." I straighten with interest. "A chance to ask questions."

"That he's unlikely to answer."

I tap the side of my head. "I'll take a look."

"Bad idea, Violet. You know that skilled witches can find an imprint of anybody who's entered another's head. That's how people get caught."

"Perhaps I'm prepared to risk that."

"Then I wish Rowan was here to stop you."

"As if he could."

Grayson shakes his head. "Sawyer must suspect our involvement in events, including Rowan, as everybody knows he's one of your guys. And possibly Leif, as he was with you last night. I'm glad he's safe."

"Leif will always be safe with me." Grayson arches a brow again and I blink at what I just said. "If I've asked Leif to help me, it's my responsibility to ensure his wellbeing."

"Then I hope that extends to us all, Violet."

"Grayson, I don't believe you're stable enough to help—" I'm arrested by the door to Mr. Willis's room opening, especially since the man standing before us isn't Mr. Willis or Sawyer.

"Hello, Grayson." The tall man smiles. "And Ms. Blackwood. Do come in."

"Josef," he mumbles in a returned greeting.

This wiry man with midnight black hair is a strong member of the Petrescu line—as is Grayson, their faces sharper than many vamps, with their mesmerizing green eyes. When Josef looks into mine, they're as unreadable as his expression. I hold that gaze until he looks away.

As I continue to look at the vampire, emotions swirl around my chest and stomach. Tangling in peoples' lives involves mixing with their own complicated relationships, good and bad. I once had none, these days I'm hit by complex links to people left, right and center.

That link to Grayson evokes a worrying response to this creature.

But still, Sawyer *and* his attorney today. Interesting.

This time Grayson and I are forced to sit opposite Sawyer at the mahogany desk in the borrowed room, whereas Grayson's uncle stands to his left, seemingly distracted by what's outside the arched window. We're on the academy third floor and although he'd easily jump uninjured, I'd still happily shove Josef out.

Grayson's edginess unfocuses me further, the guy weakened by his uncle's silent intimidation. Part of me wants this man dealt with for his unjust and violent behavior towards Grayson; I'm determined to implicate him for his as yet unknown connections to everything threatening us. The problem is, the desire to act against Josef is closer to vendetta than detective work, which will not assist.

And how can I ask Sawyer questions with Grayson's uncle in the room?

Sawyer greets me too, and I return a curt hello, irritated because neither of these men are Dorian.

"Is this about the item we allegedly stole or another matter?" I ask Sawyer.

Kai? Fires?

"The item," he replies.

I nod. "Was said item a protective talisman?"

Grayson hisses air between his teeth, but I ignore him and carefully study Sawyer's reaction. "No," he replies.

Hmm. The truth. I slide a look to Grayson's uncle. Sawyer must be aware Josef and Grayson are related.

"Do we need to play the three guesses game?" I ask. "Because Grayson and I have no clue what we're accused of stealing."

Josef gazes at Grayson, who steadfastly avoids his eyes.

"As I said, the item is of sentimental value to my wife. A necklace. The jewels look expensive, but they are not. The necklace isn't worth anything." Sawyer raps his fingers on the desk.

"Did your father request you steal the item?" asks Josef and fixes his attention on me.

Why decide to tell us what we allegedly took *now* and not before?

"My father doesn't wear jewelry and my mother isn't one to adorn herself in frivolous items," I reply.

Unless this *is* a magical item. Has Dorian looked into Sawyer's wife's family history yet?

"Violet wasn't the only kid at the party capable of opening the safe with magic," says Grayson. "And why would she steal something like that?"

"Rowan, perhaps?" suggests Sawyer. "Do I need to involve him in our meeting?"

Yes. Why exactly *hasn't* Sawyer involved him?

"This is ludicrous," I say. "As with all other crimes I'm accused of, there's no evidence."

Josef leans over and speaks quietly to Sawyer, pointless with a hybrid and vamp and their superior hearing. "And the other matter?" Josef whispers. "Kai."

"Is he okay? Kai wasn't partaking in social activities last night, when he's usually in the center of everything," I reply.

"You certainly are verbose, Violet Blackwood," says Josef.

"I find I have plenty to say, Josef." And the more words that leave my mouth, the more seconds I have to form my thoughts. Long and complicated sentences can puzzle people too, which helps.

"Kai claims you mind-controlled him," says Josef.

"Excuse me?" I sit straighter. "I'm aware that's illegal and am avoiding illegal activities. Again, I am not the only witch capable of mind-control."

"What action does he claim is mind-control?" asks Grayson.

Sawyer scratches his head and side-glances Josef.

"The car crash?" I suggest. "And that isn't an admission of guilt, merely proof that I'm *au fait* with teen gossip. I expect Kai wants to avoid culpability for his stupidity by pointing fingers."

"Kai told me he saw you at the wake," says Sawyer. "Or rather, you interfered with him attending."

"Nobody went to Rory's wake," I say.

"Yes, you all did. I instructed him not to before I went to work that day. Kai ignoring me is one issue—that you caused trouble for him is a bigger one."

I'm silenced by confusion. "Who saw him at the wake?"

"You, apparently. Forced him to drive under the influence to hide your actions."

Does Sawyer not remember going to the lodge? Has someone affected his mind? Josef resumes his gazing through the window.

"You went to work that day? At the factory?" I ask.

Josef looks back. "Mr. Sawyer's movements are none of your concern, and we are the ones asking questions, not you. Now, tell us where the jewelry is."

"This is ridiculous," I retort. "Why are you *really* targeting us, Mr. Sawyer? Why do you suddenly need your attorney?"

Placing both hands on the table, Josef leans across to me. "Is Kai your next target?"

"Again, ridiculous. Mr. Sawyer's son is inconsequential to me. As is his wife's jewelry collection."

The door to the room opens, the new arrival not knocking to announce himself. Sawyer's annoyance is cut dead when Dorian walks into the room and slaps a manila folder on the desk.

"Good morning, *gentleman*," he says.

Josef Petrescu noticeably shifts closer to the window as my imposing father brings all his powerful energy with him.

"We weren't expecting you to join the meeting, Dorian," says Sawyer evenly.

"Nice to see you again, Christopher." Dorian flashes his charming smile. "I do apologize for not attending town council meetings recently."

"I understand. You're a busy man." His own smile is thin-lipped.

"Yes, but with all the commotion happening recently, I feel we need more involvement by either myself or the supernatural council." Dorian sits on the edge of the desk and flicks through the file without revealing anything to others.

"In town affairs?" asks Josef stiffly.

"I've avoided too much *interference* in case I'm found to favor my daughter, but these issues spread across three jurisdictions now. Mine, human, and shifter." Carefully, he opens the folder and pulls out a photograph. "I'm aware you have a Petrescu attorney, Christopher, which is concerning enough, but I also understand that you've witch influence on your business or life. Or both."

I can't see the image clearly from here, so fold my hands in my lap and pay close attention.

"This man." Dorian taps the paper. "What role does he play in your life?"

"Don't answer," says Josef sharply.

Dorian gives a bored sigh and yanks out another photo to show Sawyer. "And this one."

There's a definite odor of human perspiration growing in the room as Sawyer shakes his head.

"No?" Dorian taps a third photograph. "What are you discussing with both of them here?"

Josef leans across and places the photos in a pile, not looking at them. "You can't walk in here uninvited with questions and veiled accusations as if you have authority over this man."

"What?" Dorian's fake innocence doesn't fool any of us. "I have jurisdiction over the witches in these pictures. You presume I'm accusing Christopher when I'm merely ascertaining whether he and his family are safe."

"I guess Violet's inherited her verbosity from you," says Josef tersely. "The tone you used with my client *sounded* accusatory."

I'm unable to hold back. In fact, I'm rather proud that I've kept my mouth shut for this long. "Who are the witches?"

"This isn't your business, Violet," says Dorian, not looking at me. Indignance chokes from me. "In fact, perhaps you should leave while I discuss this with Sawyer and his *attorney*."

"But—"

"*But* you are suspects in recent crimes and I don't want my own investigations compromised."

I open my mouth, but words won't come. *His* investigations?

"My client isn't prepared for you to hijack his interview with your daughter by using distraction techniques," says Josef. "If you wish to discuss the witches, we'll arrange a time and meeting."

Dorian reaches for the photos and his nails linger on the back of Josef's hand as the two meet in more challenge than an attorney and his client's accuser. "I don't believe we've met," says Dorian softly.

"No, otherwise I'd remember," says Josef with an air of calm that doesn't match his new aura—that superiority crashed out of the room as soon as Dorian barged in.

"Oh, undoubtedly Mr. *Petrescu*." Dorian's smile shows too many teeth to be friendly. "Now, where should we meet to discuss the situation?"

"I'll consult with my client and be in touch."

Dorian casually places the photos back into the folder and walks around the desk to face Josef. "Where should we meet?" he repeats. "3PM. I'm too busy to plan my day around others, but will allow you to suggest the location."

"Why do you want to talk to me about these men?" blurts Sawyer. "What do you mean my family's under threat?"

"Your attorney made it clear we're not to speak on the subject, Christopher." Dorian folds his arms across his chest, holding the folder against himself.

"No. There's a reason you're looking for them. The deaths? Is Kai in danger?" Sawyer looks at Josef, who vigorously shakes his head.

"Do you know where Oz is?" I interrupt, and Dorian growls at me.

I've reached into Sawyer's mind over the last few minutes and the same magic fingerprint is on his mind as Leif's, but less splintered. Although not revealed to me, I've just seen the photos Dorian showed Sawyer imprinted in his thoughts—two of the images are the witches who accompanied Oz last night.

Does Dorian know who they are?

Maxwell and the lodge aren't in Sawyer's mind, but could be beneath a shimmering layer of magic I can't pass through.

"Oz who?" asks Sawyer, convincingly clueless

A muscle tics in Dorian's jaw, his eyes darker. I meet my father's stare. I've interfered and for all I know my mother isn't around to help against his temper.

"How about *I* decide and make this simple for you, Christopher. Your factory. 3PM," says Dorian.

"Eight PM," replies Josef sharply. "I've things to do myself, as does my client and we need to be prepared for your not-an-interrogation."

Find the witches and warn them, I'll bet.

Dorian gives him a long look. "I can't attend at that time. Tomorrow? Same time?"

I jerk upright. Dorian's giving them time to leave. Hide. *What* is he doing?

"That's fine with me," says Sawyer hastily.

"Of course." Josef smiles. "I can spend a day in town." He looks to Grayson. "Catch up with my nephew, if he doesn't have plans already?"

Dorian shrugs. "Fine. Violet and Grayson. Wait outside while I finish making arrangements."

That's a tone I don't argue with, but I still frown, lips thinning further.

Grayson stares at his uncle, then stiffly stands and is through the door before I am.

Chapter Twenty

VIOLET

"WHAT THE HELL'S HAPPENING?" Grayson asks and pulls me to one side as the door closes.

There's a long wooden bench against the opposite wall where students who've committed misdemeanors await their fates at the headteachers' hands, and I walk over to sit.

"Hopefully Dorian's found something, and even more hopefully he'll share this information with me." I look to the door. "You should leave before your uncle appears, Grayson."

He stands in front of me, hands in pockets. "No point. Everything's worse if I avoid him."

"You'd go with Josef knowing he'll hurt you?"

"You sound horrified, Violet. Almost as if you care." There's no teasing, only an expressionless tone.

"I do care when confronted with people who hurt and bully others."

"Not the ones who receive the hurt and bullying?" he asks.

As I stand, we're closer than we've been in a while, but not as close as in the closet. "I care what happens to you, Grayson. I don't want you to get hurt." His eyes brighten. "I don't want any of my friends getting hurt."

Grayson laughs softly. "I would be upset at the 'friend' part, but as I'm promoted from acquaintance, there's hope yet."

"What on earth does that mean? Your biggest focus right now is your uncle dragging you away to do who knows what." I swallow. "That can't happen. I'll ask Dorian to stop him."

"I'll be alright. I might even find some useful clues for the investigation," he says lightly.

I'm suddenly aware my heart rate increased and as I look at Grayson, the same response as to Leif last night jumps in. "Everything isn't all about my investigation, Grayson."

He steps back and mock gasps. "What?"

I clench my teeth. "Didn't you listen? I don't want my friends to get hurt."

"Because that's unjust?"

"Because I care about them!"

The words fall from me before I weigh up whether to speak them, and they're as big an escape as when the hybrid burst out unprompted. That *man* in the room looking at Grayson the way he was, glancing between us and projecting hatred that only grew when Dorian walked in, tore through to open the other side of me.

And again, the same visceral reaction to when Leif's fear touched me yesterday fills my body. Exactly like my worry for Marci's intentions with Holly have buried into my mind and nag at me.

How can I live alongside people and not begin to consider their lives? Some do things to help each other because they're good people. I'm *not* a good person and can't fully understand these people's choices and behaviors, but I have some capacity to help those who *deserve* help.

Yet that's logic, and I'm responding to Grayson illogically.

My draw to Grayson already saw me protect him against Dorian at my house, and I *want* to keep Grayson from harm just as he wanted to protect me in his accidentally murderous way. And I will. Not using the hybrid side who could easily out-fight Josef Petrescu and leave the man a torn mess in a pool of his blood. No—in a careful, planned, but still permanent way.

The door opens. "How wonderful to see our families reforging a friendship," says Josef as he looks between us. "Unfortunately, as partners in crime, but a charming show of trust between the two children."

Children. *Ugh.*

Dorian runs his tongue along his teeth. "I want Grayson at this meeting, Josef," he says evenly.

"And *I'll* attend," I add, quietly seething when my father doesn't respond.

Sawyer walks by giving curt goodbyes and Josef pulls himself straight. "Come along, Grayson," he says, as if speaking to a puppy.

"Not speaking to your client first?" asks Dorian. "Alone."

"And waste precious time with my nephew?"

A tightness seizes my chest as Josef takes Grayson by the elbow and guides him away from us, Grayson not saying goodbye. Something opposite to my last response to Grayson walking away washes over me, and I fight rushing after them. *Grayson can't leave.*

Dorian watches them go and turns back to the room. "Now. I'll explain what I've found and what you are and are *not* to do."

Grayson and his uncle disappear around a corner, and I blink away my thoughts and fear before following Dorian back inside Mr. Willis's office. The photographs are again spread on the table, and Dorian stands back, rubbing his chin as I sit and look at them.

"This witch is Grant Underhill. He works locally, another businessman—accountant—so his connections could be valid. Except he's also friendly with *this* man." He taps an image of someone I've never seen. "Adam Woodlake. He's registered as a duo—elemental and mind magic—and works in a completely unrelated industry and town. There's no reason for his connection to Underhill and Sawyer, yet..." He taps a third photo of Sawyer sitting in a restaurant with both witches. "Here they all are, meeting."

"And Maxwell?" I ask.

"Nobody has that first or surname, and your image from the

lodge isn't clear. Sawyer never reported the fire, and my men found no body. A witch scrambled Sawyer's mind." I look away. *I know.* "Violet. I hope you didn't invade his head."

"*You* did!"

"I had someone check the lodge," he says, ignoring me. "No body or signs someone's repairing the damage. Perhaps Sawyer hasn't visited since he's 'forgotten' about that day?" Dorian pushes his tongue against a canine. "We don't have anything to go on, Violet."

"Shifter connections?" I ask hopefully.

"There's a contract of shifter rights to part of the land bestowed by Sawyer. One of the witches—Underhill—witnessed the deeds, as did Josef Petrescu. I'm investigating whether he's an attorney to both men. I've failed to find anything useful about Woodlake."

I flop back in my chair. "*No* shifter connections?"

"There are, because supes were involved in the deal for the land between Sawyer and shifters." Dorian gathers the images into the folder. "I'm unsure if this is a case of a human who's found themselves in trouble after something went wrong with witches he trusted or if they're helping him with something in return for... something." He huffs. "Whichever way, this involves shifters."

"Maxwell intended to murder Kai," I remind him.

"Like I said, shifters are involved, and the necromancers are connected to Sawyer's witch buddies. Neither of that pair are necromancers, as far as we know, but we could also be wrong." He opens the door again. "Either way, the human's bitten off enough to choke himself to death, and if the witches don't end Sawyer, the shifters might."

I lower my voice. "You need to find what happened to Rory's body. And to Oz."

"Mmm. Ethan's trying to gain entry to the settlement." He gestures at me to leave. "Either Oz will kill, and the witches will leave a Blackwood-runed victim, or he'll be the victim, as Rory was. The witches no doubt took his body to hide their tracks."

"Can't you find and talk to these three witches? Where do they normally live?"

"Overseas, yet these photos are recent. No UK address. There's also no knowledge of them at any addresses we have on file."

"What do we do now?" I ask Dorian as he escorts me out. "How do we find Oz or—"

"His next victim?" interrupts Dorian. "We can't, Violet. I suggest you stay on campus while I look further into these witches. Hopefully your Petrescu 'friend' might bring some information back from his visit."

"If Grayson *comes* back," I say. "You do know what Josef does to him?"

"Yes, Violet. That's why I don't trust the kid." He fixes me with what I can only call his 'dad stare'. "Are you... involved with the Petrescu boy?"

"Grayson. And he's a friend. You know that."

"He hasn't taken your blood."

I huff. "*No.*"

"Your blood is extremely precious, Violet," he says quietly. "You know not to share."

"With a Petrescu? *Yes*, Dorian," I say wearily. "Rest assured that although I may entertain others touching me, I do not entertain the idea of sharing my blood."

"Touching?" he asks sharply. "In what way?"

"Seriously, Dorian?" I retort. "And what were your extra-curricular activities at eighteen?"

He leans towards me. "You know the answer to that, as does every other bastard out there, especially ones who want to challenge me." Dorian licks his fingers and smooths down my hair, and I growl at him treating me like his little girl. "You and I could have a father-daughter chat about boys and staying safe." He laughs at my horrified look. "But we both know that the only safety concern is for the boy's life."

As Dorian steps back and adds more condescension with his smile, I return an unruffled look. "Well, then. How fortunate I don't *consort* with *boys*." His smile slips. "But I will bear your words in mind, father."

I startle as Dorian's fingers curl around my upper arm. "Never, ever allow that Petrescu to take your blood, Violet Blackwood."

"Because that's a threat to my life or to your pride, Dorian?" I ask. "You're behaving as if an intimate relationship between your daughter and a Petrescu is worse than several murder accusations against me."

"Intimate relationship?" His voice thickens with animosity. "Stick with the witch."

If only he understood. The quiet and seemingly unthreatening Rowan could take magic from me that's a bigger threat to Dorian than sharing my blood with Grayson. Grayson stated he doesn't want power. Rowan clearly told me he does and already touched the shadows—and one time without my involvement.

"Dorian," I say softly and place my fingers on his warm hand. "When will you learn that teaching me to be like you was never a smart idea? Because Dorian Blackwood never once listened to what another told him to do—or not to do. Therefore, you'll struggle with me too."

Air hisses through his teeth. "What's happened to you, Violet? You're not the girl I left at the academy that day."

"Yes. I am. Only now I'm embracing that girl in order to do or not to do what I want." I smile. "Thank you for insisting I attend Thornwood Academy. I'm learning a *lot*."

I do love when I render my father speechless.

It's a talent only my mother and I share.

Chapter Twenty-One

VIOLET

GRAYSON DOESN'T RETURN by the evening.

I spend the afternoon with Rowan and Leif talking through developments with Dorian, Sawyer, and Josef. As I suspected would happen, Leif's lost the memories that intruded last night, and I silence them with my frustrated outburst. We both know I'll need to invade Leif's head again, but today our concern surrounds Grayson—and Oz.

Although we know it's too late for Oz. Realistically.

I may've ignored some of what Dorian said, but did stay on campus to wait for Grayson and remain in the public eye. Dorian appears to miss one major point here—what if the next murder is *on* campus? Our investigations so far show there's no immediate threat to witches—especially with Grayson absent— and it's unlikely vamps will be targeted either.

One meeting today ended with no movement forward, but I *can* work on Holly. Dorian requested I follow up the Marci and Holly leads myself since his interference would be more obvious.

More than happy to.

I saw Holly earlier but had no time to talk, when she returned to our room following another stay at Marci's and felt the need to stammer out an apology for yesterday evening. I informed her I don't expect apologies as I don't hand them out myself. She left, worried she'd be late for class.

I'm now confident that Marci was the witch with Holly who sought a scarf while I sought to avoid contact with Grayson.

I snooped in her closet again shortly after I returned from my meeting. At first, I convinced myself that Holly added the new layer of clothing to the floor to make my search more difficult. Five minutes into a deep dive beneath pants and sweaters, I discover nothing but Holly's lack of organization and untidiness. As with last time, the mess niggled, and I resisted temptation to replace clothes on the hangers.

Where are the runes and spellbag?

And what do I do with my potion? Because this room isn't a sanctuary any longer.

I've no time for pointless classes this afternoon and return to the notes I've now removed from the wall. After half an hour, I'm happier that I have a 'to do' list:

1. Attend meeting with Sawyer
2. Find Kai
3. Persuade Dorian to share all his findings with me
4. Discover Holly's secret

I don't notice Holly return until she speaks.

"Are you busy this evening?"

I turn in my seat and gesture at my work on the desk, then turn back. "Yes. Why?"

"I've a Spring Ball committee meeting," she says.

"You don't need to inform me of your movements, Holly." I slide out the paper with the code I'm still working to decipher. Dorian and Eloise now have a copy but no helpful solution.

"You should come with me to the meeting," she continues.

"Repeat those words to yourself and consider how non-sensical you sound."

"I need you to come, Violet," she urges.

Carefully placing down my pen, I turn fully in my seat and regard her, where she stands still in uniform looking every inch the innocent bystander in my car crash life. "Why? Do you need input on the color scheme? You know you're asking the wrong girl, Holly."

"Please. Just this once. We need your advice on something else. Not color scheme."

Why does she look at me earnestly as if I even *have* advice pertinent to a school dance? "What? Ask me now?"

"I'd really appreciate if you came with me," she presses.

Holly has never insisted I attend one of her meetings before. If I'm not going to the dance, why would I care about organization? "What's really happening, Holly?"

"Marci can explain." I shake my head, confused. "She leads the committee."

Marci? Ah yes. 'Head' of this committee. If Marci's involved, I'm invited for a reason. I am not stupid.

Holly's handing me an opportunity on a plate and I'm protesting? Joining Holly in her social circle assists me in investigating other students' connections to my two new suspects. Especially Marci.

"Where is this meeting?"

"Pendle House."

Not a classroom in the common area of the school? Hmm. Interesting. "I'll join you. Once."

Pendle House? Perfect. I'll call in on Rowan afterwards and inform him what we do next.

SOMETHING DAMPENS HOLLY'S usual exuberance as we walk through Pendle House hallways—strange for a girl who's friends with everybody. Some we pass say hello to Holly, whereas I apparently don't exist.

Holly pauses at an arch at the end of the hallway and takes a surreptitious look around her. She opens the oak door to a set of stone steps, which spiral downwards into another part of the building. Basement? Holly's jitteriness and the meeting's location intrigue me further.

"Why do you meet in the basement?" I ask.

"Privacy."

"For a dance committee? Top secret discussions on font for the posters?" I scratch a cheek. A meeting in a basement in Pendle House. Curious and increasingly suspicious. "Don't presume this'll persuade me into attending the dance," I warn her.

"I still have time to persuade you."

I swear that's a smug smile in response to my grimace.

Holly leads me down the steps, where arched alcoves in the gray stone brick, lit by iron lanterns, run alongside. Another short hallway, this one unlit and with a slate floor, leads to another door. She pauses and knocks, rapping her knuckles in a rhythm. Secret code for a dance committee? Good grief.

The door opens and Marci faces us, a large burgundy book in her hand. Her face lights up when she sees me, the weirdest part of the whole evening.

"Nice work, Holly," she says. "Hey, Violet."

That almost sounded friendly.

"Black. Horror theme. Perhaps accent with blood red. Skulls," I inform her.

"Excuse me?" Her smile drops.

"Theme. For the dance. Unless there's another reason you want me here besides my advice."

Marci chuckles. "Violet. Come inside before somebody sees."

I pause. "Isn't this a little overkill for a student committee?" Both girls look at me in an indecipherable way. Should I waste energy on mind reading?

Holly sighs. "Violet. This is more than a committee meeting."

Marci steps back and opens the door further. I peer into the circular room. In the center, three girls sit around a white painted circle containing basic runes, and red candles in bronze sconces on the walls flicker to highlight their faces.

Not unexpected for a room beneath the academy's witch house, but an odd place for a human. "Holly? Is this a coven?"

Chapter Twenty-Two

VIOLET

ALTHOUGH HOLLY'S link to Marci pointed at a witch's influence, I'd discounted anything further. In my short time at Thornwood, I've watched witches and other students interact and there's a definite 'them and us'—almost a social *faux pas* to include humans in anything magical. Hence my suspicions why Marci befriended Holly and broke the unspoken rule.

But this? I don't need any more persuasion and march into the low-ceilinged room then wrinkle my nose at the pungent herbal smell.

Three witches—Marci and two who she introduces as Nita and Zoe. I dart a look from girl to girl. I may've seen them around campus, but the blond and the dark-haired witches weren't at the bowling alley or Kai's party.

There's plenty of magic energy humming around but also a dull aura similar to Holly's after the breakup with Ollie, but harsher. Was Nita strong-armed into joining the committee too? Because something's off about her. She's picking at the edge of her academy blazer and the sad aura would interfere with any magic attempts.

"What's this?" I ask. "Are you *really* organizing a dance, or are you a coven?"

"Both." Holly wanders into the room and sits beside Nita before taking her hand and whispering something. Nita nods and sucks in a shaky breath.

"How are you in a coven, Holly? You're human," I say. *Oh, please no...* "Aren't you?"

She nods. "Honorary human member."

Zoe chuckles.

"Of a secret coven? Or is this a general meeting room for witches to practice magical homework?" Marci smiles at me. "I'm guessing the former if you're semi-hidden in the basement and lie to everyone that this is a committee meeting."

Marci nods. "Few people want to be involved with the committee."

"Yeah, Marci's known to be bossy," puts in Zoe. "Unofficial head girl."

I lock gazes with the girl who decided to treat me with rudeness and disdain last night, and all but accused me of the murders. "Why am I here?" I ask Marci. "You made public your evident dislike for me and your suspicion more so."

Marci sits by the circle beside Nita. "I can't be seen as a supporter, Violet."

"Of me?"

"Yes. Nobody on campus should be seen to support you. No witch, anyway."

I narrow my eyes. "And you want me to join your 'committee'? A coven whose sole purpose is to use magic for frivolity? And other humans; vamps. Where is *their* involvement?"

"Marci has strict criteria for meetings and who joins us. Most choose not to be involved due to how overbearing she is," says Zoe.

"Well. I'm not joining a coven, especially one led by someone who thinks they're superior to me." But my curiosity grows by the moment. Most irritating.

"We've some information to share with you," says Marci. "Helpful information."

"And what do you want in return?" Is this another Rowan *quid pro quo* situation? "I don't share my magic."

"Your help in finding the killer." Nita's voice is thick and wavering, a more extreme version of Holly when she lost Ollie.

Oh. Holly *has* told them about my investigations.

Tread carefully, Violet.

Nita attended the memorial but wasn't one of the weeping girls. But still... "Were you one of Wesley's girlfriends?" I ask. "A secret one, since the guy hated supes."

She shakes her head and struggles to speak.

"Rory," says Marci.

"Excuse me?"

"Nita and Rory. And *that* was secret," explains Holly.

Finally sucked in enough to discover more, I join their circle. This changes everything—there *is* a connection between the murders and the academy.

"Nita and Rory were romantically involved?" I ask for confirmation.

The witch couldn't be more opposite to him—the diminutive girl with her long black braid and pretty face compared to his huge bulk, and a nose broken several times. Neither can I imagine the guy who attacked me at the memorial would ever talk to a witch, never mind... whatever else they did together.

"Yes. We dated the last few months," says Nita.

Dated after he died? Died the *first* time. "And was he friends with any other witches?" I ask.

"Marci knew him—she chaperoned me at first in case..." Nita waves an arm. "Shifters have a reputation and most hate witches and humans. We first met at—"

"Don't care. Please keep to the point."

"Violet," whispers Holly and gives me a familiar stern look.

Holly's still staring. Good grief, why does this happen all the time? I watch Nita wring her hands together again and sigh. "I'm sorry that you lost Rory in such a shocking and undoubtedly painful—" I begin.

"So, about the witches," interrupts Holly as Nita's eyes well.

"He worked for some other witches. Odd jobs. Laboring. Cash in hand," says Nita.

"Oh? Who?" I ask.

"One of the families over in the next town. Grangeton. They're demolishing an old house on their land to build a new one. Some shifters work there," says Nita. "Rory didn't know that the owners were witches at first or would never have answered the ad, but they paid well. Work's hard to get in this town."

Oh. *Oh.* "Do you know the family?" I ask.

"No. Only their name. Brightgrove."

"Minor family," puts in Marci. "Older couple."

"What magic do they practice?"

"The woman's elemental, according to Rory. Not sure about her husband. They didn't see him much," says Nita.

"I'm guessing *you're* not mental magic skilled," I say as much to myself as Nita. Because if she were, Nita would know Rory lost his mind. Literally.

She shakes her head. "Mine's fairly weak. Humans bred into our line and my parents are elemental born."

"And you?" I ask Marci.

"I'm best with alchemy, but also have elemental magic skills," she says stiffly, as if I should know.

Again, no mental magic. "Who else worked at this house?"

Finally. A shifter link to witches. "Oz and Trent," says Nita.

Oz. *Oz.*

"Not Viggo?"

Marci snorts. "No way. Viggo never knew or he would've lost his shit with them all. At first we thought Viggo killed Rory—he's vicious."

"But he had a large number of alibis for Rory's exact time of death," says Zoe. "He was interviewed too."

"And Viggo wouldn't kill Rory," says Nita. "Rory was an Ursa and part of the inner circle."

"What do you know about Trent?" I ask. "Did you meet him? Is he friendly?" Is *he* a construct?

Nita looks at me in disgust. "This is about finding Rory's and

Wes's killers."

I suck my lips together. If the recently deceased Maxwell was correct, Rory killed Wesley. And Oz killed Rory. If he isn't permanently deceased, is Oz next?

"Did any kids from the academy labor for this family?" I ask.

"No. So that's not the connection between Wes's and Rory's murders."

"And have you discovered anything that might link them?" I frown.

"Only the runes, and the way they were killed," says Zoe warily.

"Oh. You subscribe to 'the Violet Blackwood did it' theory?" I make to stand.

As I do, Marci tosses something into the circle we sit around.

A pendant

A very *familiar* pendant. I kneel and take hold, examining to confirm my suspicion—small, coin-like with a leather string through the hollow center. "Who does this belong to?"

"Rory. He couldn't wear the necklace around Viggo, but he was supposed to wear it when around the witches on site," says Marci.

"A couple of weeks ago, Rory stopped wearing the pendant altogether," says Nita. "We had a fight about it, and he got weird —we didn't see each other much after that."

"The witches are involved!" I say triumphantly. "You gave Rory a protective talisman. How did you *know*?"

"More of a just in case," says Nita. "Those elderly witches wouldn't kill anyone—they barely practiced witchcraft in their lives. But Rory was paranoid. He needed the money, so Marci helped out by creating one."

"*You* made the pendants? Why would you give one to Wesley if he attacked witches on campus?"

"Wes?" Marci frowns. "I never gave one to Wes."

"Kai?"

"No. This is the only one I charmed. To be honest, I wasn't sure I had the shape or spell correct." She slants her head. "I studied the older texts—my father's a historian."

Older texts? "*You* wrote in the academy book! A code?"

"No, but I deciphered what I think you're talking about." Marci smiles.

Wesley and Rory. They both wore pendants but weren't wearing them the nights they died. Sawyer implied Kai lost his— he wasn't wearing one at the lodge.

"I told you I had useful information, but I'm only telling you this because if you didn't kill Rory, I want to help you find who did. For Nita's and Holly's sake," says Marci.

"Why Holly's?"

"Because Holly's in danger from associating with you." Marci takes the pendant and twirls it in the air above her hand. She used a light tone, but her expression is as dark and heavy as usual when she's around me.

"Marci wants people to think she suspects you and is protecting me," explains Holly quickly when I growl. "But she doesn't think you're guilty."

"Yes. Holly could be in danger, Violet, but not from you," adds Marci.

"And because we're investigating Rory's death too, we can help each other," says Nita.

"But nobody can know that we're associating with you," says Zoe sharply. "Or we're all linked and in danger."

My head spins in circles. "Right. Do you know where this house is?"

"What's left of it, yes." Nita rubs her cheek. "I'd meet Rory there some nights."

"At night? In an old house?" I frown. "What on earth for?"

"Privacy," says Holly curtly.

"There isn't much of the house left now," says Nita. "But Rory started spending more and more time at the place— became obsessed by the money he was earning, and I saw less of him."

Once the necromancers killed him.

"Did he spend this money on anything interesting?" I ask.

"No. He saved. Rory couldn't start flashing the money around or people would ask questions."

"You could ask your father to look into who the witches are?" suggests Marci. "We've started, but haven't gotten far."

As if I'd tell them. How can I trust these girls?

"Why not tell me all this sooner, Holly?" I ask. I'm about to blurt that I know of her items in the closet, but it wouldn't help if she knew I snooped and suspected her.

"Because we didn't want anybody to know in case it threatened us in some way," repeats Zoe. "Especially if anybody discovered the truth about Rory and Nita."

"What about the police?" I ask. "Didn't you tell them?"

"Tell them what? That Rory had an illegal job, and witches might be involved in the murders? That wouldn't help with the tensions between the academy and town." Nita shakes her head. "My parents are prejudiced against shifters too."

"Oh!" I straighten. "Do you think they—"

"No!" She looks at me in disgust. "They live hundreds of miles away and know nothing about me and Rory."

I've so many questions but many I can't share, even though they're sharing with me. Mention Sawyer? No. But I'll look into connections between this elderly couple and Sawyer. Perhaps discover another between them all and the witches Dorian identified.

"Will you work with us to help Nita?" asks Marci.

"Why? I have the information now. I don't need you." Nita's eyes narrow until they almost disappear. "Um," I slide a glance at Holly. "And also because you'd be in danger?"

"*I* want to bring these people to justice," says Nita, voice rising. "This is *my* fight."

Good grief. "Alright. But how could we possibly work together if you don't want anybody to know you're connected to me?"

Holly's face fills with too much glee for a situation where we're discussing murder in the presence of a grief-stricken girlfriend. "That's simple. You can join the Spring Ball Committee."

And have Marci commanding my actions? Over my temporarily dead body.

Chapter Twenty-Three

VIOLET

I STAND with Rowan outside the low, green-painted gate and regard the front of the house. Ivy clambers around the wooden porch and up the dark brick, swallowing the windows of the two story building. The older Victorian style home isn't as large as the mansions on many of the old witch estates, but still stands out as an embodiment of a bygone era where witches had more wealth. Although set on part of a founding witch family estate, most of the land was sold to humans who've built a modern housing estate nearby.

Not waiting, I open the creaking gate and step onto the slate pavers running through the neatly tended front lawn bordered by bushes with tiny blue flowers. I'd expect sounds from the renovations, but the only rumbling comes from passing car engines on the main road a few streets away. In fact, the whole area is quiet, save nearby warbling birdsong. Is this good or bad? Whether there're people working on the renovations or not, we'll take a look. If nobody's at the house, we can sneak away to snoop. If the residents *are* home, we can field them with some mental magic.

Are there any remaining workers? Such as Trent. I'll take a

wander into the minds of anybody working outside, should they still have one.

We've looked into the resident family further, and there's nothing suspicious about the people who own the house, or their connections. They've lived in the home most of their lives, and all their children and grandchildren are accounted for and unsuspicious. Although the couple are old enough to remember a time where Confederacy and Dominion battled for supremacy in the supernatural world, they've also no past links to the rogue Dominion.

They're just one of the families who blended into human society and kept away from conflict.

But—interestingly—the owners recently returned from overseas, where the elderly couple had swapped the perpetual rain and gloom of England to a life in the agonizingly sunny and warm Mediterranean.

Overseas. A link to the suspects?

Naturally, my decision to visit the premises led to arguments and attempts by Leif and Rowan to dissuade me. Ridiculous. This is the biggest lead yet and although we communicated our findings to Dorian, time is running short. The witches already covered up Rory's situation. They know I've seen them, and we've no idea how they might use Oz next. Or how soon.

Where is Rory? Disposed of?

If these renovations are a massive and unlikely coincidence, then best I discover now—by visiting. This time, Rowan comes with me and not Leif—he wants to keep away from shifters and I'll definitely need Rowan's magic help. The fake reason we're using to gain entry to the premises is flimsy, hence we'll use magic to wipe memories of the visit.

Rowan passes through the gate and along the pathway to a white wooden porch, the entrance marked by a heavy, door painted a bold green to match the gate. A large brass bell with a chain serves as a doorbell, which rings loud enough for half the street to hear.

The door opens and the moment the older woman's eyes land on me, I speak. "Hello, I'd like to ask you some questions."

I frown as Rowan shoves me to one side. The elderly witch peers at me through silver-rimmed spectacles, and her creased face becomes more crepe-like as she does. She's wearing brown slacks, and a knitted, lilac cardigan that sets off the purple tinge to her white hair.

"Pardon? My hearing isn't particularly good."

I clear my throat and raise my voice. "I'd—"

"We're from the academy and would like to interview you," butts in Rowan.

"About your fam—"

"For a history assignment."

"Will you stop interrupting me?" I grumble.

"History?" asks the woman.

"We wondered if you have any old photos or drawings of the estate as it once was," explains Rowan. "We've an assignment to study all the original witch estates in the area."

"Are you looking for work? You're not suitable," she says loudly to Rowan. "We need lads with muscle."

How rude. "Rowan has a keen mind even if he is physically inferior to some other males," I say and offer him a smile that he most certainly doesn't return.

"Wow," he mutters. "Thanks, Violet."

"Pardon?" asks the witch.

Oh, joy. Did she hear Rowan's earlier question? "Can you show us some photographs?" I ask loudly.

"I'm sorry, there's too much noise out here. Come inside."

Noise? Is she imagining things?

I take a step forward as the woman turns.

Rowan catches my sleeve. "Let me do the talking."

"Why?"

"Really? You need to ask me that?"

I swallow a retort. Persuading Rowan to join me took more effort than usual. He can't leave. "Then ensure you ask the correct questions and in a timely manner."

"Then promise not to speak to anybody unless absolutely necessary," he retorts. Our eyes meet in a familiar stalemate. "Don't growl at me, Violet."

I stalk into the hallway where a tall dark wood grandfather clock faces us, bronze pendulum swinging to count the seconds in loud tick-tocks, and Rowan follows closely.

"Everybody's very interested in my house all of a sudden."

"Oh?" I almost bump into her as we enter a tall-ceilinged lounge room filled with light from the bay windows that look over the rear of the property.

The strength of lavender in the room hits me. Not only the scent, but the woman must love the flower and color because there's a definite theme that extends beyond her hair and clothing. When I'm old, will I obsess about violets?

No, because age isn't anything to worry about. I glance at a photo of an elderly couple on the stone mantel above a spotlessly unused iron fireplace—the woman and her husband in their wedding attire. How odd to think Rowan will age and I won't.

Something odd tugs at my chest as if Rowan pulled me with him as he steps forward. He's my witch bond. How does *that* work for me with a non-immortal?

"Is your name Lavender?" I ask.

"Elizabeth, my sweet," she replies. "Do sit. I'm making tea. Would you like a cup while we talk?" Elizabeth doesn't wait for an answer as she walks through her lavender painted door into a kitchen.

No exchange of names? Suits me.

"Lavender?" asks Rowan quietly.

"I agree, overkill on the color."

"No, you asked—" He shakes his head. "I suppose you confirmed she's one of the Brightgrove couple."

"Right. Check the dresser drawers," I say and point at the massive piece of furniture dominating the room, covered in a plethora of fine China animals and a vase of lavender sprigs. "I'll take a look out the back of the house."

"We can't start ransacking the place, Violet," says Rowan sternly and perches on the edge of an overused, brown-cushioned sofa.

"And we don't have time for cozy chats. This is a fact-finding mission, Rowan." I blow air into my cheeks. Where do I start?

"Good grief. What's that doing here?" I take a sudden step behind the sofa Rowan settled on, as a fat, not-China calico cat eyeballs me from where it balances precariously on top of the dresser.

"Are you scared of cats?" asks Rowan.

"There was once an unfortunate incident regarding a cat and —" I cup my mouth to hide my reply from the cat. Who knows? This could be a familiar. "Necromancy."

Rowan's mouth curls as if he's about to laugh at me. Well then, he's the first person I've ever met who finds necromancy *amusing*.

I startle as the cat springs from the shelf, continuing to eyeball me, then wanders away, tail upright as if giving me the middle finger. The woman reappears with a rectangular silver tray containing a ceramic teapot decorated with flowers, and matching cups and saucers. A plate of cookies rests beside a small silver milk jug, and she places her bountiful offerings on the low table in the center of the room.

"Tea?" The woman sits and picks up the teapot.

"I'd rather not poison myself," I say. "Do you have any photos?"

"Violet." Rowan's teeth are clenched. "I'm glad she can hardly hear what you're saying. Let me speak."

I watch as the woman pours tea into a cup she sets in front of Rowan. "Don't drink mysterious brews at a witch's house," I mutter. "Please consider that this could be someone linked to murder."

"'Mysterious brews'. That's clearly ordinary tea, and I'd detect if it wasn't." Rowan chuckles. "But yeah, okay."

A loud shout followed by laughter carries through the partially open bay window. I shall take a look out there while Rowan works on the witch, since he insists on performing the interrogation.

"I feel unwell. I require some fresh air," I announce and turn to leave, before lowering my voice. "Please try to stay alive until I return, Rowan."

Before anybody comments, I leave the house via the door we

entered through and pause. Yes, there's magic around this house, but nothing stronger than I'd expect for two elderly witches.

Where's the woman's husband?

I skirt around the side of the home, avoiding walking past the window near Rowan and the woman. The building undergoing renovation isn't far from the house, brick built and at least a century newer than the main residence. The roof's intact, but one side of the house demolished. My boots crunch over discarded wood and drywall as I wander to where a dumpster is filled with broken orange brick and splintered wood. From my hidden vantage point, I peer through a frameless window.

Workers gutted the majority of the building's interior, including removing carpets. So far, there's no attempt to rebuild or remodel with no scaffolding or sign of fresh building material nearby. Although plastic sheeting replaced the carpets and, to be frank, looks better than the stained and highly floral ones in the dumpster.

Voices and music come from the rear, and I edge along to investigate who's here.

Definitely shifters—two men who've decided they no longer need their shirts, the pair's skin and jeans covered in gray dust. Which is Trent? Who's the other?

One has long curled hair pulled from his face, possibly brown, but the dust streaks it gray; the other guy sports a shaved head. They sing along to their awful music while demolishing a wall with bare hands.

Shifter labor—cheaper than hiring machinery.

Rowan made me promise not to speak to anybody unless absolutely necessary. His definition of 'necessary' differs from mine, and I stand, preparing to quiz the pair.

A second set of voices come from inside the building, and I duck back behind the dumpster, watching and waiting for people to descend the still intact wooden staircase. Instead, two men walk through a doorway leading from a room I looked into that they were definitely *not* in.

A cellar? Blood magic? We need to return at night once we've gleaned information from the witch indoors.

I edge back behind the dumpster and watch as the two men approach the shifters.

One's older—the witch husband from the photograph inside the house? And the other... *From the hospital*. The one Dorian identified as Adam Woodlake. He may look less officious in khaki cargo pants and a pale green shirt than when wearing the gray suit, but the man scanning his surroundings with a calculating gaze is unmistakably the same witch.

I clutch my phone tighter. I *knew* there'd be a connection.

Adam greets and then speaks to both shifters as bank notes exchange hands, but disappointingly he doesn't use their names. They grin and nod as Adam also gestures inside the derelict building, informing the pair he wants the walls that divide two rooms taken down by the end of the day.

My phone fills with images as I point and click.

How long have shifters worked here? Surely a house this size could be demolished quicker than the length of time since Rory died.

But the *witch*. Excitement surges in my chest. I have proof of a link between the murders. *Finally*.

As the older witch continues to instruct his shifter workers, Adam walks a short distance away and takes something from his jacket pocket. I've barely time to register that the brick-like phone matches the other one I'm carrying before said phone vibrates in my pocket.

My eyes widen as the whisper-silent buzzing continues.

I have my evidence. We need to leave before either witch sees us. My teeth grind. If the witches hadn't appeared, I could've spoken to the shifters and easily extracted more information.

"Maxwell. What the fuck is going on?" asks Adam.

But I definitely need to get away.

"Where were you last night? Your four-legged friend is drawing attention. What the fuck did you to do him?" Adam stares at the ground, pushing at a lump of brick with the toe of his shoe. "If this is because you don't like the price we agreed, you get nothing. Meet me at the house tonight and sort the situation before I do."

157

Rowan can't move as fast as me and the woman in the house will *definitely* tell this guy that we visited if I don't get into the house and mind-wipe her asap.

I've now confirmed the message received the other day was for Maxwell. My detective heart fills with joy as imaginary lines connect people in my mind. Now to discover who these two shifters are. They could've attended the fire the night Wesley died, as I couldn't see the whole group in the dim, but they weren't at Wesley's memorial with Viggo.

The moment the Adam's back is turned and he strolls to rejoin the group, I sprint back around the front of the house. No time to call or text Rowan.

I burst back inside to find Rowan chatting to the witch, who's all smiles—but no photos. Where are his powers of magical persuasion?

Don't act weird. Don't act weird. "Your cat attacked me."

The witch's smile drops. "Pardon?"

"Vicious creature." I look at Rowan, wishing for once we had bonded telepathy. As planned, the witch stares at me. "We're leaving. We never visited you."

"I'm sorry, what?" she asks.

Good grief. I didn't factor in the difficulty of mind-wiping a half-deaf witch. "I said, we never visited you. The tea and cookies are for the shifters," I say loudly. "That's why there're three cups."

"Yes. They don't usually like my tea, but do enjoy the cookies." She rises and picks up the tray as I continue to play around with her mind.

Rowan finally stands, and my jaw almost slams to the floor as he turns. Is Rowan actually *eating* a cookie? I'd expect this behavior from Leif, but honestly, they're not even *nice* cookies. Not a tempting chocolate chip in sight.

"What's happening? Did the shifters see you?" he asks.

"The witch from the hospital is outside," I hiss and slap the cookie from Rowan's hand. "And good grief, Rowan. *A cookie?*"

Panic finally crosses his face, and he pursues me as I rush towards the front of the house, then yank open the front door.

"I hope that magic worked on Elizabeth or we've a serious problem with our investigation." The door closes behind with a thud as I continue to hurry away. Rowan catches up and I slice him a look. "Don't expect any sympathy from me if you just ate a cookie laced with an unpleasant substance."

Chapter Twenty-Four

GRAYSON

WHY AM I not surprised that Josef chooses to 'catch up' with me while he's in town? And why am I also not surprised when that catch up isn't a casual lunch but a visit to a familiar place?

The outside of the old cottage looks no better in daylight, weeds struggling through what was once a pathway to the door, and the gardens overgrown by dandelions and grasses, the yellow almost adding a prettiness to the surroundings. Brambles invade the rose bushes and although a handful of white ones managed to grow, they're almost obliterated.

I spent way too much time here when Josef locked me away from the world, which means I'm suspicious when he doesn't drag me into the house and the lock the doors behind us. Josef's buddies aren't with him, and we pause in the untended gardens rather than enter, but I remain suspicious.

"Lovely afternoon for sitting outside, don't you think?" he asks. "Imagine never being able to do this like your poor parents and those before."

Josef brushes dirt from a faded wooden bench and sits. I hate him. I hate his make-believe nice guy, all sharp suits and flashy smiles; the man who uses his mental abilities to further burrow himself into human society. I fucking hate what he does to me, but most of all, I hate that I look like Josef Petrescu.

"Expensive suit," I say and nod at him.

"The unfortunate trappings of my job." He smiles. "How are you, Grayson?"

"Better than I presume I'll be at the end of this conversation." I remain standing at a cautious distance, hands in pockets.

"How's Ms. Blackwood?" he asks, and cold trickles along my spine when he doesn't confirm or deny that he'll injure me. "Are her investigations progressing well?"

"I'm not involved. The witch she hangs out with doesn't like me." Josef slants his head and I summon images of Rowan's dislike the same way I showed Rowan images of Josef's abuse. Not a total lie, even if we're friendlier now.

"Then you need to get *that* person out of the way." Josef examines his manicured fingernails and pulls a face. "Witches. They're causing me a lot of trouble. Or rather, trouble for my *client*."

"Sawyer?" He knows about Maxwell. "Why?"

"I warned him not to become involved, but witches are clever bastards—no complex magic needed if they're playing on a man's ego. You can help fix the problem, Grayson."

"How?"

He smiles in that way I know means danger's coming. "Witches are blackmailing my client. They've threatened his son."

I reel as he swipes aside one of Violet's theories, specifically the one I'd hoped would get this man out of my life. "You're not working with witches against Violet?"

"Grayson, *please*," he says in disgust. "You know I never work with witches. You still haven't told me—how is Ms. Blackwood's investigation progressing? Proved her 'innocence' yet?"

I rub my cheek. "Violet hasn't killed anybody."

"Shame. But I'm sure that situation will change now she's become unhinged." Josef flashes his teeth. "Grayson. I'm Sawyer's attorney and know everything that occurred at Kai's little soiree. Violet sounds rather volatile, and a reliable witness told me she took great interest in your blood."

"Violet never touched my blood, and neither did I touch hers."

I never expected this development, as convinced as Violet that the murders were partially connected to the Petrescus. The moment I discovered Sawyer worked with witches *and* my uncle; the picture seemed clearer. Now everything's muddied. Unless Josef's lying.

I hold my ground when Josef rises and slowly walks over, as he does when he likes to hear my pulse beat harder. "But you bring out the *worst* in Violet, correct?"

"Violet isn't exactly like her father. She controls herself. Violet hasn't and wouldn't hurt anybody."

"Such faith, Grayson." He's close enough that I hear his pulse too, the slow movement of an ancient's blood. "I need her to hurt someone. I want Violet to kill the witches who're threatening Sawyer—the ones I believe are involved with these killings."

"What?" I ask hoarsely.

"Well, if the witches are trying to frame Violet for murder, makes sense she'd like to eliminate them." He smiles. "Self-control or not, the need to eliminate enemies *is* a Blackwood trait."

"She's proving her innocence, not attacking people." I shake my head. "I'm sure Violet will deal with the witches, but not by killing them."

I flinch as he pats my cheek. "Poor, naive Grayson. Has Violet put a spell on you?" I tense at his mocking. "If I ensure she 'finds' these witches, *you* ensure she kills them."

"No."

He blinks slowly. "You don't use that word with me, Grayson Petrescu."

"I can't *make* Violet do anything."

"Incorrect. You can coax out the side Violet's father encouraged her to hide. The one that *everybody* needs to see in his daughter. The same side Dorian artfully hides but which will appear in full force when his little girl's threatened." Blood whooshes in my ears; what the hell's happening here? Does Josef know about the shifters? The necromancers?

"How can you arrange for witches to meet Violet if you're not connected to them and their killing spree?" I ask suspiciously.

"Not meet *Violet*—Sawyer. Or rather, a chance meeting between the witches and Sawyer's little boy, whose death would be a great inconvenience. Humans tend to lose their focus when a precious child dies. I rely on Sawyer's influence over the town. I can't let that grip on his power slide, which would happen if the witches succeeded in killing Kai and caused the man to lose his mind."

I stare at the moss growing on the wooden picket fence, the fresh spring air suddenly no easier to breathe than the musty house. Do I accept Josef genuinely isn't involved with these witches and the murders? Sure, he dislikes the race, but he hates Dorian more. This could still be a way to manipulate a situation for revenge against Dorian without getting his hands dirty. But a coincidence that the witches and Josef share the same aim? I'm doubtful.

What now? I slide my eyes back to his stern face, hoping to hell our catch up doesn't last longer than one afternoon.

"What are these witches' names?" I ask.

"Dorian has the names, but he won't find the men easily, even if Sawyer tells him everything."

Evasive. "Why are they threatening Kai?" I ask.

Josef sighs as if I'm a small child trying his patience and takes his seat again. "Sawyer bargained with witches in order to cement his status in the community. A spell here and there to keep himself one step ahead of rivals, and other magic to ensure protection from the shifters. Really, Sawyer should be protecting himself against the *witches*."

"And Sawyer didn't keep his end of the bargain with the witches? Is that what's happening here?"

"Evidently he did not. Sawyer refuses to tell me everything about this agreement with witches or what's causing them to threaten Kai, and the witches blocked his mind from mental interference." The hardness in his expression spreads to his eyes. "Luckily for Sawyer, these witches require more competent hitmen than the shifters—they've missed the target twice."

Josef doesn't know about the necromancy.

But there's a lot not adding up here. He must know these witches if he has enough influence to arrange a meeting.

"You'll arrange for witches to meet Kai but instead Violet will be there?" I ask. "And you want me to take Violet to the meeting so she'll kill them before they have another chance to target Kai?"

He nods. "And Violet's always with that witch or human which will give her an extra incentive to kill, as I'm positive the witches will attack one of them. With any luck, those boys might help."

"You'd make enemies of witches just to frame Violet and help a human?"

"I've no fear of witches, and Sawyer's a very useful human, Grayson." He flicks his tongue against his top teeth.

"Your plan won't work now that Dorian knows their names. He'll catch the witches himself, or at least have them under surveillance by now."

"Which is why time is of the essence, Grayson." I shrink back as he's abruptly in front of me again, sharp teeth centimeters from my nose. "That Blackwood bastard killed the man at the pinnacle of our family line and pushed Petrescus into the gutter. Oskar Petrescu led our society and kept abominations like him under control. Now the Blackwood is in charge, dangerous supes could roam the world. Such as his *daughter*. Dorian doesn't deal with these threats in the way Oskar did. He will not keep us safe. That will be his downfall."

"I'm aware of our family history, Josef, but times change."

"And change for the best?" His eyes glint for a moment. "Did you know Oskar wanted to stop Violet from existing? End hybrids?"

The sunny day cools. "Kill her?"

Josef attempts to catch me off-guard and pierce my thoughts, and although I slam a barrier against a memory of her dying at the lodge, I bet he doesn't miss my heart lurching as I desperately dampen down the response to his words. "No, Grayson. He would've killed the hybrid before the abomination took its first breath."

My sharp breath betrays me as the horror of Josef's news hits me straight in the gut. A distant relative of mine wanted to kill an unborn child? And Josef wonders why our family's hated by Dorian. I don't know the full Petrescu history and avoid looking too far into their past deeds. Many don't believe stories about the Confederacy's more extreme actions, instead blaming everything on the Dominion's terrorist work.

I never wanted to admit that the blood of sadistic tyrants runs through me. What really happened to Dorian, and Violet's other parents before Oskar died?

"I've taught you to honor your family name, haven't I?" he asks lazily, a smug awareness on his face now he's hit a weak spot.

"By using violence and torture to keep me from attacking people?"

"Yes. Now let the Blackwood kill these interfering witches before Kai comes to harm. Keep your hands and our family name clean." He nods. "And thus, eliminate the Blackwoods once the world sees them for what they are."

I brave holding his gaze in challenge, which is never a sensible move. Nor is my next one. "No," I say.

"Again, that word, Grayson." He moistens his lips. "You already know I can kill you. I've no aversion to making that death permanent if I don't feel you're committed to your family name."

Josef intends to terrify me into obedience. Again. If we'd had this conversation inside the cottage, the memories of my death would be harder to push away. The scent of my blood still lingers in the cellars, and the cottage's smell of mold and decaying wood would evoke images of the day. But outside, I've a freedom that Josef thinks he can steal, and a mind he wants to bend to his will.

"Now. Listen while I tell you exactly what I expect from you," says Josef. "I can't alert you to a time and place until the last moment, obviously, since you might pass this information on." I regard him silently. "Time will be short, and when you encounter the witches, rest assured I'll be close by to ensure the plan comes to fruition. Let the girl kill. Do not stop her. Subdue her afterwards."

That's impossible.

"This is my chance to get to these witches before Dorian. Do not waste the opportunity, or your life, Grayson."

How fortunate for him that I'm drawn to Violet and her to me. And how unfortunate for him I'm unable to escape how deeply she's affected me.

Josef knows I'll walk straight to Violet and inform her what was said here, and that she'll tell Dorian.

What does the man know?

Chapter Twenty-Five

VIOLET

AS THEY'RE HELPING US, Rowan insists we tell Marci and the other witches about our fateful visit to the house. Only Marci agrees to meet at short notice, so I'm forced to join Holly and Marci for coffee with Rowan at my side. We leave Leif out of the meeting after reporting back to him. Again, too many of us together could be noted if there's someone within the academy involved.

And Grayson? Not back, and the crawling across my skin intensifies each time I think of him with Josef. Unsafe.

I don't often frequent the academy cafeteria but have been known to join Holly. News already spread—probably due to Holly—about Marci embracing me into the dance committee. I stay tight-lipped rather than make a snarky comment to the still-smug Holly and she reminds me that's a reason to be with Marci right now. Violet Blackwood and Rowan Willowbrook's relationship also became of interest, and apparently Violet must always have one of her guys with her for protection.

Ludicrous.

Nita refuses to attend as she's particularly paranoid about

being seen with me, and the meeting's too short notice for socially in demand Zoe.

The moment we tell Marci our news, I'm vindicated in my protest to Rowan that this meeting wasn't a great idea. Marci shoves the coffee cup hard across the table and red spots appear on her cheek. I wrinkle my nose at Rowan, somewhat aware of her displeasure as she bounces a look between him and me.

"Why the hell did you go to the house in broad daylight? Couldn't you wait until the evening?"

I scratch a cheek. "I wanted to speak to the shifters." *To assess their state of body and mind.* "For any information they may have. The shifters wouldn't work at night."

"And what did they say?" she asks icily.

"Nothing. I decided to leave instead." I sniff at my coffee before taking a small sip from the tall cup.

"Then what was the bloody point in going?" snaps Marci. "Somebody could've seen you."

"They did. The witch whose cookies Rowan unwisely ate." Marci's jaw slackens. "But don't worry, we wiped her mind. We don't believe she's directly connected, either."

"I never took a bite of the cookie, I accepted one out of politeness," retorts Rowan.

"A witch *saw you*." Marci interrupts and sinks back and wipes a hand down her face. "Now I wish we hadn't told you about the house. I thought you'd be more careful."

Again, I've remained economical with the facts. Marci isn't aware of the witch's phone call or arranged meeting, and most certainly unaware about Maxwell and the constructs. This is a 'need to know' basis. I refuse to simply accept and believe Marci's innocence, particularly considering her dislike of me.

Holly remains silent, watching and absorbing, waiting for the moment she needs to jump in. I promised her I'd pull back on any words or behavior that could cause tension, but I'm unsuccessful so far.

"We need to locate the shifters and witches who may be involved, and quickly. Now I've evidence, I'll pass my findings on to Dorian who can locate the shifters to assess their wellbeing and apprehend these witches. Then authorities can interview them all." I smile. "Simple."

"Simple?" She chokes a laugh.

"Yeah, I doubt the witches will allow anybody to find them easily," says Rowan. "Let's hope Dorian's chat with Sawyer and Josef brings us closer to more facts."

Josef. I blink away images of Grayson injured by the sadistic creature; my stomach suddenly unsettled. Why hasn't Grayson contacted me to let me know he's safe?

"All Dorian needs to do is find and apprehend the witches. Even if they're skilled in mental magic, Dorian's men will be superior and can trawl inside their heads for the truth," I say.

"And what *is* the truth?" Marci leans across the table. "Because you're hiding something. Do you know what happened to Rory? Or where Oz is?"

"I can genuinely answer no to those questions," I say. If we're talking about *recently* and not his time wandering the town in an undead state.

"But you think the witches are involved in the murders?" she presses, and I nod. "Directly?"

Rowan turns to her from where he's watching those around. "At some level. Again, once Dorian gets a hold of the witches, things will become clearer."

"We *will* get justice for Wesley and Rory," I say. "We'll find anybody who's involved, inside *or* outside the academy. Do you suspect any academy involvement? You're a bigger part of the social web than we are."

Marci taps her fingers and looks to Holly, who nods. "Did you know that Mr. Wallis left? He isn't coping with Wes's death."

"What? When?" asks Rowan.

"There're rumors around Darwin House that he's resigned," says Holly. "I've heard there's an announcement to the whole academy at an assembly later today. I bet that's the reason; Mr. Wallis definitely isn't here anymore."

"And that puts Mrs. Lorcan in charge?" I ask, and Marci shrugs. "The school is now under full supernatural control.

Rowan, did you look into Mrs. Lorcan's connections? *All* the professors?"

Holly frowns. "*You* think people inside the academy are linked to this?"

"We can't rule out the possibility, especially as Wes's murder ended the human influence over the academy—the headmaster left," says Rowan. He shifts to face me. "I researched, yes. So far, everybody I've looked into worked at the academy for a number of years. Dorian closely vetted everybody. Unless anybody's drifted into these witches' influence and is hiding well, there's nobody questionable or anyone new on the staff."

But someone *did* break into my room. Tried to frame me with runes in *Wesley's* room.

"Then we continue to watch them all," I say.

"We can't put every professor under surveillance. Not all twenty of them," says Holly.

"No. But we can monitor for suspicious activity." I'm itching to ask Rowan about his research into the students—Marci and Holly. Nita and Zoe. Their families may have ties to each other.

Rowan agrees that we can't mention anything about the necromancy or Sawyer's connections, so of course, Marci knows I'm holding back. But I'm sure she's doing the same.

"The pendant you gave Rory," I say. "Explain more about that."

"Simple protection talisman."

"Yes," says Rowan. "But why did you choose the particular symbol? Because it coincidentally matches one that belonged to Kai and Wes."

"I explained to Violet—I found the spell in one of the library books we discovered, Rowan." She tips her head. "Are you still trying to decipher the code?"

"How does Marci know about that?" I ask sharply. "Did you write it, Marci?"

"No. We spent a lot of time together in the library in the past." Marci smiles. "Much like you do. Although..." She chuckles. "Me and Rowan didn't spend all our time looking at books."

"Performing spells?" I say. "I can imagine you made a strong couple." Nobody speaks and I side-glance Rowan, whose sudden silence and tight jaw confuse me. "Yes?"

Marci chuckles. "Have I embarrassed you, Rowan?"

"No," he says curtly. "You're trying to change the subject."

Holly stares at Marci, eyes wide. "I don't think you should talk about your past with Rowan in front of Violet."

"Why?" I ask.

"Marci, shut up and just tell me what you've discovered about the code," says Rowan.

"Haven't deciphered it either," Marci replies. "The word 'circle' appears a few times. A link to the Nightshadow Circle?"

"The Circle?" Rowan scoffs. "I doubt it. That's a group of obscenely rich witches who are more bothered about outdoing each other's wealth than practicing difficult spells."

"Are these individuals a threat to my father?" I perk up. "A secret society?"

"Not secret; a prestigious organization. Invitation only and a hefty entrance fee to their annual gathering. The rest of the time, the witches network to make as much money as possible, usually fleecing humans and hiding fraudulent activity." Rowan shakes his head. "Dorian would've looked into them or any other public covens. If the Circle had any connection to Sawyer, Dorian would've found one by now."

"But they're secretive?" I continue.

"In general, no, due to families flaunting their prestige. But everyone's forbidden to discuss what happens at their annual gathering," says Marci.

"Oh?" A tingle of excitement at a connection begins. "Illegal magic?"

"I know someone who attended once." Marci's lips tug into a weird smile. "The witches dress up and wear masks, and the only magic used is to get high. Pretty much one big orgy."

"Isn't that a supe thing?" asks Holly bluntly. "Multiple partners."

"Ask Violet," says Marci, with a smirk that's somewhat reminiscent of Rowan's attitude to me in the early days.

"I haven't partaken in orgies, and I would draw the line at such behavior even in the pursuit of my investigations." I sigh. "But you're sure this coven isn't involved? Is there a record of all the members?"

"Again, I expect Dorian's on it," says Rowan. "But these rich assholes are the type who wouldn't want any upheaval or change to the status quo. The current world order suits their needs."

"How about this annual meeting place?" I ask, and my jaw clenches. "Do they have a headquarters? How did I not know about this?"

"Because there's nothing remarkable about them," says Rowan. "And if I'm wrong and there is, Dorian will discover something, Violet."

Hmm. *Everybody* is a suspect to me.

"Does this Circle allow humans to join?" I ask. "*Could* Sawyer be involved?"

Marci shakes her head. "Witches and humans don't mix." She glances at Holly. "Usually. Sorry."

Holly shrugs.

"But secret codes and hidden spell books," I mutter. "As soon as I've solved the murders, we focus on those next, Rowan."

Marci snickers. "You might not like what you find, Detective Violet."

I slice her a look. "Why? What else do you know?"

"Did Rowan tell you why he spends so much time researching in the library?" She rubs a thumb against her chin. "You know his interest isn't purely academic."

"I am *here*," retorts Rowan. "And Violet knows."

"Yes. I'm aware of Rowan's interest in achieving magical supremacy." Rowan's eyes go wide. "He initially attempted to blackmail me into helping with a difficult spell. Failed, naturally."

"Rowan thinks the code links to a spell he could use to tune into secret magic—darker, more powerful."

"Again, I am aware," I say evenly. "We have no secrets."

"Everybody has secrets, Violet," says Marci and looks back to Rowan.

"Give it a rest, Marci," says Rowan wearily.

I look between them. "*Everybody*, Marci? Even you?"

Marci's saccharin smile is beginning to irritate me as much as Rowan's smirks once did. "Seems Rowan achieved his dark intentions in another way—through whatever deal you two have. Surely you won't teach Blackwood magic to Rowan, Violet?"

Her expression's clear, curious even, as if she can't figure out why else we'd spend time together. Can't witches sense bonds between others? Interesting. "I can assure you that I will not assist Rowan with any spell that would pose a threat to the academy or the world in general. I'm well aware Rowan pushes his magic to the limits and how potentially dangerous he is."

Marci bites her bottom lip, intensifying her scrutiny between me and the other witch. "Rowan's attracted to powerful witches for a reason, Violet."

"Is this a conversation about Rory and Wes's killer or not?" he asks tersely.

"Are you implying Rowan targeted you and has now targeted *me*?" I scoff and look between them, Rowan's face now thunderous and his familiar anger flashing at Marci this time. "I'm unaware how weak *you* are, but Rowan would fail to take advantage of or use me."

"I did not take advantage of Marci!" retorts Rowan. "Our interests were mutual."

"Mutual?" She laughs softly. "Our interest in *magic*, yeah."

How very curious. Is Marci attempting to cause trouble between Rowan and me the way she attempted to with Holly? My suspicion of the girl hasn't dropped—how much did Rowan involve her in his research? She asks for help with solving Rory's murder on behalf of Nita and then appears to drive a wedge between me and others.

Did her and Rowan's relationship end badly, or is this more?

"Well, this meeting veered a little off track," I say, and stand. "I merely wanted to communicate what happened today, not begin a discussion of yours and Rowan's unsuccessful romance. Thank you for the extra information about the Circle, Marci. Something for me to work on until we next speak to Dorian."

Marci picks up her coffee cup and slurps, watching me over the top as she does. "Where's Grayson?"

"I don't track his movements."

"No, but he tracks yours." She sips again. "I'd say the guy's obsessed. How does he fit into all… this?" She gestures between Rowan and me.

Why does this girl insist on attempting to rile me as if I'm a normal person who'd care about personal slights? "I'm collecting consorts. What's unusual about that for a half-witch?"

She falters—momentarily and Holly gasps. Actually *gasps.* "Nice," replies Marci.

"Odd choice of word." I tip my head at Rowan. "I'd like to talk to Leif now."

"Don't forget the committee meeting later," Marci adds casually.

"How could the opportunity to spend more time in your delightful company possibly slip my mind, Marci?"

Rowan remains quiet as we wander away. "Sorry about Marci," he says eventually.

"Why are you sorry?"

"The stuff about me and her. You don't need to worry."

He's cautious, and I pause to turn to him. "Why would I worry? Is there anything in her past or present that would make you suspect Marci's involvement with the crimes?"

"No. And that isn't what I meant."

I arch a brow. "That was spoken rather emphatically."

"Marci's another girl who likes the world as it is and doesn't like things out of her control."

"Oh. You have a 'type' then, Rowan?" I ask, and keep walking.

"A type?" He snorts a laugh as he follows. "You're one of a kind, sweet Violet."

"One of three—don't forget my parents. Now, tell me more about this Circle."

Chapter Twenty-Six

GRAYSON

ALTHOUGH I SENT Violet a message telling her I'm okay and would be back this evening, I'm still surprised to find her waiting for me. She's sitting on the bench inside the main building, at the foot of the stairs leading up to Sheridan House.

I smile to myself as I watch Violet for a few moments, at how focused she is on her phone when the girl swore she'd never use one. Sure, Violet rarely uses the thing for anything apart from taking notes and photos—often she forgets to reply to or ignores texts—but like almost every teen she's never without her phone now.

Yet she messaged *me*. Twice. Although the second one was in annoyance because I hadn't replied.

The mouth-watering blood scent reaches me first, and I'm pissed because I prefer *Violet's* scent from when I stand close—the subtle citrus of her hair, and how her skin's warmth intensifies the smell of the ocean smelling soap she uses.

Violet lifts her eyes, detecting my blood too. Despite everything between us, I can never read this girl. Her startling gaze holds mine, face void of anything inside her mind, and as I walk over, our focus remains on each other.

Does the world retreat when I see Violet because every sense focuses on the blood union we crave, or because the girl overwhelms me by just being *her*? Thoughts of Violet engulfed me the whole time I spent with Josef, and to say I'm obsessed with her is a huge understatement. I could've scratched Josef's eyes out for mentioning Oskar's intention to kill Violet before she was born.

"Where's the blood?" Violet asks, phone screen still lit in her hand.

"What? My blood?"

"Yes."

Whoa. "You want my blood?" I ask warily.

"Good grief! Do you ever think about anything else when you see me?"

Oh yes, Violet. Plenty.

"I mean, you're uninjured. What did Josef do to you? Hidden injuries?" She pauses. "You were away for some time. I hope he didn't kill you. Death wouldn't be pleasant—as I've discovered."

"Right. No, he didn't kill me. Or injure me. Just a threat or two." I dig hands into my back pockets and look around. "What's been happening?"

No other students move through the hallways at this hour. Most are out in town or in the different student houses by now, but Violet peers around her anyway, as if someone followed. "I discovered that Holly's dance committee is a coven, and that the witches who're connected to the shifters enjoy renovating houses."

I close my eyes and shake my head. "The coven, right, we considered that. But witches... They do *what*? Do you mean the ones connected to Sawyer?"

"Can we talk about this elsewhere?" she asks and stands. "Your room?"

"Uh. Alright." But my feet don't move.

She points at my boots. "What's wrong? Are you concerned I'm using this as an excuse to attack you for your blood?"

"I should be so lucky," I mutter to myself.

"I heard that." Violet presses her lips together. "And no, you would not be lucky."

"Let's not have this conversation while we're both pretending blood isn't in our minds every time we look at each other?" I raise a brow. "Come on."

The last time Violet visited my room, she definitely wanted my blood, and her confusion and discomfort amused me. For once, I felt in control, not Violet, even if I'd just found myself beside another murder victim. This evening, Violet marches straight to the window, opens it wide and looks down at the path below, rather than at me.

"Rowan and I located a place where shifters labor for witches." Violet looks back over her shoulder. "A demolition site that Oz and Rory both worked at. We visited, and I saw one of the witches from the hospital on the premises. Also, two shifters, but no Oz."

I push my discarded blazer from the desk chair and sit. "Wow. Okay. Full story."

Violet explains everything I missed, interspersed with odd comments about 'the Spring Ball nightmare', 'that Marci girl', and a calico cat—and she seems particularly upset about Rowan and cookies.

How are things between Violet and Rowan? I don't know the witch well, but the guy's usually a loner and only Leif ever put up with his snotty, superior attitude. Now he's bonded to Violet, who treats him as an extension of herself. Because she feels vulnerable admitting he's not only a 'bonded witch' but a guy she likes and relies on?

Does Violet know this seemingly quiet guy triggers easily and has a massive temper? He can't and won't hide that part of who he is, and I've pictured the pair clashing. The result would be amusing but dangerous. Has Violet shown *him* her hybrid side or am I the only one? Although even I haven't seen the hybrid side. Not totally.

Everything she tells me backs up some of Josef's story, and I hate I'm about to extinguish some of the shine in her eyes with *my* news.

A breeze lifts Violet's hair, scattering the mingled scents across my room. "Violet. Are you standing by the window so you can't smell me?"

She pushes her tongue against her top teeth. "What happened with Josef that you should report to me?"

"You'll be surprised when I tell you," I say.

"I don't think you can predict my responses, Grayson."

I shrug. "Fine. Josef isn't involved with the witches. He wants you to kill them because they're threatening Sawyer and Kai. He's setting up a meeting to put you and them in the same location."

She remains stony faced as I outline the conversation I had with Josef. "One, I don't believe your uncle *isn't* connected. Two, I don't intend to kill the witches, because if they die, I've nobody to hand over as a culprit for the murders or necromancy."

I scratch my cheek, recalling the latter part of his demands. "Josef also wants me to subdue you until somebody discovers Violet Blackwood and the dead witches."

She slants her head. "Subdue or kill?"

I choke indignantly. "I wouldn't kill you, Violet. Apart from the fact I care about you a lot, that'd be my death sentence at Dorian's hands."

"That and you'd lose against me anyway," she says casually. "You would die."

"Maybe."

"Depending on my mood and level of savagery, yes."

I blow air into my cheeks. "The bastard also threatened to kill me permanently if I don't help with this plan."

She moves from the window towards me and tips her head back. "Then we need to deal with the threat to your life. Because either way, this doesn't look good for your health if you disobey Josef."

"Yeah. And he'll make *my* death look like your handiwork too."

She's still for a few moments, and even though Violet's hiding herself, the blood running closer to her skin betrays her speeding heart. "I would never kill you, Grayson. Not on purpose."

On purpose. I shake my head. "Dorian would be proud if you did kill a Petrescu."

"And I shall."

"What?"

"Your uncle, not you," she says. "Once the time is right."

"I hope you're joking."

Her face says not. "Did Josef say when and where this meeting would be?"

"No. Not yet."

"And you'll tell me if you hear?"

"Yes. But what if I'm lying to you about all this?" I ask. "Is there something between us that would stop you from killing me?"

"You're a friend. I wouldn't kill a friend and would also hope your affection for me would prevent you aiding in framing me."

"Sometimes you don't look at me as if I'm your friend," I say quietly.

"Would you like me to apologize for my hybrid assault on you at the party? Is that what bothers you?"

I sigh. "No. That isn't what I meant."

Violet subtly moves her hand across her face and turns away; when she reaches the window, she looks at her phone. "We should talk to the others about this situation. I need to arrange to speak with Dorian. Thank you for what I hope is your honest account of events."

"Did you worry about me with Josef?" I ask. "You waited for me. Downstairs."

Violet looks up. "Naturally."

"Not naturally for you."

Her infuriating self passes me to reach the door, where she pauses, fingers curled around the handle and looks back. "Sometimes I wonder how kissing you would feel."

I'm too stunned to grab the chance to suggest she does—or grab *her.*

"And then I conclude that I'd use the opportunity to bite your lip or tongue in order to taste your blood." Violet opens the door. "I'm no expert, but I don't think people in a romantic relationship do things like that to each other."

Again, no words.

"Yes." She nods as if finding the solution to a difficult equation. "Friends makes much more sense and ensures your safety. That is the way forward."

As Violet stalks along the hallway to tick off the next item on her list, I hold on to the edge of the door and watch her walk away from *us*. She's clueless how perfect she is to me. I'm one racing heartbeat away from pursuing Violet but remain mesmerized by the gentle sway of her hips, the subtle curve of her neck beneath her ponytail, and every other kissable—biteable—part of her. Her lips never pressed to mine, but they're in my mind as always.

How can I be crazy for such an unhinged, unavailable girl? The one who's dangerous to my health in oh-so-many ways.

Chapter Twenty-Seven

VIOLET

THERE'S a new tension between the four of us today, one I can pick up on because every one of them exudes something that interferes with my concentration.

"I'm confused why you've asked to meet Dorian at the *mall*," says Leif. "Like, this place is somewhere you hate."

"Maybe Violet prefers Dorian in public when she tells him Grayson wants to kill her," says Rowan stiffly.

"I don't want to kill Violet," he retorts.

"What else does 'subdue' mean?" replies Rowan.

Ah. That's why they're ignoring each other after our chat last night. I believed a mutual exchange of information may help with our plans and speed the movement towards success, but instead we've something unhelpful and irritating.

Conflict.

"I'm meeting Holly afterwards. At the mall."

Rowan double takes. "You're shopping with Holly? For what?"

"I have no idea and can only hope she locates the item or items quickly." Their quizzical looks continue, which is better than the earlier glaring at each other. "I'm on the dance committee. Therefore, I must partake in organizational activities."

Leif snorts a laugh, and winces when I punch his arm.

"I'm unimpressed that you find this amusing. Not only is the inanity detracting from my precious time, but Holly relishes my involvement. And there's that unpleasant *girl.*"

"What girl?" asks Leif.

"Marci. The witch behaves as if she's superior to everybody and is quite rude to Holly on occasion."

"Wow. Imagine Holly being friends with *that* type of girl," Leif replies and exchanges a sly smile with the other guys.

"I don't believe that's amusing at all. Poor Holly."

"Yes, poor Holly." Grayson and Leif swap a friendlier look, and I'm mystified what changed their terse attitude towards each other.

"At least Marci helped us," says Rowan. "We'd never know about the shifters' connection to the witches without her. I hope Dorian had a useful meeting with Sawyer and *Josef.*"

Grayson's and Rowan's gazes lock.

"Good grief," I say. "All this testosterone is choking me, and if you don't stop, *I'll* choke you both. Nobody is killing anybody."

A young woman passing by holds her daughter's hand tighter and hurries the small girl along.

"Nice one, Violet," says Grayson. "Scare the humans."

"I said *not* killing."

Dorian waits for us in a cafe at the edge of the mall, which means I don't technically need to enter Holly's territory. Yet. Sitting at a round table beneath a local landscape art piece, he's casually dressed in jeans and a faded black T-shirt, looking little different in age to me as usual. At least when Dorian wears less youthful clothing, he sets himself apart from the younger guys around.

"Is Eloise not with you today?" I ask him.

"I haven't left town since last night." Dorian watches each guy in an unnecessarily predatory way as they sit around the circular table with me. "With current events in town, I like to remind local people I'm around."

I don't bother telling Dorian that outside the academy, few humans know who he is, although they'll easily sense his supernatural 'stay away' aura. The young woman in the red shirt with the café logo who approaches certainly looks more nervous than impressed, almost spilling coffee as she places Dorian's cup on the table.

"How was your meeting with Grayson's uncle and Sawyer?" I ask.

Grayson suddenly becomes intent on reading the laminated menu. "Can you not refer to him like that?" he mutters.

"Your uncle? I'm unlikely to forget, Grayson." Dorian tips sugar into his coffee. "A rather unpleasant man. I hope he wasn't too unkind to you when you 'caught up'. He didn't comment when I asked after you."

Grayson holds the menu tighter.

Our information is best shared after Dorian shares his, as he won't be in the mood for talking after Grayson's news. In fact, Grayson should perhaps sit at a table across the café. There's half a truth to Rowan's comment as to why I chose to meet Dorian in public, and why I selected the most popular café with the largest space.

"I'm visiting him alone later," says Dorian.

"Josef?"

"Sawyer. Josef should avoid time alone with me." He glances at Grayson, but at least without a penetrating stare. "I told the man that I know about his links to the witches and need to talk about the situation."

I straighten. "And do you?"

"No. But Sawyer isn't aware of that. A quick sweep of his mind tells me he's concerned about Josef's advice, so perhaps I can find a way to the bottom of this situation." He drinks. "Kai remains confined to his home."

"Good," I say. "Make sure you ask Sawyer about the runes in his room"

"Naturally. Sawyer will tell me everything, verbally or non-verbally." Dorian taps the side of his head. "These witches *must* be in my custody soon. I need their minds trawled by my own witches and confessions 'elicited'. We don't know the extent of their necromancy, either. Numerous shifters could be unwittingly involved."

Leif shifts in his seat, fingers curling around the pendant still worn around his neck.

"Apologies, Leif, but I'm focused on apprehending the witches and then we'll look into what's happening amongst the shifters." He scratches his nose. "We can't help the kids already targeted and used, but we can nip this in the bud."

"Nip this in the bud?" blurts Leif. "This isn't delinquent behavior. It's a crime."

I nudge Leif hard. *Bad idea.* Dorian's shown a calmer side over recent events, but he's unlikely to stay that way if challenged.

"Yes, Leif," he says through gritted teeth, showing too much canine for comfort. "But my daughter's safety comes first." His savage look drills into poor Leif's face. "I will do everything necessary to protect her. *Everything.* Is that clear?"

"More than crystal, Dorian," I interrupt. "And Leif's stressed. He's no experience of necromancy."

"None of us has," says Rowan.

But Dorian's focus shifted again. "Why's Grayson more nervous of me than last time we met?" He slants his head. "Has something happened between you and him, Violet? Does he have your blood?"

"Good grief, no," I mutter.

"So?" He arches a brow.

Grayson runs fingers repeatedly through his hair, silently forming the story in his head but not sharing. I sigh. "Grayson won't hurt me, even though someone asked him to."

"Fuck, Violet," says Grayson hoarsely.

"Excuse me?" growls Dorian. "Explain."

"Well, Josef—" I begin.

"Let Grayson explain," says Rowan quietly. "Less bluntly."

I rest my hand on top of Grayson's slender fingers, the cool of his ring against my palm. My gesture mutes him further and Dorian hisses air between his teeth.

"Again, I require a guarantee that you won't hurt Grayson, Dorian." My father often has a glare worthy of a petulant toddler—which I once told him and regretted the decision. The exact look he has now. "Grayson has information about the witches that I saw at the house."

"Is that so?" asks Dorian darkly. "Friends of Josef's? Is that why Sawyer wouldn't speak to me about them in his presence?"

Grayson finds his voice again and cautiously relays his tale to Dorian, repeating what he told Rowan and Leif last night after meeting me. To his credit, Dorian listens and doesn't interrupt. He taps his manicured fingers against the side of his cup.

"Josef Petrescu is not an idiot and yet that plan stinks of idiocy. He knows Grayson will tell you, Violet, and then me. He's intending to lure me into a situation." Dorian nods at me. "You are not to approach anymore witches or locations where they might be. If you see anybody who's connected, or if Josef contacts Grayson, you contact me immediately."

"But—"

"Violet." His warning growl runs over everybody at the table. "I will confine you to the estate if you ignore me. I'm close to locating and apprehending these witches. Your work is done."

I choke. "No. There's a bigger picture. I want to keep investigating. The shifters, and—"

"Once I apprehend the killers and hand them over to human authorities with their confessions, yes. For now, no." He sets down the cup and looks from guy to guy. "And your *acquaintances* will ensure you don't go against my wishes, if they know what's good for them."

"They can't tell me what to do," I retort.

"Do you want them to stay safe, Violet?" he retorts. "Your Petrescu friend in particular would be wise to listen to me."

"Absolutely," says Grayson stiffly.

Speaking of petulant toddlers, I rest back in my seat and give Dorian a well-practiced daughterly scowl.

"Now, where is this phone you neglected to give me the other night?" He holds a hand out, palm upwards. "Any further communication from these witches needs to come to me."

Yesterday evening, when I called to explain some of my day, Dorian questioned me about how I knew the witch left a message for Maxwell. When I answered, I had to hold the phone away from my ear as he yelled at me. At that point, I suggested he meet us today rather than risk the outcome if I informed him of Grayson's news too.

"Violet, I'll meet Sawyer tonight. Then I'll locate the witches —I already have men visiting the house you mentioned and the lodge, in case either of those are the meeting location. I'm also looking further into the house owners' affairs and background. I'll deal with the witches, and I can move on to look for whoever's overseeing this doomed plot against me."

"We."

"Phone."

Glaring, I retrieve the phone from my sweater pocket and slam it on the table, which he takes and shoves into his jeans pocket.

Dorian stands and takes the black jacket he doesn't need to wear from the seat beside him. He's always one to disguise his supernatural traits in human company—none would walk around in the rain without a jacket and the gloomy weather demands one.

"Don't disobey me, Violet."

"We," I repeat through clenched teeth.

"Do stay safe everybody," Dorian says and smiles before walking away.

Rowan opens his mouth to say something to me, but pauses as I turn my sour face his way. None of the guys need any hint as to my mood.

The chances they'll say the wrong thing to me are almost as guaranteed as the chance I'll ignore Dorian and continue my investigations.

Chapter Twenty-Eight

VIOLET

THE MALL. I swore I'd never visit the place again and now I've had two engagements here in one day. My bad mood following Dorian's authoritarian behavior became decidedly blacker when Leif jokingly suggested retail therapy with Holly might calm me down. Grayson and Rowan wisely remained silent as they all left the café before my storm cloud burst on them.

Leaving me to my retail *trauma* with my dear friend and roommate.

Holly bounds ahead with her usual bouncy enthusiasm and I trudge behind until we arrive at a third set of escalators heading further into the heart of my personal purgatory.

Thirty excruciating minutes later, I'm still here, now standing in the narrow aisle of a store stacked with linens and assorted homewares.

"I heard that many sensible people shop online," I say pointedly.

"Where's the fun in that?" asks Holly.

"Where's the fun in *this*? You've spent half an hour comparing colors and trimmings on these... whatever. There's a minuscule difference in shade and texture, even with vamp eyesight." I huff and look around. "Can we go now?"

"Soon." I pull a face as she rubs the material against a cheek.

"And how does this item fit the Goth theme that Violet Blackwood has mind-controlled the committee into using before she conducts her massacre at the dance?" I ask.

Of course, the news I'm involved rippled around the academy faster than the speed I could run from all this.

"Everybody knows that's a joke." Holly rubs her fingers between two separate but almost identical fabrics.

"Perhaps I *should* dictate the theme since there's only *one* shade of black," I say pointedly.

"Oh, but think about the different laces you'd need to choose from," says Holly with a sly smile. "Plus, the candle colors. Style of the skulls. Everything coordinated."

Blowing air into my cheeks, I look the other way. Floor to ceiling shelves between the wall and the piled linens are stacked with glasses, everything from slender flutes to fish bowl size, some painted in gold or silver, and others with glass etched into intricate patterns. If Holly starts searching for more 'inspiration', I'll be forced to raise the volume of my protest.

Holly looks up, material draped over her arm, having finally chosen her table-runner sample.

"Surely Marci's advice would've assisted more than mine," I say, grabbing Holly's cheeks in one hand and turning her face away from another shelf distracting her.

"There's something else I need your help with choosing." She slaps my fingers away.

"Not the glasses!" I ask in horror. "There're *dozens* of options. Please. Enough. You've paraded me as a 'helper' to back up our story; I want to leave. I've arranged to meet Rowan and Leif."

"No. Not glasses." *That* expression. The way Holly's eyes gleam, her mouth slightly curled as if avoiding a full smile. Exactly how she looks when believing she has an edge over me. "A dress for the dance."

I balk. "You don't need me for *that*. Good grief, I'm pleading with you not to take me into another store. I have no sense of fashion and could not assist your search in any way. Ask Marci."

"No, silly. For you."

"I don't need one. I'm not attending." I mentally calculate the quickest route from the mall.

"Violet. You're a committee member. Of course, you're attending."

I study her now undisguised 'gotcha' look. "Your sweet and friendly act doesn't fool me, Holly. You are, in fact, a ruthless criminal mastermind."

"What?" Her smugness slips away. "You suspect me? What have I done? Didn't we explain the items in my closet?"

"You planned to ensnare me into this dance committee in order to strong-arm me into partaking in the event." I narrow my eyes. "Have I not made myself clear on the subject?"

"Well." Holly taps her lips. "There *was* your comment how you'd rather be flayed alive than attend the dance. And also, the time you told me you'd rather be locked in an airless room with nothing but venomous spiders for company."

"Not enough clarity?"

She chuckles. "You'd better choose which of your guys to bring with you."

I can't help the snarl that escapes; one loud enough to earn a look of alarm from the elderly lady beside me. The snarl that grows when Holly adds, "And choose your dress."

"I shall do neither, Holly," I retort. "Now get me out of here before I'm tempted to mind-control you off the upper floor balcony."

FEW PEOPLE FOUND interest in the boutique homewares shop, but we step out into a mass of shoppers. Holly's territory confuses me, and everybody here resembles mice running round a maze trying to find the place that dispenses food. Or in their case, consumer delights.

I immediately stride towards the elevator that leads down to the bowels of the mall and Holly rushes to step in front. I pull myself to a stop as she faces me.

"Violet."

I regard her unblinkingly. "Holly."

"Please come with me. I promise not to force you into a dress. If you want to wear your usual clothes to the dance, that's okay." She smiles hesitantly. "But you could help me decide? There's too much choice."

"Come with you on the off-chance I'll see a dress and swoon at the idea I could wear the thing and look pretty?" I arch a brow.

"Just a look?" she continues. "Please."

"Don't start whining. I hate whining. That's why I'm happy with a life free from siblings."

"I was *not* whining." She pauses and blinks. "Free from? Did you kill a brother or sister for annoying you?"

I run my tongue along my top teeth and look at her impassively. "What do you think?"

"Omigod, Violet." Her eyes go as large as one of the fishbowl glasses.

Honestly. This is as bad as her initial belief that I ate children. "I don't have a whining sibling, Holly."

"Anymore?" she whispers.

I *could* allow Holly to continue believing that I'm capable of fratricide, but I'm more generous to her than in our early encounters. "Do you think the world has room for another Violet Blackwood?"

"You did kill!"

"Good grief!" I choke. "No. My parents ceased reproduction after one spawn. I once asked why, and they told me 'complicated reasons'. I presume I'm the complicated reasons."

"Would you've liked a brother or sister?" she asks.

"Do *you* have one?"

"An older sister. She isn't at the academy. Ivy never attended."

"And do you like said sibling?"

Holly pulls a non-committal face while I try to picture her

sister. "She was mean to me when we were younger, but we get along okay now."

"Sounds excruciating either way. I'm perfectly content as an only child and the world should be too." I pull my phone from a pocket to check the time. "Can we leave?"

She tips her chin. "You *are* coming to the dance, Miss Blackwood, otherwise no more assistance with your investigation."

"Quite the little blackmailer, aren't you? Do you think that's wise behavior?" I ask and smile to myself as worry lines her face again.

I may be surrounded by mice in a maze, but remaining in one spot makes me a sitting duck, despite the wide plant pot filled with invasive Yucca plants beside my head. The Darwin House guys I've avoided since Kai's party are resting against a metal barrier opposite. One that would prevent them from accidentally falling from the balcony if a particularly dark-hearted person felt tempted to shove them. The pair sip soda drinks through straws as they watch us.

Naturally, I return their scrutiny. Like me and Holly, the guys aren't in uniform, blending further into the townsfolk around. Holly's continued chatter about clothing doesn't reach my ears, as I have my hearing trained on their conversation. I meet Logan's eyes and he pulls himself from the railings, drops his cup into the nearby trash, and walks over. Notably, he remains at arm's length.

"If you've unfinished business and are looking for Grayson, he isn't with me today," I say.

"The guy might've confessed to murder, but someone's lying," Logan says gruffly.

"Grayson?" I ask in disbelief.

"No. The shifter dude," puts in Raul.

I sigh. "Would you know the name of the specific 'shifter dude'?"

"One of Viggo's crew. The one who collapsed at the bowling alley in front of *you*." Logan's lip curls. "Yeah. We heard all about that."

"Oz? Confessed? To what?" We remain at a wary distance from each other—wary on his part.

"Killing Wes and Rory." He sneers. "Allegedly."

"Oz *confessed* to killing Wesley and Rory?"

Logan nudges his friend. "And she says *we're* the dumb ones. Yes, he did," he says to me slowly, as if speaking to an imbecile.

"Where is Oz?" I ask.

He scoffs. "Where do people usually go when they confess to crimes?"

The station. "No." I rub my forehead. "That makes no sense."

"Why? Because the Blackwood bitch did it?" says Raul.

Oh, for goodness sake. "Raul. I'm confused why you'd speak to me in such a manner, considering my response to your unwanted touch at the party." I pull myself closer to his height. "Luckily, Grayson came between you and my teeth. I'm unsure Holly could manage the same." I turn to Holly. "I need to leave."

Raul finds the common sense to shut up. Logan does not. "Oh, and another thing before you go," he says with a hint of smugness, and I turn a weary gaze his way. "They arrested Leif too. Apparently, the guy was Oz's accomplice."

In a single second, Logan smashes through my carefully constructed reality, where everything slotted into place, and my friends remained safe. I have no words, only an image of Leif clinging to his pendant earlier.

"No," says Holly in hushed shock. "That can't be right. Leif didn't do anything."

"How can you know that?" asks Raul.

"When did this happen?" I demand. "I was with him an hour ago. News evidently travels at the speed of light in this town."

Logan shrugs. "Poor guy—taken advantage of and screwed over by you."

I'm reeling, this development beyond anything I expected. The human authorities wouldn't have any evidence. *Would they?* And Oz. Why would the witches put him in a position where supe authorities could look into his empty head?

"Is there new evidence against Leif since the last time cops interviewed him?" asks Holly, as if reading my mind, and clutches the bag closer to her chest. "Leif isn't friendly with shifters. Why would he help Oz? And why would Oz kill one of his own friends?"

"Do *I* look like a cop?" retorts Logan. "All I know is the pair killed Wes and Rory."

Raul crosses his arms over his puffed out chest. "Now there's proof the animals can't be controlled, any shifter that walks into town's looking for trouble."

"Especially anybody connected to Rory or Oz. Like the shifter asshole who leads them," adds Logan.

"Maybe Viggo instructed Rory?" suggests Holly. "And Oz?"

"No," I reply. "Incorrect."

"And you could only sound so sure if you were involved," says Logan in triumph.

"Shifters rarely kill each other unless there's an issue within their packs. *And* Viggo doesn't like Leif. Leif avoids shifters. There's no way he's involved."

I startle as Holly pats my arm. "Don't worry, Violet. Leif will be okay."

"I'm not worried. This merely expedites my need to locate the real killers," I say, half to myself.

"Yeah, at least Kai can leave his house now someone's arrested," says Raul. "His parents are paranoid someone will kill him next and won't let him out."

"No!" They stare at my vehement tone. "Kai should not leave the house."

"I heard he's grounded for the DUI," says Holly hastily as Logan's brow draws together at my vehemence.

"His parents don't watch him 24/7. Can't cage Kai." Raul smirks.

"Good grief," I mutter. "Is the guy stupid? If Kai's father's concerned for his safety, Kai should pay attention."

"Why the sudden concern?" asks Logan.

"Because Leif and Oz aren't responsible!" I look at Holly. "I need to find Rowan. He doesn't know what's happened, or he would've called me."

"We should've sorted the shifters months ago," says Logan darkly. "If they come into town now, we will."

The world threatens to crack further as the fault line between shifters and humans widens by the moment. "Why is excessive violence your solution to conflict?" I ask. "Is it not enough that they arrested Oz if you believe he killed Wesley?"

Logan steps forward. "Yeah? There won't be justice for Wes. Just you watch. The shifter elders will step in and take Oz back to their stinking settlement. At least your boyfriend will get what he deserves unless he pleads his shifter side, and the elders take him too."

No. *No.* What's happening here?

"Yeah," puts in Raul. "Wait until Kai hears. Then the fun will begin—it's the shifters' fault he's grounded."

"Uh. The DUI?" Holly reminds them.

I'm barely listening any longer, mind in overdrive what I'll do next. Leif *was* at the scene the night Wesley died, but I'm positive he didn't touch the guy. Leif's memories proved that. Others need to see into Leif's mind too—see the truth.

A thought buzzes around like an insect. The witches took Oz from the hospital and hid him. Why would they then allow their construct into a situation where authorities will discover his true state?

I catch sight of myself in one of the many mirrors that run through the mall. A girl dressed in black leggings and loose cotton and lace shirt to match, the long silver pendant hiding a blade resting against her pale skin. Dorian Blackwood's darkling daughter with her aloof persona, the notable blue eyes watching the world in a different way to how these people do.

A deceptively delicate and pretty girl with a love of telling the world exactly what she is and why they should keep away from her.

Isn't the answer clear? If the Blackwood runes couldn't implicate me, my vocal pride that I'm a necromancer will.

Chapter Twenty-Nine

LEIF

OZ HAS no mind because he's a necromancer's construct; mine's blank after being blasted out of reality. One minute I'm preparing to meet up with the others again, the next I'm hauled into a cop car and thrown into an interview room, confused as hell.

Who set me up? Shifters or those bloody witches?

I've sat at this bare table in the interview room for what feels like hours, repeating my denial again and again, as a gray-haired detective and a younger, friendlier faced one play good cop/bad cop with me. Senior Detective Wagner and Detective Harding. They interviewed me once before, after Wes's death, but last time with witches present who confirmed every word was the truth.

Now, no witches and no chance these men will believe me.

The two detectives inform me Oz admitted to killing Rory because he wouldn't keep quiet about the three of us murdering Wesley. *And* that I should think myself lucky because Oz would've murdered me next. How can I say Kai's the one under threat without sounding sus?

So, I repeat my denials, one eye on the clock that seems to

never change time, positive the detectives will let me go when I've nothing to give them.

Until Wagner smugly plays his ace and shows me video footage from the night Wesley died. I stagger mentally further back from the world as I numbly watch his laptop screen. I'm in the woods with Rory and Wesley. There's a scuffle between the pair, the camera barely picking out what happens in the dim, until the growing brawl becomes growls and slashing. There're no voices, nor is there any sign of the witches from my memories, only thick trunks and branches obscuring the scene.

The camera pans around to me, standing a few meters away, silent, staring.

And when I rush forward, that's all these detectives need. To the world watching, I'm joining in, not trying to stop the attack.

I wipe both hands down my face. "I didn't do anything."

"Oz's phone footage says otherwise." Wagner rests back in the chair, arms crossed over his chest, paunch straining against his beige shirt. The 'nicer' detective remains silent.

"I tried to help," I say, keeping my voice stronger than I feel right now.

"Uh huh. So that's why you immediately reported the crime after the fact?" he asks, then pretends to search through some papers spread on the desk. "Because I don't have any record of a good Samaritan helping out a dying boy."

"I couldn't remember, that's why!"

Wagner exchanges a look with an impassive Harding. "If you couldn't remember, how do you remember *now*?"

"No. I couldn't remember until—" *Violet* "—recently."

"And whose idea was it to deflect attention by drawing a Blackwood rune?" asks Wagner.

Harding tuts. "And then befriending Violet Blackwood and leading her on a wild goose chase. Or was she involved too?" I look back at the clock. "Do yourself a favor, Leif. Tell us everything."

"I'm not even friends with shifters!" I protest, then drag a hand through my hair.

Wagner leans forward. "The shifters want to deal with this

'in house', as it were—for us to release Oz to their custody. But since one of the victims *and* a suspect is human, we're staying involved."

"And the supernatural council?" I ask and straighten. They'll know what Oz is—see his empty mind.

"No involvement at this point. Mr. Blackwood's *so* insistent that his daughter isn't involved. We've no witch or vampire suspects in custody, nor was one of his own murdered, therefore, he can keep his nose out."

My mind whirls. "But witches could look into my mind. Into Oz's mind. They'll see the truth."

Harding looks at me as he taps the phone in a plastic bag beside the laptop. "I believe we have the truth here, Leif."

How? How has this footage only just come to light? Where'd Oz's phone come from?

But I know the answer—the witches filmed the death and chose their moment to 'anonymously' handover the phone evidence to the authorities.

"I've no reason to murder Wesley."

"You thought he was Kai. Oz told us."

"I had no reason to murder him either! This is insane. I didn't *do* anything." I jab a finger at the laptop displaying the footage. "I was *helping*."

"The rune, Leif. Was that the Blackwood girl? Because if so, we could involve the supernatural council. We'd be obliged to," says Harding slyly.

I sink back again. "Where's my attorney? You can't do all this without one. I have rights!"

"Like Wesley's right to stay alive?" asks Wagner.

"Who was next on the list, Leif?" pushes Harding.

"By your deductions, *me*," I retort. "I hope you're watching Kai if that's who Oz intended to kill."

I need to talk to Violet. Dorian. *Somebody*. Can Ethan help? His connections with the shifters?

"What about the witches who took Oz from the ER the other night?" I ask. "Isn't that suspicious? He was seriously ill."

"Oz was under the influence of illicit substances," says

Wagner. *Under the influence, yeah. Drugs? No.* "That's a common problem we have with teens in town, especially shifters."

I lean forward, forearms on the table. "I'm not a shifter, but I'm beginning to understand why there's constant trouble between them and humans. They're not the only violent, drug-influenced part of the town, but shifters are made to feel like they are. I think you're being incredibly narrow sighted to discount witch involvement. What's Oz said about *that?*"

Wagner presses his lips together. "That's information one of you will share."

I eye them both. Rory. They've barely touched on his death. Where's his body? Because if the detectives knew the wake never happened they'd say something, surely.

"The witches who took Oz from the hospital!" I urge. "*Why* would they?"

"Nobody took Oz from the hospital."

"Jesus!" I hold both palms against my forehead. "Someone in this town is covering things up. I saw the witches take Oz! I was at the hospital. Don't you have security footage?"

"Yes, Leif, but there are mysterious gaps in the time stamps, as if someone tampered with the recording. No witches on camera, but Rowan Willowbrook and Violet Blackwood were with you. Do you think we need to question them next?" Harding asks softly.

"What about DNA? Mine would be on Wes's clothes." I pause. "Or Rory's."

"Funnily enough, we struggled to find any DNA." Harding moistens his lips.

"Because witches were involved," I half-shout. "Why aren't you listening to me? Have they screwed with your minds too?"

"Witch involvement? *Hybrid* involvement. Runes. DNA removed. Tell us how the Blackwood girl is involved and help yourself."

I fight sneering at them. "You think Dorian would keep out of this if Violet's dragged in again? Sure. Bring Dorian in now. And his mind-reading witches. Tell them to look into Oz's empty head!"

Harding tuts again and looks to his colleague. "And Leif says *we're* prejudiced against shifters."

I slump back. "I'm not saying any more. But you have this wrong. Your pieces don't fit together."

Silence falls and I rub my perspiring palms against my lap, before sipping from the bottle of water a staff member brought me over an hour ago.

"Leif. Video evidence is a large piece of the puzzle and fits perfectly. Now we need somebody to give us names. Oz couldn't draw a witch rune as intricate as the one on the bodies."

"Witches," I say through gritted teeth.

This is useless.

I know I saw Wes's murder because Violet helped me find that memory, but I'm also positive I stumbled across the scene when running from my fight with Viggo. Wrong place, wrong time that led to the witches messing with my head rather than killing me? Or am *I* the one set up?

As the detectives take me back to the small cell to consider if my next home will be the county jail, I picture Violet and her recent responses to unjust treatment of others. There's nothing Violet can do or say that stands against the evidence on that phone.

I hope to hell that when the hybrid girl descends on the sheriff's office, Rowan accompanies her.

Chapter Thirty

VIOLET

I'M NOT HERE to steal evidence and pay a side-visit to the morgue this time, but I am dealing with the same woman, who's well-practiced in preventing anybody passing. I'm under strict instruction by Rowan *not* to use a spell on her mind and risk a stay in a cell too, but the temptation rises the more times she refuses to let me see Leif.

"I'm still not sure we should've come here, Violet," says Rowan.

I turn away from the unhelpful woman who watches us closely. "Did you honestly expect me to do anything different?"

"No," he mutters. "Will you let me speak to the receptionist? You're... agitated."

"I am not," I snap, pulling at a thread on my sweater sleeve.

"Uh. Violet. The bond along with your whole demeanor tells me otherwise," he says cautiously.

"If I were agitated, I wouldn't *listen* to somebody. I'd simply attack them."

Rowan glances at the round-cheeked, officious staff member who's now completely still, eyes wider. "Can you at least be quiet until I've discovered where Leif is and what's happening?" he snaps back.

Clenching and unclenching my fists, I stalk towards the metal bench that spans the wall opposite and to the left of the area I'm trying to pass through. Amongst them, a middle-aged woman sits stiffly, clutching a small black purse on her lap, and looks as ready to explode as I am.

No memorials today, so the station fills with more bodies and accompanying noise than my last visit. The situation's made worse by my close proximity to so much talking and shouting, all of which grates on my remaining nerve.

I cross my arms and lean forward to look towards a closed door at the end of the entrance hallway. One person in uniform went through earlier. Is this where the humans are holding Leif?

Why?

Rowan has his elbows on the woman's reception desk, leaning in to speak and she's ignoring him, tapping her keyboard. We're getting no more information from her. I bounce a look around those gathered again. Are Oz's parents here? Leif's mother? The pissed woman beside me is definitely human, but Leif's mother lives a few hours' drive from the town, which means she won't be here yet.

Rowan returns and throws himself onto the bench beside me, bringing a whole load of his own agitation. "They're keeping Leif here tonight. That's all she'll tell me."

"Why? Logan said *Oz* confessed."

One of the detectives who enjoyed sausages at the memorial BBQ appears from behind the focal door at the end of the hallway and halts when he sees me. I'm on my feet and over to the graying man, who's shrugging on his black suit jacket, before he can take another breath.

The detective barely flinches, greeting me with the usual disdainful look in his hazel eyes. "My, you can move fast, Ms. Blackwood."

"Why have you arrested Leif?" I demand.

"Because he's a murder suspect."

"Leif would *never* murder someone," I say. "He isn't capable."

"Everybody's capable, especially someone who's half-shifter."

Our locked gaze doesn't break. "I can assure you that I've met enough killers to identify the type who would or would not kill. Leif is not one. Release him."

The detective scoffs. "Your delusions of grandeur continue, I see."

He looks behind at Rowan approaching too, and instantly, I shove into the detective's mind. I'll deal with the consequences if he notices, and at least if *I'm* arrested, Dorian will appear to help. I'm pissed that he hasn't replied to my messages yet and half-expected my father here. Where is he when I need him?

In the man's mind, I catch a glimpse of a laptop screen displaying footage taken in the dark woods, then quickly withdraw before he feels the tickle from my intrusion. *What the...?*

"Where's Dorian?" I ask him.

"Not required. This is a shifter and human investigation. Unless those under his jurisdiction become involved, the man stays away."

"Witches are involved! I'm calling my father," I announce.

"Do what you like. He has no influence in this case. Unless..." He lifts a bushy brow. "*You're* involved."

"You are an idiot," I state loudly. "All of you. When you interviewed Leif, did he tell you about the witches at the hospital?"

With a tight smile, the detective takes my shoulders and moves me to one side, earning himself a low snarl. "You're not the sweet little thing your appearance suggests," he says, leaning down to speak close to my ear.

"Anybody who thinks I'm sweet fools *themselves*. I'm entirely clear what and who I am. It's also becoming apparent I've superior intelligence to you, *Detective*."

Rowan's hand slides into mine and squeezes, a move which becomes more familiar each time: 'shut up, Violet'.

"Your mouth will cause you a lot of trouble one day," says the detective in a tone I'm to presume is menacing.

"I don't believe my mouth will cause the trouble," I reply. "More likely my teeth and—"

"Violet's upset," interrupts Rowan.

"I heard Ms. Blackwood finds her 'other side' harder to control recently," says the detective. "Do be careful."

Is he speaking to me or Rowan? I narrow my eyes at the back of his head as he turns and walks away. The stuffy space becomes more airless as two mountainous men now stand close to the desk. Their surly expressions don't change as the detective approaches.

I wrinkle my nose at their potent scent. Shifters.

They're not as big as either of my shifter fathers, but almost as broad as Ethan. One stands taller with more self-importance, his hair thick and wavy, falling into his eyes. Both have a somewhat wild appearance, and the other, with his blond ponytail, looks around as if everybody else is either prey or predator. Not that I'd expect a single human in here could take them on.

Elders?

"Where's our boy?" snarls the taller man, and everybody's eyes cut to them.

"You must be Oz's father," says the detective and extends a hand.

"No. I'm the Ursa chief and Ozric is under my watch." His gravelly voice resonates with the primal energy within him, the way Ethan's does. "Hand our boy over."

"Perhaps we should talk about this privately." Despite his even speech, the detective's perspiration grows.

"No. The situation is simple. Ozric is one of us; you do not decide his fate." The pony-tailed shifter holds his ground as the detective nods at the woman behind the desk.

A warning to prepare for trouble.

"With all due respect, Ozric is over eighteen, and confessed to killing a human. Therefore, we'll charge him under our laws," says the detective.

"Have you ever noticed," I whisper to Rowan, "that when people say, 'with due respect' they mean the exact opposite?" He glances at me in confusion. "Or even what respect is due. It could be hardly any."

"What are you talking about?" Rowan shakes his head at me.

The entire station, probably including those in the morgue, would hear the current argument between my favorite detective and the shifters.

"Right. We should leave," Rowan whispers.

"Is this not an interesting twist, Rowan?" I ask. "Almost as if someone's planting a larger wedge between the two societies?"

"And Leif?" he says in a hushed voice. "He's in between already. What if the elders try to take him as well?"

I jerk my attention away from the human/shifter confrontation. Leif's biggest fear—shifters taking him. Forcing Leif to live by their rules. To become one of them. The surging compulsion to keep Leif safe from injustice moves through me as readily as with Grayson.

Or more?

I'm picturing our group without him. Picturing *me* without him. The guy who's hard bodied but soft-hearted and plays arcade games to give the dark-hearted girl strange gifts. The one who asked me for help with a vulnerability that touched a side I'd ignored. Leif, who'd do anything to help me too.

"I agree," I say. "We leave."

"Bloody hell, did you actually tell me that I'm right?" splutters Rowan.

I sigh. "Make the most of the occasion because you rarely are, Rowan."

The heat from the elders radiates unnaturally, pheromones that only other supes can sense hog the air. I don't look at either pissed elder, but smile extra-sweetly at the detective as I pass the trio.

"Wait!" yells the leader and the second shifter stands in front of the door, his frame filling every inch of the doorway.

"Excuse me. I'm leaving," I say.

"You're that girl," growls the elder behind me.

Raising my eyes to the ceiling for a moment, I pivot to face the angry man. "'That girl'?"

"The Blackwood girl. Your fucking father interferes in our business too."

"Dorian? He keeps out of shifter business." The man's eyes almost disappear behind his heavy scowl. "Oh! Ethan. Apologies, I'm so accustomed to Dorian as the one bad-mouthed, I sometimes forget my other fathers aren't popular in some circles."

Deep-set, hazel-brown eyes flicker with a wildness that points at his bear heritage, a silent warning to me that he's not one to be trifled with. The elder slants his head. "*You're* involved in all this. What did you do to Oz?"

"Good grief!" My voice rises. "The single-mindedness of everybody in this vicinity astounds me. I am trying to *help*. Ask that detective—he knows I'm conducting my own investigations." I wave a hand. "I have a question for *you*. Where is Rory's body?"

"Violet," whispers Rowan in horror.

"Burned. As is our way," the elder says.

"Wrong."

"Violet!" urges Rowan again.

"What did the witches do with the body?" I tip my head far back in order to look into the mountainous man's amber eyes. "Witches have screwed with shifters, and lives are in danger, *and* you are simply too thick-headed to realize this."

"*Your* life is in danger if you keep speaking to me like this," he growls.

"Oh, no. Despite this loud threat witnessed by the people gathered, any attempt to kill me would fail."

Rowan's now holding my arm in both hands, attempting to pull me away, but I dig the heels of my heavy boots into the tiles.

"Mark my words, Oz will die next." I step back and address the detective. "And then Kai."

"Omigod, Violet!" I stumble as Rowan yanks me hard, catching me off guard. He shoves open the door and drags me outside into the cooling afternoon. "What the hell did you say that for?"

"Because it's true. Unless the humans investigating the

murders... what's your phrase? Get their heads out of their asses, we really will have a serial killer on our hands."

Rowan locks his hands behind his head, elbows at right angles, his face whiter than the moment I told him about Leif. "And *you* just gave the detectives Violet Blackwood's kill list."

"Don't be ridiculous. I didn't mean *me*."

Rowan shakes his head, face losing more color. *Oh.* "We're definitely running out of time now your big mouth landed you back on the suspect list."

I snort. "The humans have no clue what they're doing. Neither do the shifters. Witches hold of all the cards and are smugly playing their hand. However, nobody beats me at games."

"In this case, they might," Rowan glances back at the station. "I'm bloody terrified for Leif."

"Leif has his talisman. The detectives won't allow the shifters to take Oz, or Leif—the woman on the desk just hit a panic button."

"Yes, but—"

I pause. "Yes, but, I'll free Leif tonight. Problem solved." For some reason, Rowan doesn't respond, nor does he appear to listen to my plans as we reluctantly walk away.

Chapter Thirty-One

VIOLET

ROWAN'S as taciturn as Leif often is on our journey back to the academy. Understandably, as Leif's incarceration *is* a concerning development, yet one we can deal with. But even as we walk into the academy grounds, Rowan doesn't speak, and I give up on sharing my plans about what we do next. He's hunched over, hands in pockets with an air of the old Rowan with his self-absorbed barrier between us.

"Right. Let's discuss our plans. Holly's coming back to the academy once she leaves the mall. She'll ask too many questions that'll interfere with my thinking, so we can choose between your room or the library," I announce.

"We're not breaking Leif out of his cell, Violet," Rowan says evenly. "If we get caught, that's a crap load of trouble neither of us need."

"We won't get caught," I reply. "I've already thought about this. What we'll do is—"

"Stop!" Rowan holds up a hand, palm out. "No."

The word skitters across my frayed nerves. "Pardon?"

"I said, no, Violet." His steel-blue eyes are harder than I've

207

seen for some time. "I won't help you. We need to be more logical about this."

As I clench my jaw, a muscle twitches in his and we refuse to break each other's challenge.

"Very well," I say eventually and turn towards Darwin House.

I've barely taken any steps when Rowan shouts after me, "Is that it? No discussion?"

"What is there to discuss? You've told me you won't help. That's a clear statement." I continue walking. Perhaps Grayson can help instead if he's around and is amenable? Although there *is* always the risk he might extract someone's internal organs.

"Talk to me." Rowan sprints by and spins to face me, cheeks mottled red.

"Have you changed your mind?" I ask.

"No."

"Then I'll speak to you later. I've things to plan." I sidestep. Rowan does the same. I'm struggling to understand the energy coming from him. He's upset about Leif, naturally, but why aim that frustration at me? "If you don't want to help—"

"Leif's my best friend, Violet," he interrupts, voice strained. "Of course, I want to fucking help, but in the *right* way."

"How is our releasing Leif and hiding him until we solve the murders *not* the correct way?" I shake my head. "What if that awful shifter elder finds a chance to take him?" Rowan digs hands deeper into his pockets and continues to glare. "Don't give me that look, Rowan. I'm beginning to decipher what it means."

"The 'my girlfriend really is crazy, and I don't know how much longer I can stop her doing crazy shit'?"

"Girlfriend?" Rowan's energy grows more erratic, and I sigh. "Your agitation greatly outstrips mine earlier."

Rowan swears. Several times, then walks away, towards the cloisters that lie between Darwin House and the main building. "Go find Grayson. Maybe you'll listen to him," he calls as he goes.

"Why? Does he have some information for me?" I ask hopefully.

"Bloody hell, Violet," Rowan yells as he stops and turns back. "Do you ever think like a normal person?"

"Was that a rhetorical question, Rowan? Because you're well aware of the answer."

"Taking evidence on the day of Wes's memorial and the toe removal? Unwise, but I helped. Breaking through security to take a whole person? I'm drawing the line."

"Then how do you propose to help Leif?" I ask evenly.

"Sanely. With a human attorney for Leif. Help from your fathers."

"You trust that human authorities can beat whoever these witches are?" I scoff. "Fine. You don't need to help, Rowan. I understand if you want to avoid trouble."

"*Trouble?*" His voices rises in pitch. "The day I'd never avoid trouble again is the day I met you, Violet. And now we're fucking bonded!"

I snap my head back. "Yes. I'm acutely aware of that situation. And I don't appreciate the yelling, Rowan. Go away and calm down."

Instead, Rowan swears—at *me*—and drags me towards the edge of the covered cloisters, close to where I encountered Grayson the Vigilante. Something in his aura triggers hairs to stand on my arms and not through any emotion—from his sparking magic.

"I don't appreciate you implying that I'm turning my back on my best friend if I don't do what you say," he says through gritted teeth.

"Rowan. Calm down. Your agitation will lead to an unfortunate magical incident, and Leif isn't here to intervene."

This time, I stumble as Rowan grabs my face in both hands. "Will you just speak to me *normally*, Violet? Stop hiding behind words."

"I'm not. And your grip on my face is unwarranted," I reply as my cheeks squish.

Magic pulses through his fingers like the beat of his heart, intensifying the sharp frustration passing between us. This isn't Rowan's gentle and tentative touch from the evening we discussed our joint power—this is the guy I watched conjure lightning.

The witch who absorbs my shadows.

The moment that magic hits my mind, I yank Rowan's hands from my face and send him backwards to slam into the wall as I did the day he invaded my room.

He sneers at me, eyes sparking silver. "Oh, here we go. Violet Blackwood doesn't want to discuss a situation or listen to criticism, so she lashes out."

"Good grief. This public display after a minor argument is ridiculous." He remains pinned to the wall by my spell, but the magic he shared with me runs through my veins, mingling with my own.

"Stop talking to me in that way," he growls.

I step towards him. "Do you want me to lose my temper too, Rowan? You think *this* is lashing out?"

"You will not endanger my friend by making shit worse for him by bypassing the law. Not in this case."

"The law won't work, Rowan!"

He snatches my arm and wisps of shadow lick around his fingertips, the sparks in his eyes dulling. "And endanger *you*! Think about this. Your enemies will expect you to try this dumb move."

"Calm down, Rowan," I say and wrap my fingers around his hand, ready to pull him away. Instead, the wisps become tendrils, binding my hand to his. "Rowan!"

"The fucking witches are smarter than you, Violet. Look what they've achieved so far. Someone will find you in that station trying to break Leif out. Or Oz could die while you're there. Proof!"

"You think too much," I say, pulling my arm away as he attempts to take my hand again.

"And you don't think *enough*! You've created a world in your mind where you're invincible when a fucking fence post can kill you." His voice rises as the shadows curl further around us. "You believe you're untouchable like Dorian and you are *not*."

"Get off me," I growl at him. "That's enough."

"I'm not some weak kid who'll do everything you tell me to, Violet."

"I'm not asking you to."

Rowan steps away from the wall and my mind reels as I'm pushed back by *his* magic. "You treat me like an obedient puppy. You expect me to help without question, and if I won't agree, you ignore me." He steps closer, his spell now winding tight around us, the magic no longer held back by mine. "I will not be *used*, Violet."

"That statement is untrue and merely your perception," I retort.

"Yeah? Tell me—when have we spent time together *without* a reason that benefits you?"

My blood races with the magic he's brought to me not only through his touch, but by him triggering my own magic. Rowan's eyes darken, absorbing the earlier sparks, and his faster breaths against my cheeks aren't warm. They're filled with the cool the shadows bring.

"You even pushed me aside for Leif the other night because he was more 'use' to you."

"Why didn't you *insist* you wanted to come with me?"

"Because that would've been futile."

The witch before me seems to take up more space than he did and sucks the warmth from around us. I'm looking at the Rowan he once told me nobody knows, capable of more than they can imagine. "Rowan. Can we talk about this when you're calmer?"

"I'm bonded to a witch who doesn't give a crap about me. One I'm stupid enough to fall in love with," he says roughly.

I choke back against his energy—and statement. "You think I've *ever* allowed someone to touch me, let alone kiss me, Rowan? I'm shocked you don't realize what that meant."

"And then?" His face moves closer again. "You behave as if nothing happened."

I'm struggling for breath, heart thundering in my chest,

horrified that Rowan can lose control with such ease. But this isn't only about today. Or Leif. "I won't apologize for what I am. I don't want to fight with you."

"Do you care about me?" he demands. "Is all this bullshit about staying apart for our own good, or you hiding from yourself?"

"We had this discussion," I say, catching my own breath. "Stop *fighting* with me."

"Tell me you don't care, and I'll go. I'll accept that I'm nothing but your bonded witch and will never mean more."

"I'm protecting you. Us."

"Stop saying that!"

How? How is Rowan keeping me held in his emotion-fueled space? How's his strength surpassing mine?

"Let me go," I say evenly.

"Tell me. Do you care?" he shouts.

"Yes!" I shout back, heart unleashing and battering against my chest. "Yes, I care about you, Rowan, but this scares me. You interfere with my thinking. I can't cope with how I feel when I'm around you."

Rowan says nothing and slides a hand around the back of my neck, the touch against my sensitive nape pulling me further to his bonded energy. To *him*.

"Rowan," I warn.

Rowan's eyes drop to my mouth, his own lips still set hard. "Go on. Push me away again. Slam me against that wall and walk away."

His body isn't touching in the way Grayson's did at the party, nor am I in that crazed state of a hybrid wanting blood. Yes, I'm soaking up Rowan's magic, whether I want to or not, but there's something more.

Something terrifying.

Desire.

Closing my eyes, I hold my breath and summon a barrier to make my skin burn to the touch. Rowan yelps, and the moment he releases me, I slam a spell into Rowan's chest and shove him backwards.

Only this time, I don't keep at a safe distance from the magic pouring out of Rowan. I'm against him in a heartbeat.

My fingers wind into his unruly hair as I stare at Rowan, brimful of the emotional energy that tangled every part of me into knots. We're bonded and I *feel* him. Something inside this guy is part of me that's beyond the shadows we now share—more than our magic recognizing each other.

Like meets like.

Every minute since I discovered the bond, I've fought myself while swearing the fight is against him. I'm constantly struggling to ignore my heart and soul, paralyzed by fear that the world might slip from my control if I allow myself to feel the emotions he's created inside me.

Pressed against Rowan's body, my chest against his, our synchronized hearts tell us what we are, but it's the memory of his past touch, and the desire for more that moves through my blood. Not the magic. Not a bond.

Rowan.

Rowan's hands go to either side of my face, fingertips humming magic against my cheekbones, and his hair tickles my forehead. The question in his eyes can only be answered one way, and my lips go to his. Hard—harder than any kiss he's given me. The scent of Rowan's witch blood blooms, but I'm overwhelmed by the desire for *him*, as our mouths seal.

Rowan tastes of darkness and sweetness rolled into one, intensely swirling between us, delving past my frustration and snatching hold of an unknown inside me. This kiss is what I needed to truly understand what we are—deep and searing, rough and raw, soothing an ache I've ignored.

His soft kisses and touches from before never felt right; something bordering on annoying about the tickling gentleness. *This* kiss feels right—our bodies weak against each other despite how harshly our mouths move, tongues pushing against each other as the frustration from our argument continues to flare.

Hard fingertips push into my cheeks and my fingers remain threaded in his hair as the kiss's ferocity opens me further. I don't like people's touch, but this… *This* is Rowan whose desire that I share thrums through my veins. *This* is the touch I want. Not the cautious gentleness, but one that my darkness feeds on and loves.

And even though I pull my mouth away, lips tingling, I don't move back. I can't ever step back from the world I never imagined I'd be a part of. One where I accept emotions can create a place of safety and happiness, and where touch is natural. A place with Rowan.

"That was one hell of a kiss from a girl who doesn't like kissing," Rowan says hoarsely.

"I came to the conclusion that I don't like soft kisses," I inform him, dizzied and breathless. "That's what irritates me—not you."

Rowan coughs a laugh. "Noted. But you can't end arguments with a kiss."

"Would you rather I walked away?"

His hands slide down to hold my waist. "No."

I smooth where I've ruffled his hair. "I don't know how to behave around people, Rowan, and I especially don't know how to navigate… this. Us. I hate that I upset you because I can't think the way you do or fully comprehend unspoken emotions."

"Stop trying to control me just because you can't control other things around you and in yourself," he says quietly. "Let go."

"Oh?" I step back.

Rowan lets out a short laugh and grabs my hand, squeezing tight. "Let go of what you can. Not *me*. I want you. This."

"And you want time together alone?" I ask. "Because we do tend to irritate each other often, and I'm unsure I'm ready for where the explosions might lead if we're alone."

"Violet…" He shakes his head. "Not necessarily alone. A day together. An evening. One not associated with murder investigations at all."

I bite back, and swallow down, a protest that nothing is more important right now, especially considering Leif's predicament, but understand. The bond I have with Rowan isn't one created by fate, but by each moment we spend together that draws me closer than I wanted—or that I can keep up with.

"Do *you* want this? Us?" he asks when I don't reply.

"I cannot imagine life without you, Rowan," I tell him.

"That isn't quite an answer."

The raging magic and anger ebbed, pushed into a corner by the unity and I rest one hand against his thrumming heart. Why did Rowan not speak to me about this before? Or did he and I couldn't hear? "I held you away from me, but I never wanted you to go, and that's confusing for me. I understand I confuse us *both*, but please believe I care, even if I don't match your expectations of normality. I'm learning."

"I'll take your normality over anybody else's." He kisses the top of my head. "As long as you allow me in."

Allow him in. "Speaking of normality, Holly expects me to go to the Spring Ball, now I'm on the committee."

"Right." Rowan tugs his bottom lip into his mouth. "And you want to take *me* as you offered?"

"I did not off—" The smirk. "No, I don't want to go to the dance with you, but perhaps you could help me escape that awful fate?"

He slants his head. "You know, Violet, you always ask for dates in a very odd, vague manner."

I rub fingers across my mouth. "Would you take me on a date the night of the Spring Ball? But not *to* the Spring Ball."

"Again, odd request." He chuckles. "But sure. If I can choose where."

"Hmm. But—" He raises both brows. "Alright."

"And can I ask you something else?"

"Go ahead."

"If I try to hold your hand or hug you, could you please not react as if you're in pain?" He strokes my cheek with the back of his hand.

"And how do you know that I'm not in pain when you touch me, Rowan?"

"Oh, sweet Violet," he says quietly. "I'm perfectly aware my touch doesn't cause you pain, otherwise you wouldn't have kissed me like that."

Whatever I feel for Rowan, there's one thing about this guy

that I'll never, ever accept. He can talk me in circles to win an argument or silence my retorts—or indulge in mild coercion.

But the argument about Leif?

That isn't over. Not yet.

Chapter Thirty-Two

VIOLET

FROM OUR PLACE close to the vacant entry booth by the factory gates, I survey the Sawyer Industries factory, and the warehouse set further away across a graveled area. I'd seen the monolithic building in the distance from the Sawyers' house, but close up the corrugated metal gleams below unhelpful security lights.

Rowan's suggestion we check out the Sawyer Industries site came as a surprise, although no doubt a tactic to keep me away from the police station tonight. Still, an idea I'd suggested in the past. If Sawyer's home contains runes and magic, and witches are assisting him in some way, there must be more evidence of such at the factory site. Somewhere. The place is huge—at least the size of the academy—and I hope our magical detection won't be interfered with by tinned soups.

I'm aiming to find Sawyer's office first. Dorian told us his meeting with Sawyer took place at the warehouse, which means his office must be located there. There could be plenty to connect Sawyer to supernatural influence tucked away in the room. Rowan wouldn't find every single link between the man and supes online—nothing on the internet is private the moment it's shared. Non-public information must be hidden, as this situation is more than threats to kill Kai due to a business deal gone wrong.

Rowan and Grayson stand beside me, Grayson facing back towards the main road as he watches and listens. We waited for the final truck to leave and now only need to worry about security—human or machine.

I assess our options. Although the factory has numerous windows and several exterior doors, along with metal stairs attached to fire escapes, the warehouse appears to have a singular entry point. A spacious paved lot acts as a zone for trucks and transport vehicles to park, load, or unload goods, wide enough for two trucks to park. Annoyingly, the bright floodlights cast pools of light onto the ground, ensuring safe maneuvering of non-existent vehicles.

"Security cameras?" I ask Rowan.

"Looks like some are already vandalized, as a few of the lights are out already." He gestures at the closest part of the factory. "Saves me half a job."

"Shifters did that?" I ask and Rowan nods. "Are there any around, Grayson?"

"Nobody," he replies.

Three days. Three useless days waiting to hear more about Leif while resisting the urge to go to that station and get him. More so because authorities still refuse to allow Dorian entry, and *he* isn't pushing the issue, which led to some heated words between us. Dorian doesn't want to overstep if he may need human co-operation to apprehend the witches concerned.

Not that he's making much headway with that, either. Dorian didn't achieve his planned one-on-one meeting with Sawyer alone, since Josef insisted he attend. Josef agreed to inform Dorian if either he or Sawyer heard from one of the witches, and we all know what that means. Frustratingly, the arrests had distracted Sawyer while at the meeting, his head full of that development and there was barely a glimmer of the witches for Dorian to pick up on.

Dorian insists the meeting was 'amicable enough' and that he didn't confront Josef alone but with so much unspoken heavy in the air between them, I'm surprised.

Every supe involved knows what's really happening next— apart from perhaps the witches. And if Josef's lying, they could be aware and cooperating too. Grayson hasn't heard from his uncle about the 'co-incidental' meeting he's arranging and the more time that passes, the greater the head-thumping frustration grows that Josef might be playing us.

So now politics trumps fact-finding and prevents Dorian poking too far into human matters, but he has promised that he'll again try to gain access to Leif tonight.

I've spoken to Leif briefly. He's understandably despondent but didn't say much, worried who might be listening. The elders haven't taken Oz but have visited him several times, and there's no sign of ill health again. The strength of the emotion gripping me when I spoke to Leif stayed with me for hours afterwards, an odd aching in my chest because I'd wanted to hug Leif and promise he'll be alright. Perhaps a hug for Leif would've wiped away a little of his distress and reassured him he's important. Instead all I could do was reassure him I'll do everything to ensure he's free and safe.

How is it that only when I'm apart from these guys am I aware of how significant they've become to me? I'm perfectly conscious about how self-absorbed and selfish I am, but I'm also acutely noticing strange gaps in the world around me when Leif, Rowan, and Grayson aren't around.

Despite my promise to Rowan, and then Grayson, who annoyingly agreed with him, I'm close to ignoring the pair and going to Leif on my own. One simple blood rune spell and we'd be out of that station. Hidden. Safe.

But finding the witches and holding them accountable has to happen and interfering could jeopardize that. Dorian and his men never discovered where the witches' meeting with Maxwell was held, having waited at several locations at the allotted time. A failed meeting that'll now confirm to the witches that Maxwell is missing or dead, adding another layer of complication.

If I can't help Leif directly, I'll find something that can.

I shuffle from foot to foot as Rowan uses a spell to freeze the cameras, taking them below a temperature they can function at, and breaking the screens. He then focuses on the floodlights above the loading zone, and the area plunges into a darkness after a satisfying number of cracks.

"This way," I say and creep towards the empty loading bay, then up the stone steps to the left where there's a metal keypad on a wall by the door. A sign above reads: *Refuse to be stored in black bags and placed in dumpster*

"How very odd." I gesture. "Why would somebody not refuse?"

Rowan snickers at me. He indicates the half-full dumpster to the left of the steps. "Refuse. Trash."

"So nobody's in the dumpster?"

"No, Violet," says Rowan, still amused. "Nobody allowed themselves to be placed in a trash bag."

Stupid English language. I poke at the worn keypad. "Good. I can't sense anybody else around. Grayson?"

He steps up beside me. "I can't either, but there could be night staff inside."

"If they're human, that won't be an issue," I reply. "But I'll be pissed if we don't find anything, otherwise, I could've tried visiting Leif again."

"Who Dorian told you to keep away from," Rowan reminds me.

Muttering, I continue to press buttons in a random number order but the door doesn't budge. I crouch down and slide fingers beneath the small gap between the green roller door and concrete.

"Violet. What are you doing?" asks Rowan.

"Opening the door?"

"Can we use a more subtle entry point than a huge, focal loading dock door?" he asks. "There'll be somewhere nearby that you can vandalize instead."

Rowan blends into the darkness he created by breaking the lights, and I rush after him. One thing—I'm not letting the guy out of my sight. Last time something threatened Rowan in the dark, and threatened me too, things headed in a troublesome and shadowy direction. I can't have that distraction.

"Here," he calls in a hushed voice.

A smaller set of steps leads to a black door, again with a keypad, but easily opened with one kick of my boot. I smile at Rowan as he rolls his eyes, then walk inside.

We're immediately in a small wood-paneled office space, a dark wooden desk and chair with a laptop, and a narrow metal filing cabinet. Notices with lists and dates are pinned to the wall—nothing of note. No magical items or energy.

Rowan squints through the darkness. "I don't think this is Sawyer's office. His would be much bigger and better furnished."

"And I doubt he wears the perfume that's lingering," I reply and pick up a framed photograph from the desk.

Two boys in school uniform posing for the annual class photograph. If the academy commits such atrocities, I will not be involved. Nobody's taking a photo of me in that preposterous, ugly uniform. Holly already warned me about a photographer at the Spring Ball. Thankfully, I'm sneaking away from that one with Rowan.

"Definitely not his office." Rowan takes the frame. "These kids are too young, and Kai doesn't have a brother."

"Any word on Kai yet?" asks Grayson from the doorway. "Has Holly heard anything or seen him around since the arrests?"

"The idiot's resumed his social activities, but so far no clashes with shifters," I reply. "Holly told me the shifters stay away from town. At least they have sense."

"They were probably told to by the elders," says Rowan, who now flicks through a filing cabinet. He pulls out some papers. "Inventory. Orders. Nothing else."

"Nothing magical in here," I say as my annoyance flares.

Grayson cautiously opens the second, unlocked door opposite our illegal entry point, and peeps out. "Warehouse floor."

I join him, pushing the door wider. Row upon row of metal

shelves reach from the concrete floor to the corrugated ceiling, an impressive 75 feet tall at least. The high ceiling is reinforced with steel trusses and the large, unlit industrial lights hang down.

The shelves are laden with neatly labelled boxes, and the aisles wide enough for the small forklifts stationed close to the inside of the roller door

No sound anywhere.

Confident there's nobody here, I step out, boots tapping on the polished floor as I wander the aisles and examine the identical boxes. Most are cardboard and stacked on shelves constructed from metal rebars.

"If we're looking for magic, this'll take forever," grumbles Grayson. "There could be anything hidden in the warehouse."

Rowan stands at my shoulder. "I can barely see anything—you two have vamp sight."

I pull at the small, black rucksack he carries over one shoulder. "Flashlight?"

"Why did you bring a bag anyway?" asks Grayson, as Rowan sets the rucksack down and retrieves his flashlight. "A picnic for later?"

"Ha ha. No. Because my pockets aren't big enough."

"For what?" Grayson frowns.

"I don't know. In case we actually find something we could use for psychometry."

Grayson's mouth parts in an 'o'. I already knew—makes total sense to me. The flashlight not so much when he could create a witchlight, but Rowan insists he doesn't want to use more magic than necessary.

Despite our hushed voices, words drift upwards. A metal-floored mezzanine wraps the warehouse walls above and I wander towards the clanging steps, the others following. Glass-paneled rooms at the top offer a clear view of the entire warehouse floor, and I approach a black door.

"Sawyer's?" I suggest. The door handle won't move at my first attempt. "Locked."

"Warded?" asks Rowan.

The wood splinters as I yank away the handle. "Evidently not."

"Can you stop breaking things, Violet?" he says in exasperation.

Ignoring him, I walk into the room.

The spacious area obviously serves as both a working and relaxing area, the L-shaped mahogany desk central at one end, along with a plush leather sofa, a couple of matching armchairs, and a glass coffee table at the other.

"Oh yeah, this is Sawyer's," says Grayson, pointing at a row of certificates on the wall. To the left of the desk, matching shelves display awards for business and golfing prowess. I examine the cupboard beneath the shelves, also not runed, and discover bottles of whiskey and cut tumbler glasses inside.

"I can smell him," I say, but also sense magic similar to his bedroom. "Look around. Anything with symbols?"

Grayson crosses his arms and walks along the floor, studying each framed certificate, while Rowan picks up and examines each award. Perhaps there're unusual etching on one of the silver golfer figurines. I close my eyes and attempt to home in on the magic energy in the air.

My gaze drops to the rug, bright blue and printed with the Sawyer's Soups logo, a bold red font with no incorporated symbols. Still. I blow air into my cheeks and crouch down, placing a hand on the rug.

"The magic comes from low down. Check the drawers," I tell Rowan. "Grayson, can you stand in the doorway in case someone followed us from outside?"

"You think they did?" Rowan pauses, face filling with alarm.

"I expect someone's watching us," I say casually. "Don't worry. I told Dorian we were coming here. Although… I might've given him the wrong time. We have an hour."

Grayson places a hand on Rowan's shoulder. "Don't stress. There's plenty of places to hide."

"Hide?" I scoff. "Let's see what *Sawyer's* hiding. Then, we leave."

I roll back the rug with Grayson's help, disappointed to see unmarked floorboards. The rug extends beneath the desk, and I narrow my eyes, remembering the nightstands in the bedroom.

"Grayson, help me move the desk," I say and effortlessly lift one end. Between us, we relocate the desk to the opposite end of the room as if moving an empty box.

More floorboards are beneath the newly revealed part of the rug. "There must be something," I say. "Can't you sense it, Rowan? Turn the picture frames over. Anything on the back? Magic from touching them?"

"This is taking too long," mumbles Grayson, darting to the doorway again as me and Rowan lift away each picture.

We locate a safe behind his college graduation certificate, easily opened and containing nothing, which is as suspicious as if it had been filled with secret documents or items.

"Ugh." I look around the room. "Move the other furniture."

"Sawyer will notice someone rearranged his office," says Rowan.

I shrug and give the leather sofa a light shove, easily sliding it in front of the relocated desk. "He might think it's the witches. Or Dorian."

"Violet," Rowan says.

He points at the flood beneath the sofa's original position, and a buzz of excitement runs through me. Circular runes are burned into the wood, each one no bigger than a thumbnail. "Yes!"

Flames flicker at my fingertips as I crouch and reach towards the runes. "Bloody hell, Violet. Don't set fire to the place," protests Grayson.

"Please don't insult my ability to control magic. I'm merely searing the wood to wipe out the runes. They'll be holding something behind." Both look over my shoulder as the runes momentarily glow orange before the cracks where the floorboard joins others glimmers white beneath. "Grayson?"

Rowan steps back, staring as Grayson's nails grow longer and stronger. "You can turn hemia that quickly?" Grayson flashes Rowan his canines in answer. "O-kay."

He leverages the floorboard away and they join me in kneeling to peer inside. A shoebox sized container is tucked in the small, dark space, and I dart a hand in to remove it. More runes decorate the gray metal, roughly scratched with a blade, and magic emanates from the box to my fingers.

Chapter Thirty-Three

VIOLET

"IRON," I say and smooth a hand across the lid. "That's why the magic's faint."

"Before you ask, we're not taking the whole box," warns Rowan.

"Do you know the runes, Violet?" asks Grayson.

"Unfamiliar, but useless, whatever they are," I say and trace one of the circles and intersecting lines with my finger. "These look like an attempt at a spell by a non-witch." I casually pull open the lid.

Folded papers rest at the top of the full box, and I pass them to Rowan as I delve below. A yellowing envelope contains a series of photographs, which I pull out and flick through. A young couple in various close-up shots. The black-haired girl's pretty features could be fortunate human genetics, or she could be a lamia vamp. Same with the tousle-haired guy—good-looking but in a classical human way and not the almost-too-perfect that gives a vamp's features a slightly 'off' look. Or are they witches?

A love heart is inked in blue on the back of one photo. Pursing my lips, I also hand the guys the pictures, then take hold of a deep purple piece of torn silk cloth. Something's inside, and

I unwrap it to reveal a small, spiked silver tiara jeweled with prominent amethyst oval gems. Rowan crouches and takes the tiara from me, closing his eyes momentarily before shaking his head. "Nothing. Dead energy."

"Not literally, I hope," says Grayson.

I take the tiara back and shove it in my pocket.

Rowan now holds the envelope and stares at one of the pictures. "Is that the academy behind them?"

The two teens stand together, holding hands, beaming at the camera. They're dressed in formal attire, the girl in a long, purple dress that reveals every one of her perfect curves, the neckline scooped low enough to be on the edge of decency, and the thigh slit almost to her backside. Good grief. Is this what girls wear to formal occasions?

"She's wearing the tiara," says Grayson.

I examine the purple, silky material in my hands. "Is this part of the dress?"

"Whoa. Okay." Rowan pulls the torn material from me. "Either this literally is dead magic energy or I'm getting a bad personal feeling about what this is."

"Take that photo. Leave the rest." I attempt to remove the picture from his hand, but he keeps hold. "Rowan."

"Did I just see you pocket the tiara?"

"We need a more focused psychometry spell on this object. You said that's why you've brought the backpack."

"But taking something this hidden and significant…" He sighs and holds a hand out. "Fine."

Delving back into my sweater, I hand the tiara to Rowan, who re-wraps it in the purple cloth. "Do you recognize the people? Are they witches or humans?" I look closer. "Is one Sawyer?"

"The photo's from years ago. They'd be old by now. Older than Sawyer."

"Humans didn't attend the academy back when people took those type of photos," says Grayson. "And nobody knew about supes existing—any human staff were mind-wiped."

"But supes and humans would mix," I say. "Local reports

about attacks that could've been vampires or shifters existed. I can't believe no supe formed a romantic relationship with a human without telling them."

"That can't be anything to do with Sawyer," says Rowan firmly.

"Why not? He has a weird relationship with supes. What if that family connection goes back years?" I ask. "We take the photo, cloth, and tiara."

"No body parts?" Grayson asks.

"I haven't delved deep enough to see if there's any mummified…" I pause and narrow my eyes. "Sarcasm?"

Grayson gives a tight smile and I tut at him.

"Maybe don't joke until Violet's checked," says Rowan.

"Oh, crap, I hope not," mutters Grayson.

My fingertips run along the base of the iron box, but semi-thankfully there's nothing more inside. "What are the other papers?" I ask. "Do we take those?"

"Deeds." He bites his lip. "But these aren't signed by the witches, Josef, or Sawyer."

"Deeds for the land?" asks Grayson.

"Maybe? Too complicated for me to figure out right now." He takes his phone from a pocket before placing the papers on the box and photographing. "I don't think we should take everything."

"Why not?" I ask.

"In case the rucksack gets lost or damaged?" he suggests. "Then you'll have nothing."

He's correct, but I won't tell him that. I watch as Rowan puts the papers and envelope with all but the one photo inside the box and carefully places it back beneath the floor. "I'll ward this properly," he says. "With my runes in place, it'll take the owner longer to get inside and see what's missing."

"Owner? Sawyer owns the box. Who else would hide something under floorboards, in his office, in his factory?" I ask.

Rowan stands and holds out a hand to me. "Come on, Nancy Drew. Nice work, but let's tidy up and go."

His mouth tips into a smile, a shared memory of our first

search for clues in the woods when co-operation was the last thing on our minds. Back then, we were lost for answers, but now I'm certain Rory killed Wesley, and Oz killed Rory. But the shifters aren't the ones the humans should bring to justice— they're undead pawns. The witches need apprehending and confessions forcibly extracted to discover why this is happening before relations between shifters and humans explode into a war.

And before Leif suffers any further.

I've still time before Dorian's expected arrival, and once we replace the furniture, we rapidly head back down the metal steps onto the warehouse floor.

A banging door echoes through the aisles and voices bounce through the air between us and the exit.

Rowan swears and veers behind a shelf with me, Grayson beside us both in a single breath. I bite my lip and pull Rowan so we're in the gap between the tall boxes of tinned soup, pulse rate rising. This isn't Dorian; his energy would blast into the place in seconds.

Witches followed us, aided by Josef? Good. We can finish this.

But something's wrong. Grayson looks at me and mouths 'human'.

"Not witches," I whisper to Rowan.

"Sawyer?"

I scramble up the shelves and wind my way between the boxes in the direction of the voices. When I look down from a hidden vantage point, my heart lodges in my throat.

Kai with his friend Dale, bundled in black clothes and over-sized hoodies.

"Good grief," I mutter and crawl back to inform the others. "Kai's here."

"This is not happening," mutters Rowan. "What the fuck is he—"

A second set of louder voices enter the warehouse, these new arrivals not caring who hears them.

Something thuds on the floor close by. Grayson, who'd climbed too, now stands towards the end of the aisle and glances back at me. He doesn't need to say the word, since the scent announces their arrival.

Shifters.

"Oh, no," I say through clenched teeth. "No."

"What?" urges Rowan.

"I can smell shifters."

Rowan's whole body goes rigid. "No way is this a coincidence."

"Back behind the boxes. Call authorities. Don't move," I tell him.

He leverages himself backwards and I creep along the floor towards Grayson. His face is grave, and he shakes his head before jabbing a finger towards the direction of voices.

Kai and his friend stand opposite Viggo and another shifter with long-curled hair pulled from his face.

One of the shifters from the renovations. Trent?

"Your uncle?" I whisper. "Didn't he say he'd arrange for Kai to be somewhere the witches could kill him? One of the shifter workers is here."

Grayson's mouth sets hard. "I didn't know, Violet."

"Well, I bet he's their construct too, which means the witches must be nearby."

We exchange a look, but I don't say the other words: and your uncle.

Grayson swears repeatedly under his breath as Viggo steps forward, Kai doing the same. Kai's muscular, but the shifter's hulking figure outmatches him—as his friend eclipses Dale too.

"Didn't think you'd show," says Viggo, the scar above his lip pulling tighter as he sneers at Kai. "Thought you were still hiding."

"I wasn't hiding," he retorts. "And I thought this was one on one. Me and you."

Viggo gestures at Dale. "Yeah? Looks like you had the same idea as me." Then he points at his friend. "Meet Trent. You think you can take us, you dumb bastard?"

But I'm not paying attention to their male posturing, only to the vacant expression on Trent's face.

And his blank mind.

"We need to stop this," I mutter to Grayson. "Get Rowan. We stay together."

Then I step into the other guys' view before Grayson responds.

I'm looking at Kai's back, but Viggo's facing my way. He gawks as he lays eyes on me before his face becomes one massive look of contempt. "You got the witch bitch to fight your battles?"

"Much as I enjoy your insults, I would remind you I am not a witch." I link my fingers in front of myself, and subtly look between him and Trent.

Kai's head snaps around. "I didn't bring her!"

"You're fortunate I'm here," I reply evenly. "I suggest you leave, Kai, before things descend further into unpleasantness."

"Aww. A little girl to fight your battles. Hiding behind supes like Daddy?" Viggo steps closer to Kai and shoves him with a massive hand.

Kai shoves him back with both of his, but the shifter doesn't budge. "I'm here to tell you that if any animals come into our town again, I'll ensure you're locked away like your murdering bastard of a friend. Shifters aren't welcome."

"And you believe I'd listen to you?" Viggo clenches and unclenches a fist.

"No, but hurt me and your life's over." Kai points at himself. "I'm untouchable now that your kind overstepped boundaries and killed."

Trent's throaty chuckle reverberates. "You think your life matters, Sawyer?"

Chapter Thirty-Four

VIOLET

NOW ABOVE ME AGAIN, Grayson sneaks across the shelves, back towards Rowan, as I rapidly size up the situation, focusing on Trent. If Trent shifts and launches himself at Kai, what then? No way will Kai survive without me interfering. Again.

I step into the space between the two factions. Nobody moves.

"Gonna set fire to the ground again, witch?" asks Viggo.

"With the amount of flammable material in here? What a stupid question," I say. "No. I'm requesting you leave."

"This is my family's place. You're all trespassing," says Kai from behind me.

"Duh. You told us to meet you here, asshole," says Trent.

I pivot. "And what precisely were you planning to do, Kai?"

Kai's shoulders straighten. "Teach the shifters to stay the fuck away from us."

"How?" He blinks at me and I catch a violent image. "I sincerely hope you didn't plan to kill him."

Kai exchanges a look with Dale beside him, and I hear Rowan and Grayson approach from behind.

"Oh look, the witch brought her little helpers," says Viggo. "Or did you invite *them* too, Kai?"

"No! This is between us." Kai glances at me. "Leave."

"You don't think the shifters work alone, do you, Kai?" asks Rowan.

"We do," snarls Viggo.

I take a step towards Trent and his mouth twists with disgust, nostrils flaring as if I've polluted his airspace. Our gazes lock and I push into the mind behind his amber eyes. What if I can take hold? Stop him shifting?

But there's nothing in his head to latch onto. Beyond blackness; a dark void.

Yet unlike Oz's mind at the arcade, red sparks hiss and spit in the recesses of his mind as if a firework failing to light. There's a whispering inside that darkness, a low voice speaking in a placating tone.

Hairs involuntarily lift on my arms as I step back again. The dark magic within this construct radiates in a way I swear other witches and shifters should sense too.

I glance over my shoulder. "Did you call the police?" I mouth at Rowan, and he nods. His rucksack's missing too. Hidden, I hope. I turn back to the group. "Kai. Please don't cause more trouble for yourself or risk harm. I believe your life is in danger."

"Help me kill the bastards then," he says simply. "Or was your boyfriend really involved and you've come to help the shifters?"

"No fucking way," spits Viggo. "She's the real killer!"

I hold a palm over my forehead. "Why can't anybody focus away from me to what's happening around them?"

Rowan tries to take Kai's arm but he side steps. "Come with me. We'll wait in one of the offices."

"No. Prove you're on our side," snarls Kai, looking at Viggo. "Help me teach the shifters a lesson."

"Good grief," I mutter. "A lesson? The only lesson happening here is in natural selection—a human who doesn't possess enough self-preservation to continue his family line."

Naturally, Kai looks blankly. "Huh?"

I dart a quick look at Grayson—drawing in Kai, Dale, and Viggo is possible mentally, but not Trent. He needs removing from the situation in case there's a witch nearby to prompt him into action.

"Kai. Go with Rowan and wait for authorities before this ends badly," I say.

"No."

Good. Grief. I throw myself at Kai's mind too and bounce back. Is he wearing a new pendant beneath that shirt? Because his mind resembles the state from the party. In that moment, Viggo lurches at Kai and I dart between them, almost knocked off balance by Trent attempting to shove past. "Stop!" I shout.

Can Viggo shift yet? *Will* Viggo shift? Because the feral scent from *Trent's* shifter side grows beside me. He straightens his shoulders, eyes zoning in on Kai.

"I said, stop!" With both hands, I shove Viggo in the chest and his mouth goes wide, roaring at me as his whole body slams against a shelf a few meters away. A box crumples, and soup tins spill to the ground to his left.

Kai barks a laugh in triumph and marches over to grab a can of soup, lifting it above his head, arm drawn back.

Rowan grabs the tin from him. "Kai, stop!"

I'm too focused on Trent whose changes are no longer subtle, the skin on his face stretching and contorting, a thick layer of fur begins to sprout as if he's suddenly growing a beard.

"What the fuck?" stammers Dale as Trent's lips swell and then recede, revealing large, sharp teeth. "That's cheating."

Grayson chokes. "Cheating? This isn't a fucking game, you moron."

Trent lunges, and again, I throw myself between the shifter and Kai.

"Run!" Rowan shouts at Dale. "Tell the cops exactly where we are. I called them."

Trent's transformation wipes away any bravado Dale still possesses, and he skitters away, sliding on the smooth floor as he rounds the corner.

Viggo's back on his feet, propping himself up on the edge of a shelf with one hand.

"Can you trap Kai?" I ask Rowan as I lunge at and knock Viggo back to the ground. "Rune circle. Barrier. Something."

A guttural yell pulls me right back to the night at the lodge and away from attempting to intervene between Kai and Viggo. Now shifted, Trent aims straight for Rowan. I yell and barrel forward but don't reach Rowan before the bear pounces.

I feel the slash as if it were against my own skin and the raw, primal thing I promised I'd keep subdued roars to life as loudly as the bear. Someone drops from above and Grayson lands on the bear's back, hooking his hands either side of the jaws and separating Trent's teeth from their hold on Rowan's shoulder.

"Don't fucking kill him, Grayson," rasps out Rowan, hand going to his ripped shirt. He presses a palm on a shoulder, and the hybrid Violet winds further around my calm and logic as blood seeps through Rowan's fingers. I snarl, muscles coiling, teeth and claws ready to join Grayson's hold on Trent. "You too, Violet."

Grayson tussles with the thrashing bear, who's now turning on him, and his hemia transformation comes quicker than at the lodge. Taunting Trent, Grayson dodges and springs onto a shelf, pausing for the shifter to catch up, before hopping to the next.

Rowan shuffles to lean against a shelf, hand still on his shoulder and I rush towards him, heart stuttering. He's bleeding —but not as badly as Trent intended.

"Violet!" he shouts, eyes widening in his pale face as he looks behind. "Kai!"

I spin. Kai takes advantage of my distraction and, as he raises the can again, I'm too slow. The metal thuds against Viggo's skull, the skin on his forehead splitting open. He yells and grabs a can of his own, before rolling away from Kai's next attempted hit.

Viggo slings a can at Kai with an unnatural force, and this time, I catch the projectile. Momentarily, Viggo pauses and stares at my dexterous move before his attention switches to Kai again.

I side-glance at the idiot human crouching to take a soup tin in each hand.

"Good grief!" My other arm shoots out and I circle one hand around Kai's throat, lifting him from the ground.

He chokes out, fingers clawing at my hands instead. "What the fuck happened to your face?"

"I'm not as pretty when I'm pissed," I growl out. "And someone hurt Rowan."

"*They* did!" he rasps and attempts to point at Viggo.

"Drop the tins, Kai." He hesitates, and I keep one eye on Viggo, who's concentrating on his opponent. "Death by soup can is not a noble way for either of you to die," I shout at the pair.

"Put me down," he chokes out.

The whack to the head might not have killed or knocked out Viggo, but he's weakened enough to struggle with staying steady, body swaying as he clutches a can and figures out his next move.

At least that move doesn't include attacking Rowan, who watches through pained eyes. "Don't kill," he says again. "I'm alright."

Yes, but Rowan's in pain, and gripped by terror. Not for himself—that I might lose myself to the fury and kill. That he would then lose me.

"Viggo," I snarl. "Stop and leave."

He hesitates as I attempt to capture his mind; Kai struggles against my tight grip and I can only hope that Grayson's dance with Trent continues until I can subdue the bear too. Is Trent acting on Viggo's suggestion or the witches' influence?

"This has nothing to do with you," rasps Kai.

A leather cord peeks from his neck, and I slice through with my fingernails, ripping the pendant from his throat. "Look at me," I say through sharp, bared teeth. "I am pissed that I saved your life once, only for you to endanger yourself again because you're as bone-headed as your rivals. Go."

A noise like an earthquake rolling through the warehouse interrupts, and I glance at Rowan again. He shakes his head and I jerk mine around in confusion. The whole rack of boxes behind Viggo collapses forward as a bear leaps through the center, smashing the solid metal shelving as if breaking through sticks.

Time pauses as Viggo screams, tins cascading from the broken shelves like a waterfall of metal. Some bounce from him and I'm too slow to stop anything as the whole shelf collapses across the aisle, hitting one opposite, the boxes piling on and crushing the shifter.

"Fucking hell," chokes Kai.

Throwing Kai to one side, I dash towards the stunned bear, who's now staggering from side to side, shaking his head. The collapsed shelf blocks our way from the aisle to the exit and Viggo's not visible at all beneath the chaos.

"Your ultimate aim, Violet Blackwood?" asks a smooth voice.

Chapter Thirty-Five

VIOLET

I WHIRL AROUND, attempting to locate the witch who spoke, eyes immediately zoning in on the pool of blood where Rowan sat moments ago. Who set this up?

"You killed Viggo, and now you're about to kill Kai, little necromancer. All with the help of your Ursa construct," continues the mocking voice from somewhere in the warehouse.

Kai's on his hands and knees, unable to get purchase as he slips in the Viggo's blood on the shiny floor. "Is Viggo dead?" he shrieks. "Did you kill him?"

"Where are you, witch?" I snarl. Every sense is sharpened to finding him, and locating Rowan's heartbeat, also aware how sluggish Viggo's becomes. But what can I do?

"Rowan!" I shout and spin in a circle.

Kai manages to scramble to his feet and clambers over the barrier created by the fallen boxes and tins. He's halfway up the fallen shelf when he swears again, turning to face me as he halts and points to the other side. "Who the fuck are *they*?"

I ignore how Kai flinches when I scramble after him and crouch on top of the boxes. The two witches—Grant Underhill and Adam Woodlake. My heart explodes, magic lashing my veins, and primal fury seizes hold as I spot Rowan on the ground beside them. Unmoving.

"What have you done?" I scream at them.

Did they injure him further? I'm on the first witch in half a breath, knees on Adam's chest and claws at his face. Rowan's blood scent fills the air and I pant heavily, every cell in my body wanting to strike, but deep in the heart of me I know I can't. He's the link to freeing Leif.

"I've got you!" I snarl. "If Rowan's hurt, I'll kill you but not tonight. Not yet."

The second witch's laugh cuts short as someone blurs down from a shelf above. Through my red-misted, hybrid vision, I witness a dark-haired vampire tear through Grant's throat.

"Grayson!" I shout, claws still at Adam's neck. "Not again!"

The vamp's facing away, and he turns after dropping the witch to the floor.

Not Grayson.

Josef. "And now she's killed a witch too," he says.

Below me, Adam coughs a laugh. "Nice double-cross, Petrescu. But you've got the wrong guy."

"I merely informed you that the Sawyer boy would be here tonight," he purrs. "And presumed you'd follow. How fortuitous that Ms. Blackwood chose the same evening to break into my client's factory and has interfered in your plans."

Fortuitous? My stomach sickens. Grayson told Josef? No. Rowan suggested our visit.

As Josef steps towards me and the witch, I spring to my feet and swipe at Josef instead, protecting the witch that my vengeful side wanted to end. "Don't touch anybody else!"

"Stop!" Adam holds his hands up, palms out. "You want her caught? No need to kill me. Grant's death triggered her fate."

"I didn't kill him," I snarl. "And I won't kill you. I know all about your shifter 'workers' at the house. The necromancy. You murdered people and you'll pay!"

"Won't even kill as revenge for Rowan's death?" asks Josef smoothly.

"Rowan isn't dead," I grit out.

"Yet." Josef smirks. "You can only take on so many people at once, even as a hybrid."

"Now that one of us has died, Oz's memories will trigger," says Adam, weakly. "Supe authorities will involve themselves in the investigation and see inside Oz's mind. A very clear memory of what you did that night Wesley died, Violet. The construct you created. The influence on Leif to hide your crimes."

"What? I wasn't there!"

Adam smirks up at me. "You've never planted false memories in someone's mind?"

"You're lying!"

Dipping my head, I fight against the girl who'd rip Josef apart, avoiding looking at Rowan, only reassured he's okay by his heartbeat in my ears.

"You've lost either way, sweetheart," says Adam.

"Who's doing this?" I shout at him. "There's someone else. Someone bigger."

"Isn't there always?" Adam chuckles.

Josef claps his hand, a gleeful smile on his malevolent face. "This is better than anticipated and all I had to do was follow. We have a number of deaths here," says Josef and gestures at Viggo and Grant. "Not enough though." I cringe as Josef strikes out at the witch, kicking him beneath the chin until his head snaps back. Josef glances at me. "Don't worry, I won't kill him. That's your job."

Where's Grayson? I lift my head and inhale, desperate to sense him too. Maybe he left to warn Dorian. And the bear... "Where did Trent go?"

Josef shrugs, but his expression's less casual. "He got away. My bastard nephew helped the wrong person as usual. This would've been over much quicker if you'd killed Trent for attacking Rowan."

"You do know the police and my father are on their way?" I tell Josef.

"Yes. But there's still time."

"Kai's safe," I spit, pointing at bloody footprints leading away from us. "Your client *will* be impressed."

"Mmm." Josef steps closer and I prepare to launch myself at him, but he merely darts to one side and looks down at Rowan. "Why aren't you helping your bonded, Violet? Playing for time?"

"If you value your life, do not touch Rowan."

He pouts. "You'd kill a Petrescu, and witches, and shifters. Dear me, you really are out of control. Just look at the state you're in."

As I stare at the vamp, wiping the blood leaking from my nose, stories of my father tumble into my mind. Some speak of his infamy for slow, sadistic torture; others how he could pull apart person after person in a room before anybody catches up to what's happening. Heads smashed, throats opened, and Dorian's high from his actions spurring him on.

But Dorian was created and taught to be that thing by others; an experiment that backfired because they gave him something they shouldn't. Intelligence. Dorian ended every threat to his and his families' lives and continues that behavior to this day.

Josef Petrescu. The witches. They all rely on me to be the same as Dorian, and here I am—in a warehouse with a crushed shifter, and a dead witch bleeding out. Whoever's at the pinnacle of this attack on the supernatural world, these aren't the only victims they want. Even if arrests happen tonight, this is not over.

"Kill the witch!" shouts Josef. "I need the shifters back in my control. These witches need to know I'm a step ahead of their pathetic plans for a coup."

I shake my head, wishing I could shake away the images of Dorian. I wasn't created to be a weapon, but I've a part of him seeded deep in my soul by birth. And right now, my bond to Rowan feeds this part and the hybrid flourishes. Everything I can see Dorian doing in my mind? If Rowan's dying, that'll be child's play compared to what I'll do to these men.

Rowan isn't dead. Rowan isn't dead. I repeat the mantra as the hybrid nudges, telling me I should kill the witch anyway. *End Josef. They deserve to die.*

I've no chance at rationality anymore. Especially not when

Josef hauls Rowan from the floor like a rag doll and spins him to face me, one sharp nail against a jugular. "Let's hurry this up."

Every sense hones razor sharp as I face off Josef. "Do you think you'd survive if you killed a hybrid's bonded witch?" I snarl out.

He's waiting for me to pounce, but I'm preternaturally still, calculating—how and where to strike, the moment my speed could catch him unaware.

Take out a threat to my father. My world. Me.

I can't. I can't. I can't.

Ragged breaths saw from me, and I switch my focus to Rowan. My father could move fast enough, but Josef's reflexes would almost equal mine. Rowan would die before I touched the vampire. Rowan's injured but breathing, and as I will him to open his eyes, my stomach lurches when he does. There's no signs of the sparks from his elemental magic, nothing moves magically within the warehouse. He's too weak.

Fire's my strongest element, but impossible to use here. Plus, if my violent hemia side is overruling the witch part of who I am, I've no chance to use shadow magic to end this. I don't have the control to use magic as quickly and easily as a full-blooded witch.

I bite my lip. But Rowan's capable of conjuring shadows without my touch. He already contains them. Leif told me shadows exploded around Rowan when I died at the lodge. I've always repressed them; never practiced—I suspect Rowan has and could use them now.

No. Rowan's ability to manipulate shadows can't manifest. Nobody can know or he'll become as big a target as me—not to kill, but to be manipulated. Shadows corrupt even the strongest minded witch and hold infinite power if harnessed.

I switch back to calculating where to strike Josef.

Don't kill him, Violet.

Rowan's voice heard as a distant whisper in my mind arrests me. How? We're not telepathic with our bond.

If you kill him, they win.

"What are you doing, Violet?" asks Josef lazily. "Shouldn't you act quicker?"

The wisps of shadow that Rowan showed the day we fought swirl weakly around his fingers. I snap my eyes away. Have I forgotten my other skill? Talking; distracting.

"How did you know we'd be here?" I ask. "Grayson?"

"I didn't. I discovered what the human boy planned, and it seems that the witches' pet bear told them Viggo intended to meet Kai. I never had a chance to contact Grayson, since I needed to get here and stop this attack. Looks like your nosiness helped me."

"I don't believe you."

"You don't need to."

I eye Rowan and his magic again. "Were you close with Oskar? You appear to share his bloody-minded belief in your righteousness," I say.

He clenches his teeth. "I'm an original Petrescu."

"Yes, then?" I focus hard on not watching Rowan. "You do realize that whatever happens, Dorian will kill you."

Josef sneers. "Not tonight, if ever. Now, your witch… that's a different story."

The air cools and the atmosphere becomes denser as the shadows come, but Josef shows no sign he's aware.

"Whatever you're planning counts on me *not* killing you tonight, hence you will not kill Rowan." I wipe fingers across the blood on my face and lift them up. "Yes, I've more control than Dorian, but not if you harm Rowan. Stop bluffing."

Josef's nails remain frighteningly close to Rowan's jugular, his hardened green eyes on mine. The wisps around Rowan become thicker, snaking around his arms, and I moisten my lips. Josef wants power. To see Dorian fall, which means he won't risk falling himself tonight. But why shouldn't I attack him? I can maim, not kill.

You know you'll go too far.

Again. Rowan. This time I can't help looking at him in alarm. *Are you in my mind?*

He raises a brow, his eyes now storms. *I'll sort this.*

But if you use shadows, you're at risk. Nobody should know you can summon them.

Perhaps I want them to, Violet.

As Josef's nail presses harder into Rowan, he nicks the skin—and the hybrid breaks free in my mind, reaching for Josef in a split second.

The shadows edging Rowan implode, surrounding the pair until I can't see either of them, and before I reach Josef. Josef's grip on Rowan loosens, and Rowan staggers from within the cloud, shadows consuming him too. Only Rowan sends the shadows away instead, forcing them into Josef's open mouth as the vamp flails his arms, pulling at the incorporeal attacker, choking.

In my mind's eye, Rowan's a vaguer version of himself, silent. Josef flashes a look at me, and I wince as his mind pierces mine, scratching an image across my vision before he collapses to his knees.

Grayson and a hell of a lot of blood in the warehouse somewhere.

I dart forward and grab Rowan's arm, sucking a breath as the icy cold magic eagerly greets me, turning in my direction. "No more."

"Got the bastard," he rasps out and points at the powerful vampire at his feet.

A vampire bound by shadows. The worst part isn't the energy needed to hold Josef without killing him, but that he has the knowledge that Rowan can conjure the magic as easily as a Blackwood.

Because of the Blackwood.

Rowan's magic shimmers around, not only as the shadows eating away at the environment, but as if he's surrounded by a barrier that undulates. I pull his shadow-covered figure against me, holding his face, searching his eyes. "Let the shadows go now."

"Find Grayson." He holds my cheeks in return, fingers cold as death. "Nobody will hurt me."

"Your shoulder," I protest.

"I'm alright. Nobody will hurt me," he grits out. "I'm keeping these bastards here, under control, until Dorian arrives."

I barely recognize his voice. This is the Rowan I've only glimpsed—the perfect bond to me, his potency and abilities equal to and able to absorb my hybrid's magic, the darkness in his soul a match for mine. I'm torn between relief that Rowan pulled some of the vicious desire out of me but as his aura remains clouded, my chest tightens. The humans and my father had better arrive soon because although I can trust Rowan will be safe while I find Grayson, I can't say the same for the men at Rowan's feet.

Chapter Thirty-Six

VIOLET

IF I COULDN'T SMELL Grayson's blood more acutely by the second, I *would* stay beside Rowan—ensure the witch remains unconscious, and that Josef remains choked by shadows. The metallic tang from Rowan's blood affects me more in recent days, despite the potion, but Grayson's tunnels into the hybrid's mind, feeding the desire she couldn't satisfy with the witches or Josef.

But Grayson isn't beside me. I shouldn't smell his blood in this way.

Pushing shaking hands through my hair, I focus on winding memories of Grayson around my mind, to tell my thumping heart that his blood isn't for me and he means more than that. When I find Grayson, this barely leashed part of me will surge forward, unless I hold on to how much I care for him.

Cautiously, I follow the trail left from when Grayson lured away the bear, thankful there's no blood, only upturned shelves. More boxes have tipped their contents into the aisle on the other side of the warehouse, but there's no shifter beneath these.

Viggo.

Dead. If Kai and Dale don't back me up on what happened here, I am, to coin a phrase I've heard, fucked.

I don't need to search hard for Grayson, his scent leading me as it did the night Wesley died. Only that time, the blood was in his veins. Tonight, it's spilled—Josef showed me in his mind's eye.

There's no blood trail to follow, yet I'm drawn anyway as I round a corner and find Grayson slumped against a wall towards the rear of the now-silent warehouse. But there's plenty around him. Each step I take closer, my heart thrums in anticipation of the blood that soaks his shirt.

No.

I manage to grip the edge of the nearest shelf to stop myself moving nearer, swallowing hard. He's unmoving but his heart beats, and Grayson's eyes open as he senses me. Is this how I'd react to every single bleeding individual if I didn't take the potion, or is the extreme reaction because this is Grayson? Because a whining in my head threatens to obliterate the girl clinging to the metal.

"So, this is ironic," Grayson says weakly.

"I can think of many other adjectives," I whisper.

He points at his chest. "At least the bastard missed my heart."

A long metal cylinder protrudes from below his rib cage on the left, the end slick with Grayson's blood.

"Can you stand?" I ask. "Or have you lost too much blood?" My voice cracks at the last word.

"Yeah. I'm kinda impaled against the wall by a metal bar."

"Oh. Hence the irony. I see." I hold a palm across my nose and mouth, but the action does nothing to stem the smell. "Why didn't you shout for us?"

"I did. Perhaps not loudly enough." His voice weakens and my fingers bite into the shelf. "Any chance you could take this out and I can leave? Before I do lose too much blood and face the embarrassment of someone carrying me out?"

Grayson speaks slowly, tripping over the words, wasting labored breaths. I've a million questions, including where Trent is and if Josef lied and Grayson knew about tonight, but I swipe a hand down my face instead. I've never seen anybody bleeding this profusely, and he's the last person whose blood should be near me.

"Can you wait until someone comes?" I whisper.

"Violet," he groans. "Are you seriously going to let me bleed out completely?"

"I might kill you," I say flatly.

"That's what Josef's counting on. I didn't behave. As I lured the shifter away from Rowan, I saw Josef. He wanted me to take the shifter back to you. For you to kill." He takes a ragged breath after the effort of speaking. "I'll take the risk, because I don't believe you will kill me."

The eyes that mesmerized me from the first time I met them lock with mine, only they're duller. Did I not worry for Grayson's safety when Josef had him? Find myself drawn to him the night he returned, and struggled with confusion at how relieved I was when I encountered Grayson unhurt?

How I'd wanted the teenage moment in the closet.

On wobbly legs, I creep closer, but I can only hold my breath for so long. His blood scent is a fog as tangible as the shadows were, and I moisten my lips, the hybrid heart beating to life again. I halt in shock as my boots touch the sizeable pool of blood.

"I mean, you could lick some off the floor after you help me?" he suggests lightly.

"I'd prefer the blood pulsing into my mouth from a vein." I slam a hand over said mouth. "Good grief. Sorry. Hybrid talk."

"Violet," he whispers. "I don't care. I've always told you that."

Ignoring the sticky pool beneath my boots, I crouch down to take hold of the bar, fingers slipping around the blood Grayson left with his own attempt to remove it.

"Josef?" He nods. "He has some strength to slam this through you into a breeze block."

"Petrescu. Is he dead?"

I shake my head. *Hurry. Get away from his blood.* The metal inches from Grayson's chest as I pull, and as the rebar clatters to the floor, I'm hit by what I've opened myself up to without thinking. The emerald eyes turn coal black, and Grayson's hand shoots up the back of my neck, his fingers locking onto me.

He's the vampire whose blood constantly calls to me, but that call deafened the truth. Grayson is a hemia whose veins are emptying of blood, and he needs more.

Grayson yanks me forward, but his lips barely touch my skin before I've jerked away, sliding on my ass through the blood then leaping to my feet. Grayson's eyes drop to the bar by his side, and as I lurch for it again, he knocks it beneath a shelf.

"Grayson. Snap out of it," I demand as he stands too. If he had the strength to stand, why couldn't he remove the bar? Simple answer—he could. "Grayson!"

The force with which he hits me is beyond shocking. Nothing ever touched me in this way, and I sprawl to the floor, Grayson's hips pinning me.

Rowan outmatches me magically, and Grayson physically—trust me to choose the most powerful of entities to tangle myself with.

As if I'd tangle with anybody else.

Yes, Grayson told me he had superior hemia strength, but shouldn't he be weak? Now I understand the famous Petrescu potency. He bears down on me, eyes pure black and teeth bared, and I'm almost trapped by him. I yell and jam an elbow into his face. Grayson howls as his cheekbone crunches, and I curse myself as blood also leaks from his nose. "Grayson. Stop."

He doesn't, and Grayson frees my hybrid in the one situation it's impossible for me to cage her. Self-defense.

"I'll kill you!" I shout, pushing at his face with a palm. "I don't want to kill you, Grayson."

His blood covers my hands. My hair. My skin, drowning me as if I'm beneath a pool of that blood, everything echoing apart from my heartbeat and his.

"Talk to me!" I slap him hard around the face, the noise bouncing around us, and he snatches my wrist, lips parting again. "Good grief!" I shout, raise my knees, and slam them into his chest until he flies backwards himself. "I'm a single uncontrolled heartbeat from tearing into you," I say as we both stand. The hybrid baying for his blood blackens my vision until I don't see Grayson, only a victim. "If you can run, run."

Grayson does run.

Straight at me.

I warned him. *I warned him.* Snatching his hair, I yank Grayson's head back and seal my mouth on his neck, breaking his skin with my teeth. Blood hits my tongue, my fingers crawling into his hair, across his scalp, pressing, as the primal Violet compels me. With the flow of Grayson's warmth and life, comes the taste of his darkness, as heady as the flavor. I've struck the real reason for my obsession—the very thing I avoid—feeding my dark heart.

Grayson fought against me before, but now he doesn't struggle, the hemia giving what he tried to take. Grayson's legs give way and he slides away from my mouth until I'm left holding the guy slumped in my arms, the blood from his wound pumping slowly, along with his heart.

Grayson. I drop him as horror strikes at my soul. His lifeblood mingles with mine, and the guy I tried to protect is now *my* victim at my feet. Grayson won't die. Not permanently. But all I can see in my mind's eye is Josef killing Grayson. Grayson never allowed me to see that memory, and I was pissed that he shared with Rowan and not me. So, as we sat outside the lodge that afternoon, I peeked. I saw what his uncle did to him.

I'm as abhorrent as Josef Petrescu.

Dropping to my knees, I place my hands on Grayson's clammy face, touching his translucent skin, as I count his barely there breaths. My lips press against the wound I made, and the blood now sickens me, as I tremble with disgust.

Dorian would never hurt someone he cared for. Eloise told me the first time he took her blood, Dorian did so with permission.

I'm not my father. I'm worse.

"Grayson." I say against his skin. "I'm sorry."

Through all the mingled pleasure and shock filling my body and mind, other parts of *us* drift in. The time we pressed together in the closet, where I inhaled the same warmth as now. I've touched and been close enough to Grayson to connect with him in the way I've secretly wanted. To share affection, not blood.

But in the end, this is all we are to each other.

I don't want authorities to walk into this warehouse and find me over Grayson's almost-dead body. Not because I already need to explain away Viggo crushed beneath Sawyer's stock, or the dead witch, or even whatever's happening around me as the distant sirens approach. No. Because I don't want anybody to see what I hide from the world and promised would stay locked away.

I pointlessly lash out as someone hooks me under the arms and pulls me away from the dying vampire. My father hauls me to my feet and spins me around. He seizes my cheeks and jerks my head from side to side, then turns over my hands to examine my wrists.

"His blood?" he asks tersely.

"What?" I blink away the remaining red mist.

"On your hands. Face. Everywhere." I nod mutely. "Did he take yours?"

No. But would I have given Grayson my blood if the guilt had continued to eat at and consume me? Did I want to know if Grayson taking from me felt as euphoric as taking from him?

"No, he didn't."

"Good."

I retch, wiping at my lips and rubbing my tongue against a rough coat sleeve. "I'm a monster," I say hoarsely as I meet Dorian's glacial eyes. "Look at him. I did that to someone I care about."

He loosens his grip on my arm and cups my jaw with a broad hand. *Tell me I'm not a monster. Tell me.* "Don't worry, sweetest girl. I'll fix everything that happened tonight."

Even Grayson, who I don't dare look down at?

My awareness snaps from the small space I'm lost in and to where Rowan walks around the corner, jacket still torn, shadows gone. He strides over and halts, not because Dorian stands close to me, but as he spots Grayson on the ground.

"Violet. What—?"

I half-throw myself into Rowan's arms, wanting him to hold onto and remind me that I can care for someone, however strange and rough that affection is. Remind myself that I helped people tonight—Kai, Dale… Death still stalked me here, but never took over. As my grip on him grows, Rowan struggles for breath, but he embraces me as tightly.

"What have I done?" I choke into his blood-soaked shirt.

"Everything will be okay," he whispers, but his fear is palpable.

Nearby, other voices and movement pull me further back to the scene. Is this over? Or about to get worse? Dorian can get into that witch's head. He can certainly extract the truth from Adam one painful way or another—but was the witch truthful when he spoke of the trigger in Oz's mind that'll falsely implicate me?

Rowan smooths my hair and struggles to hide his alarm—I'd little blood on my face when I walked away from him, now I have a lot and it's obvious whose, since Grayson is hardly breathing. Subconsciously with guilt, I touch my lips and dip my head as Rowan moves to kiss me. I'm not kissing Rowan with Grayson's blood on my face.

Grayson's blood on my face.

One of the detectives approaches and the smugness I expected isn't evident, his face clammy and pale. His attention immediately drops to Grayson before he beckons to me. "Come along, Ms. Blackwood. Let's see if we can find the truth this time."

I slide a look to Dorian, who nods curtly. *Don't worry, sweetest girl. I'll fix everything that happened tonight.* "Dorian. Please help Grayson. I know he's a Petrescu, but he doesn't deserve this."

A storm passes over Dorian's blue eyes before clearing to the brightest blue sky, and he smiles. "Of course. I'll ensure he's taken care of, Violet."

If only I knew which part of Dorian that smile and words came from, and exactly how he'll take care of the guy I can never touch again.

I grip onto Rowan's hand and numbly walk as he leads me away.

Chapter Thirty-Seven

GRAYSON

EVER THE SLIPPERY BASTARD, my uncle and his mind skills allowed him to worm his way from authorities at the warehouse. All it took was Rowan and Dorian's distraction when they came to me and Violet. Josef alleged to the detectives that he became aware of Kai's plans at the last moment and called authorities while also heading to the warehouse to intervene. The first responders' confusion by the whole scene when they arrived— injuries and deaths; witches and shifters—aided him in avoiding closer questioning.

Nobody has seen Josef since he left the warehouse leaving his mind-washing, bullshit excuses behind.

Despite Dorian's protest to the humans, my uncle isn't a suspect because he didn't have a direct hand in the murders. And as Sawyer's attorney, Josef has a longstanding relationship with an important council member who'll vouch for him. I'm still on Josef's hit list—when he saw me in the warehouse luring Trent away from Rowan and Violet, he struck, furious at my betrayal. How the hell was I to know he'd come to the warehouse too? I didn't even realize the witches had arrived at that point.

How much was Josef aware of before he walked into that

warehouse and saw me battling Trent? Did Josef know Violet was at the warehouse with me and Rowan? Because something doesn't sit right—someone followed. Somebody knows.

Trent attacked Rowan, not Kai, and turned the witches' plans upside down. And this time, the shifter's attack triggered my instincts to ensure Rowan's safety—to help him and keep Violet from losing her shit.

I got the full story from Rowan a couple of days later—once Josef realized Violet wasn't on the verge of killing the witches, he ensured one would die, then hedged his bets she'd get the blame. Josef knew time was short, and that authorities would arrive, otherwise he might've been more the calculating, the strategic bastard he is.

Again, bigger forces at work. Watching. Waiting.

Well, they failed, whoever the fuck is behind this. Josef never got to the Blackwoods—Violet or Dorian—and the night ended with one of the witches alive and taken into custody.

News also traveled to me from Rowan that Kai filled in the gaps about what happened at the warehouse. After some disagreement between humans, shifters, and supes, Dorian hauled Adam away to extract the *actual* truth from the witch. Dorian got his confessions about witch manipulation of shifters, but Adam told Dorian nothing about Josef's involvement with the culprits and their plan to kill Kai.

The necromancy angle remains secret for now—Oz 'conveniently' died before witches examined his mind and the humans were happy with the story that the witches mind-controlled shifters. The evidence showed Rory kill Wesley; that was enough for them. Funny how humans will do anything to save face and insist the town's 'safe' rather than appear incompetent. All the humans cared about was solving Wesley's murder and claimed that Rory's and Viggo's deaths are 'the shifter elders'' issue.

Sawyer remains allegedly clueless why his son was a target, despite Adam stating Sawyer 'owed him' for past services he didn't pay for, but that nobody else was involved in the plot. Again, Sawyer brushed aside whatever these services were, apparently reassured nobody else is a threat to Kai now the witches are dealt with. Dumb. No wonder the race gets screwed over so much. Still, that suits Dorian, since he wants the humans out of the picture while he tears down whatever's happening.

I can't imagine what political shit hit the fan or what this means for the accords between the town, supes, and shifters, but I'm betting that shit pile is building. Violet's right. Even though Dorian's failed to get any other names from Adam, there's someone higher up behind this.

The humans freed Leif once his memories were found to be clear, but he hasn't returned to the academy. Trent is either AWOL or hidden by shifters—Dorian will need to step in to find him and also investigate how far the necromancy goes. How far this *plot* against him goes.

What a fucking mess.

As intended.

And guaranteed that Violet will involve herself in more investigations.

Violet.

I ask Rowan about her when I don't hear anything, worried that she or the guys suspect my involvement. He told me no, but agrees that everything seems too big a coincidence. Rowan tells me Violet's spending a lot of time alone and refused to leave Thornwood to join her parents. Violet does eventually reply to a text I send, but only after a week, an unusually normal—but abnormal for Violet—exchange. I ask how she is; Violet replies she's fine, apologizes, and hopes I'm recovering.

When Rowan tells me she's thrown herself into helping Holly with the Spring Ball organization, I know she's not coping.

I spend time recovering at my parents' place, who're absent as usual. I've healed from death before, so recovering from semi-death is easier, although perhaps it's a good thing the human staff worried about the half-starved hemia vampire and left.

I'm away from Thornwood for two weeks, long enough for everybody's excitement about events to fade. I also tell Violet I'm headed back on the day I return, but she never answers the message, and neither is she sitting at the bottom of the stairs to Sheridan House now, as she was when I returned from Josef.

My teeth grind as I stare at the spot she waited for me that day. Josef genuinely thought Violet would kill me; that my response to hemia blood loss meant I'd attack her and the night would end with my own death. After all, why would a Blackwood allow a Petrescu to live? How could a threatened, hybrid Violet Blackwood overcome her true nature faced with a vampire whose blood she's obsessed by?

Good question and one Violet needs to answer.

Few people register me as I cross campus. I'd expected a different feel to Thornwood now that the human headteacher left, but focus seems to be on the upcoming dance. How easily humans hide themselves in the mundane to pretend that they can live in safety.

I wait close to Darwin House to watch for Holly or Violet. Well, didn't Violet inform me I'm a stalker once before? Holly hurries out an hour after the classes that I never attended finish, and the light remains on in the room she shares with Violet. I cast a glance upwards, like a crazy Romeo looking for his deranged Juliet. Warring families? We all know how that one ended.

Other humans pass me, leaving the building, and I draw my hood across my face and scoot up the steps. I'm not *not* allowed in here, but considering my vigilante treatment of Wes's gang a few weeks ago, striding in, head high, isn't wise.

My shoulder knocks a poster for the Spring Ball, tearing the paper from the pins, and I take hold. I've never attended but I'm going this year. Rowan told me Violet is—if I can't talk to Violet tonight, she won't be able to avoid me there.

Light still filters beneath Violet's door and I cock my head. Silence. My heart lodges in my throat when I pick up her hazy mix of delicate fruits and tangy blood. I barely remember my attempt to take Violet's blood, but the girl who took up residence in the corner of my mind the day we met now permanently lives there, day and night.

I take a steadying breath. This proves she has me in a

chokehold—I'm nervous. Has my blood changed anything for Violet?

As I lift my knuckles to rap on the door, the thing flies open, and I catch a brief glimpse of Violet before she shoots backwards to stand in the center of the room.

"Grayson."

Violet looks no different, the same carefully arranged mask and heart-rending eyes that meet my own, and as usual there's the same sudden speed to her pulse to match mine. She's dressed in a baggy black sweater and leggings, hair scraped from her face, make-up free, and I chew down the desire for her that gnaws at me.

Closing the door, I rest a shoulder against the frame and regard her impassively. Violet returns the favor, unblinking, back straight. A giggle comes from a room along the hallway. A shout from the grounds outside.

Silence between us.

"For a girl who insists she always speaks her mind and doesn't care what people think of her words, you're rather quiet," I say softly.

"In this instance, I believe I should utilize my newfound skill to control my tongue."

I flick the tip of my own tongue against a canine. "Why haven't you answered my other messages?" No response. I peel myself from the wood and take slow, deliberate steps towards her. "If you're avoiding talking to me, Violet, you must know I'd come to you in person."

"Undoubtedly." Not a single physical response, no change in her face or stance, and her heartbeat returned to slow and steady.

"Why do you think I'm here?" I ask and stand over her.

"To talk, I imagine, as that's a favorite pastime of yours." There. A single flutter of her pulse, a tiny whisper of something held back from escaping. "Or to request an apology."

"You already gave me one. Short and as sweet as ever, and on a phone screen."

She blinks. Just once. "Your response to that message disturbed me."

"Disturbed you?" I raise a brow.

"'*I don't mind*' was a rather odd response to someone who apologized for bringing you to the brink of death."

"Mmm. Imagine the Hell I thought I'd arrived in when I opened my eyes to Dorian's face."

She lifts her head. "He helped get you somewhere safe to recover, away from human or witch blood."

"I know. Then he left me with a gentle pat on the head. Expressed how happy I should be that I hadn't taken your blood—because that would've killed me."

Her brow pinches. "No. That's incorrect. You're not a witch. Vampire blood only kills witches."

"I'm pretty sure your father meant that if I'd taken your blood, he would've taken my life."

"Ah." She's entirely too casual, not treating my words like the joke I'd hoped.

"I'm happy you attacked me, Violet."

"Excuse me?" she blurts.

"I'm glad you chose to attack me." She doesn't budge as I edge closer.

"A friend would've helped you that night, Grayson. I am supposed to be your friend."

"You defended yourself against my attack on you."

"I could've walked away to request others' help. I did not because the hybrid wanted blood. Your attack brought out my self-defense, and I used that as an excuse. I was lost." She pauses. "Afterwards, I felt like a monster."

"I'm a monster too, Violet," I say quietly.

"You're not like me."

"And you don't know me despite the constant reminder I'm Petrescu. I've drained people to the edge of death due to lack of control. I won't deny that I chased the euphoria and didn't care." She blinks again. "Don't you remember saying I'm worse because I didn't act in self-defense when I killed Maxwell?"

Violet remains still as I edge even further into her personal space.

"You would lose control eventually and I'm happy I took the brunt the first time. I'd rather I experienced what you're capable of—and proved you're able to stop," I continue.

"I could've killed you."

"Temporarily." My mouth tips into a smile. "That's presuming you weren't angry enough to tear my heart out?"

She shakes her head. "The blood."

"At the warehouse, my uncle placed you in a position where he wanted you to kill, and you held back. Rowan says you allowed him to act rather than takeover and lash out. You controlled the hybrid, Violet, but she was still close to the surface. If you hadn't attacked me, you may've hurt someone else." She looks away. "I'm sorry that I attacked you too, but also glad."

"Obviously sorry, as the move didn't end well for you."

Our gazes lock again and frustration bubbles in my chest at how unreadable she is. Rowan's right—Violet moved back from the world after taking so many steps towards us.

"And how was my blood? As you imagined?" I ask casually.

Violet turns away and sits on her chair, beside a desk covered in familiar handwritten notes. She sits on her hands, while my own dangle by my side. Lost. I had two options when I walked in here tonight—come on strong and challenge the challenging girl or take a softer approach.

Now what do I do? This isn't Violet. She's unsure of herself on a whole new level.

"Why are you ashamed, Violet? You're part-vampire. Hemia. No different to a shifter losing themselves to their 'other'."

"It's very different," Violet's rising voice skitters across my nerves.

I take a sharp breath but push on. "And Rowan? I know he's taken your shadows. That you can lose part of yourselves to each other. Isn't that the same?"

"No, Grayson, because I have control."

"Control," I say harshly. "Violet Blackwood is always in control."

She lifts her eyes. "Until I'm not. This is different to Rowan —bonded witches are programmed not to harm each other. If I worried about his life, I'd stay away from him too. When I'm with Rowan, I'm spun into his darkness and he meets the edge of mine, but blood is a whole different level, Grayson."

"Then tell me one thing—why did you stop?"

Violet tugs her bottom lip between her teeth, pupils dilating. "Because…" She shakes her head. "Because I could. I stopped for the same reason as I waited for you that evening you returned from Josef," she says quietly. "Because you mean something to me. Because I care what happens to you. Because I care *about* you."

"And I don't want you to keep away from me because I remind you what you are. I didn't die, but it would kill me if I lost you over this," I reply.

She stands. "I'm not ready to talk about these confusing things, Grayson. I am glad you're safe and would prefer you remained that way."

I don't make a single move from the spot I'm in. "When I'm tortured by thoughts of you, they're not your attack, or the bloodlust, but an obsession to know how *you* taste. To kiss you. Seems your dark little self filled my world with enough color to blind me against how dangerous this is."

For an aching heartbeat, Violet doesn't move, but her pulse flutters beneath her skin, telltale pink flushing her cheeks. My stomach drops as she walks towards the door. "I want you to leave. I can't be alone with you."

"What? Didn't you hear what I said?"

"Yes. What happened changes everything for me, and between us, Grayson," she says gently. "I could lose you in so many ways."

I'd told myself this will be the last time I'll repeat myself. The final time to ask her to understand. To look into *her* heart and see if any part beats for me as mine does for her.

And I'm pissed. Pissed at Violet's denial more than her rejection. Not taking my gaze off Violet, I walk to where she stands by the door before she can move again.

"You think I look at you differently now? Fine, you didn't ask my permission, but what happened is inevitable," I say coolly.

"This wasn't a snatched kiss," she protests.

"Yeah. I'm glad because I want to remember the first time you kiss me." Her eyes go wide as I touch her cheek. "Because whether you bite my lip or tongue, or neither, that kiss is inevitable too."

"I wouldn't."

"Kiss me?"

"Draw blood again."

"So, you would kiss me?" I tip her face. Violet takes a shaky breath. "Something in the shadowed heart of me absolutely and totally lusts for your blood, but I'd take a single kiss over that."

She doesn't move, as if I'm the one using a spell rather than the magical retaliation I'd expect from Violet. I move my mouth closer, lips hovering near enough that I can taste the sweetness on her breath.

Violet doesn't move, telling me everything without saying anything.

"This is how it's going to be then?" I whisper. "A fight for control?"

"Against you?"

"No. Against yourself."

"You want to know how I felt taking your blood?" she says stiffly, not moving her torturous lips from near mine. "Like I wanted everything. All of you. That I didn't care if you did the same to me. Now that I have that blood inside me, I want more —*she* wants more. Not me. I don't want to lose myself to the hybrid or lose you."

"But that isn't the problem, is it, Violet?" I say moving my lips close to her ear. "We're past that. We're past everything we were because you have Petrescu blood inside you now. My blood."

"I'm painfully aware of that."

I look back to her. "Is this because you think I want *yours*? I don't. I've no idea what your blood might do to me physically and I've a clear idea of what your father *would*."

Violet's pulse heightens, that precious blood flushing from her cheeks to neck, her scent sending the world hazy. She doesn't move, driving the frustration deeper. We're close—closer than the time in the closet when I should've just bloody kissed her.

There's no clever retort or threat, but Violet does exactly what I expected. The thing she does the best.

Holds back.

Laughing softly, I cup Violet's face and briefly press my lips to hers, knowing she'll hit me with either her fist or the truth. Violet's energy becomes shakier, but she doesn't let that control go, even though I feel in my bones that her protests don't come from fear she'll hurt me, but that she'll lose herself.

"Everything's changed," I whisper and move away. "Because the Violet I first met would've broken my neck by now, yet here we are."

That stillness. The silence.

But the desire? Hers screams at me.

"Then you still have time to leave before I do that," she says hoarsely.

With a shake of my head, I step back and yank at the door handle. "I'll respect what you're saying and what you want, but this won't be easy."

She blinks back to the here and now, disoriented by my sudden shift. "Again, I apologize."

"No, Violet. This won't be easy for *you*. I'm done—you haven't even started yet."

"Done what?" she asks.

"I'll leave you to figure that out. After all, you're the smart one."

But as I step through that door, waiting for a snarky comment, all that follows me away from her room is silence.

Chapter Thirty-Eight

VIOLET

TENDRILS OF HAIR curl around the front of my face, the rest pulled back and upwards to create a chignon. The style reflected in the mirror isn't what draws my attention. The tiara I position on my head does.

The amethyst catches the light, matching the shimmering purple I've allowed Holly to adorn my eyelids with, along with my signature black kohl and deep red lips. Holly gawks at me as she walks from the bathroom, followed by a choking cloud of perfume.

"You told me you decided to wear jeans."

"I lied." I pull up the edge of the long skirts to reveal my Docs. "But not about these."

"And... purple." She blinks. "You look so prett—"

"Stop." I hold up a hand.

I couldn't find an exact replica from the photograph despite an inordinate amount of wasted time on internet shopping sites, but the obscenely tight dress strongly resembles the color and cut. I've less curves than the girl in the photograph, but what I do have is now in plain sight, as the silken material clings to the skin it actually covers, the dress slashed open along a thigh.

"And you're wearing a tiara." The exuberance I'd expected from Holly isn't in the room, merely a quiet shock. "That's... unusual. A family heirloom?"

"Somebody's, I suppose." I straighten the silver against my lacquered locks, then glance over. "What?"

"Somebody's? Did you steal that?"

"No. Not really."

She purses her lips. Nobody I've shown the tiara to recognizes it, although so far few have seen the item apart from Dorian and some other closely trusted supes. I'd asked Dorian if I could borrow the item for Rowan to try a stronger psychometry spell when his witches failed, then 'forgot' to return it to him for evidence. At least he's partly inclined to agree that we shouldn't reveal everything we know yet.

And this tiara knows secrets.

Rowan's psychometry didn't reveal any strong images, only the girl placing the tiara on her head, but the magic barrier surrounding the headpiece has a minor crack that reveals the item hidden in a different box before the tin. This might be connected to the academy or somebody within it—the girl definitely was.

Somewhere, there's a link between the tiara and whatever's happening around me that I haven't solved yet.

Thus, I decided to replicate the girl's look for the Spring Ball and watch for any unusual reactions from students or staff. After all, the tiara's hardly forgettable with the jagged spikes ending in amethyst giving the thing more the look of a crown.

I'd hoped by wearing the tiara, I might somehow link to the magic that Rowan couldn't, but there's nothing but the dull energy I sensed the first time I took it from the box. Is there a spell on the item to stop the tiara revealing its secrets?

"I like your dress," I say to Holly when she continues to consider the legitimacy of my tiara ownership.

She splutters. "Of course, you do." Holly's chosen a shorter cocktail dress, the vibrant blue a contrast to her auburn hair that's pinned in a style similar to mine. Amongst the blue, clouds swirl and a beaded rainbow creates a hem that touches her knees. She threaded sapphire blue jewels through her hair that shine as brightly as her now excited aura.

"Yes. I do. It's very… you." I look around for the small purse I'm forced to use since I'm pocketless. "A distinct lack of pigs, though."

"Ha ha. Who are you going to the ball with? Grayson or Rowan?" she asks.

"Leif."

Her brow creases. "But he isn't at the academy. Leif went home after the police freed him."

"I told Leif he has to come, therefore he will." But he hasn't contacted me—I haven't heard from Leif for days. "And if he doesn't…" I shrug. As long as someone recognizes and reacts to the tiara, I'll enjoy my night.

"…you have other guys?" she finishes.

"I'm not prepared to meet the societal requirement to choose one person to attend with. Rowan, Grayson, and I will wait for Leif."

Holly bites the edge of her lip and nods at my chest. "They'll find you very distracting."

I frown and place my fingers against where the silver pendant disguising the blade touches the top of my breasts. If I *had* chosen the outfit myself, I'd pick more coverage, but from my research, the dress's revealing nature isn't unusual for a formal gown.

"Seriously, you look incredible, Violet." She gestures the length of me.

A sharp rap at the door startles us and I continue to study the strange creature I am in the mirror as Holly answers the door. Judging by Holly's higher-pitched voice, this is Chase and not Rowan or Grayson. Or Leif.

Chase's response to me is my first hint that I'm about to become a bigger spectacle than the day I walked into the academy. His eyes bug out. "Violet?"

"I'm in disguise," I say and meet those too keen eyes. "Shush."

"Huh?"

I'm pissed at how crestfallen Holly is since he's disgustedly drinking in my appearance and not hers. "Holly isn't in disguise," I say pointedly.

"Oh. Right." Chase turns to her. "Uh. Wow, Holly. That dress is something, huh?"

Although she smiles, I know Holly well enough to see it's false and that there's a smidgen of annoyance around her. "Yes. Can you believe this is from HauteHaven? Half off!"

Chase looks as wise as I do about what HauteHaven is. He curls an arm around her waist. "All off would be better," he says and nips her ear lobe, getting a mouthful of sparkly earring.

Ugh. "How ridiculous," I say. "That could never happen. No business could profit if giving away their products."

"What?"

Chase is not the right person for Holly. Not only is he an unpleasant individual who stares at her friend's visible flesh with all manner of inappropriate thoughts, but he's also unintelligent and easily confused.

"We need to check on a few things before the doors open to attendees, Violet," says Holly, regaining some excitement as she pushes her phone into a slim, sequined purse that matches her rainbow hem.

"And Chase is accompanying you?"

"You're not coming with me?"

"I shall wait for Rowan or Grayson."

"Which?" asks Chase.

"Whoever gets here first."

"First in, best dressed, yeah?" He snickers.

"No idea. Best dressed? Grayson probably, since Rowan isn't the neatest of people." Chase exchanges a confused look with Holly and opens his mouth, but she shakes her head.

"Don't wait too long," she says as Chase opens the door again. "And promise me you're coming, and this isn't a trick."

"I am absolutely attending the Spring Ball, Holly. I wouldn't miss the occasion for the world." Despite my best smile, Holly still doesn't look convinced.

Chapter Thirty-Nine

VIOLET

I STOMP my way from Darwin House to the main academy, Rowan matching my pace. He's barely said a word since he arrived at the room, and I struggle to tell whether Rowan appreciates my efforts to fit into the student body or not, because after one look at my dress he won't focus anywhere else but my face.

After a particularly hard stomp, water from a puddle splashes the hem of my dress and Rowan chuckles. "Ever the delicate flower, sweet Violet."

"Be careful, Rowan," I reply.

He catches my hand and I'm caught off-guard as he tugs me closer. "Do you understand the self-control I'm exercising not to kiss you stupid?"

"Common sense prevails, I see."

Rowan rubs the back of his fingers along my cheek. "Yeah, but you know I lose my common sense around you."

"And I see you managed to dress for the occasion," I say, and disentangle myself. "Although you couldn't find a comb again?"

I naturally expected Rowan to dress appropriately, but the classic navy-blue suit with crisp, white shirt and a matching tie gives him an air of something different. Neatness, yes, but he's one step further from boy to man. Not that he appreciates me calling him a boy.

His cool cotton shirt presses against my naked skin as he curls a hand around the back of my head and kisses my forehead. Rowan's hair tickles, but I'm more aware of the softness of his lips and the sudden judder of my heart. We haven't spent a lot of time together since the warehouse, but the times we have take me further away from my hesitance.

Not too far. I'm well-aware that Rowan's heavy breathing is not the exertion used in a kiss, and I'm certainly not ready to deal with the emotions inevitably involved with discovering what's beneath clothing. *Or* whatever else is involved in the process.

That said, curiosity nudges the desire forward, and as my mother needs three men to keep her satisfied, I may well inherit that lasciviousness. I did tell Rowan this, and he got a really weird look on his face and didn't speak for a minute. Regardless, my mind's elsewhere currently.

"Don't mess with Violet's hair," says Grayson from behind me. "I presume this is Violet? Hard to tell, but I'm guessing you wouldn't make out with anybody else."

I spin around and his smile drops the way Rowan's did when he first encountered my attire, apart from Grayson doesn't leave his gaze on my face, instead taking a too slow look the length of me. "Wow. Like, wow, Violet."

"If I'd known this plan would objectify me into a victim of the male gaze, I would've worn my jeans."

"Hey, even I'm not in jeans."

"Or a leather jacket." I gesture at his black suit. "Although the attire is rather funereal."

"Isn't the academy's misunderstood loner expected to wear black?" He arches a brow.

The well-cut suit ages-up Grayson too, hair pulled back more neatly than usual, but there'll aways be an aura of danger around the predatory hemia, that's somehow sharpened by his perfect form.

We've met once since our disturbingly intense meeting and neither of us mentioned what happened; Grayson back to his laconic behavior. I've considered his last actions before he left, at how close I was to letting go, but I couldn't cope with looking at Grayson and seeing the worst of what I could be. I certainly can't allow myself close to Grayson.

Not yet.

"I expected the same color scheme from you, Violet," says Grayson. "But you look like the girl in the photograph."

"Yes. Shame she had little taste." Pulling away from Rowan, I continue my march towards the academy entrance where the wide, glittery banner proclaiming the Spring Ball stretches across the entrance, lined by tiny lights.

With Rowan at one shoulder and Grayson the other, I take a step into the large entrance hall, that already contains more people than I like to share breathing space with. The walls are draped with sheer blue fabric I assisted Holly in hanging, creating the desired ethereal ambiance amongst the translucent lanterns hanging from the ceiling. The witches naturally wanted a magical and enchanting 'vibe', but I suppose we'll see how far the 'vibe' of unity works in tonight's celebrations.

The group ahead of me drops into silence as a navy blue-suited Logan double takes then laughs falsely and loudly.

"Pretending to be normal for the night, Violet?" he asks. "You're not fooling anybody."

I blink slowly and ignore him, quietly scanning faces to see if anybody focuses on my tiara.

"Nice crown. Think you're queen or something?" asks Raul.

"I am not the only person here with bejeweled hair, and certainly not the nicest." I gesture at one of the only vampires that ever bothers to speak to me, and their more subtle diamanté headpiece. "Lukas, for example."

"Let's go, Violet," says Rowan, and curls his fingers around mine as Logan steps forward. Grayson edges between us and I pull him back.

"I don't need bodyguards." I sidestep and pause briefly as I pass Logan. Voice lowered, I add, "I'm still wearing my boots that could kick you into next week, Logan."

Standing in the hallway under lights and scrutiny suddenly seems like a better idea once I step into the main hall. The mesmerizing blue wonderland continues, tiny incandescent witch lights floating above a floor where a water pattern swirls. I'm unsure *why* the ocean theme as that doesn't seem pertinent to the academy or any of the student houses, but perhaps that's the point.

I hadn't considered the assault on my ears from the band playing on stage beneath a shell-filled net backdrop in the corner, and although I appreciate the softer light from the floating illumination, this makes the room too dim for any individual to stand out.

"Before the question is asked, I will not be dancing," I inform Rowan and Grayson, and stalk towards a long table, draped in the table runner that took Holly so long to choose.

Beside flickering candles, one of the committee sprinkled the tiny silver and blue shell confetti around platters holding unidentifiable tiny morsels of food and clear jugs of blue and green liquid.

As my companions are as unpopular as I am, nobody bothers to speak to us, and Grayson rests his back against the table, holding a glass as Rowan takes one and passes another to me. Yet more shells etch the edges—I saw these in the store that day with Holly. The day I discovered Leif's arrest.

"What's this?" I sniff the contents.

"Non-alcoholic," says Rowan. "The alcohol will be shared outside."

"Good." But I place down the cup, anyway. "I need to walk around. Where are the professors?"

Grayson sips and pulls a face. "Ugh, that's sweet."

"Not bloody enough?" asks a girl with the sleekest brown hair beside him.

A group of girls—human—chose to co-ordinate their outfits —long formal dresses in the same cobalt color, strapless, and taffeta skirts touching their impossibly high shoes. Another girl giggles and nudges her. "Sienna!"

Grayson rubs his lips together and regards them. "I don't touch human blood. Too tasteless. A little like that garish necklace you're wearing." Rowan chuckles to himself. "Head towards Sheridan House. I heard some vamps are meeting up with volunteers," continues Grayson.

"I would hope not," I say. "I do not require another murder accusation to disprove."

Rowan slides an arm around my waist. "Murder? You wouldn't want to mess up your hair."

"Droll." I remove his hand from my lower back, but his touch lingers as if they remain hot against my skin. "Do you like my tiara?" I ask the girls.

"Uh." Two glance at each other. "I guess?"

"Can I try it on?" asks another and they burst into giggles. "It's *so* pretty."

I narrow my eyes as I detect sarcasm. "Nobody touches my tiara."

Again, the irritating giggling. "Nobody touches my tiara," repeats a curly-haired girl, impersonating me.

I turn away not wanting to waste an iota of energy on the girls. The item isn't familiar to them, although I never expected the humans to recognize the tiara. Along the end of the table, a group gathers, louder than others—and stupider, since the professors will easily pick up on their intoxication.

Mrs. Lorcan stands towards the entrance, elegantly dressed in teal, keeping a semi-official look with a skirt suit. She greets newcomers and I smirk to myself as the headmistress surreptitiously scans their thoughts. The headmistress pulls a witch boy to one side and, after a minor chastisement, he produces a small silver flask from inside his jacket to handover.

I've only seen the back of Holly's head as she runs in circles, obeying some command or other from Marci. Marci, as expected, delegated all her tasks, and sits at the most prominent table, smiling as some approach and congratulate her on the 'best one yet'. The girl is… beguiling. She always attracts and enjoys an audience.

Since the arrests, I've briefly spoken to Nita and Marci about events but tell them little more than is public knowledge. I've enough awareness of the effect it would have on Nita to ensure I *don't* mention Rory's undead state, and Dorian doesn't want that revealing yet anyway. Holly told me that Nita can't accept that Rory would murder Wesley and now refuses to speak about the situation.

Good because now there's no chance I'll say the wrong thing to Nita. Her information helped a great deal and I appreciate the trust Holly persuaded Nita to have in me. I'd hate to inadvertently distress her.

Marci isn't stupid. The pretty girl, who's pretending not to notice me, knows there's more to the crimes. And I've still one eye on Marci because I know there's more to *her*. With no Spring Ball committee any longer, I'll need to formulate a new plan to infiltrate Holly's social circle.

I stalk over to Mrs. Lorcan, and she startles as I clear my throat, before sweeping a gaze the length of me. "My, Violet. What a stunning girl you are beneath all that black and attitude."

Again, I can't figure out this lamia's age behind her flawless skin. Another professor stands close by, wholly focused on her ass in the tight skirt, and he crosses to whisper to her.

"Excuse me," she says sweetly.

Again, no admiration for, or recognition of, the thing on my head. I watch as the male professor and Mrs. Lorcan chat. He's an older man—must be witch or human, judging by the lines on his face and the white in his hair picked out by the light.

"Who's that?" I ask, as Rowan joins me.

"Mr. Hillside. He teaches elemental magic/geography," he replies. "Although you wouldn't know, since you've never attended his class."

"A geography teacher called Hillside?" I snort. "Well, I've no use for instruction in elemental magic, as I excel at such. Tell me, have you investigated him?" Several other adults dot around the hall, some keeping a low profile against the walls, others marching around and pausing to talk to students who're not keen to talk to them. "Have you made any further enquiries into these peoples' pasts?"

"You know I have." He nudges me. "Reckon you'll actually attend more classes now you're not running around doing detective work?"

"Undoubtedly, as my focus has shifted to the academy." I point at Ms. Reynolds from art class. "Are many human teachers remaining now the headmaster has left?"

Rowan shrugs. "I'll look into that."

"I'm unimpressed that there's little interest in my tiara so far," I comment.

Rowan drinks and gestures the length of me. "Yeah, although a number of guys are interested in more than your over the top tiara."

"Good grief," I mutter. "There's plenty of naked flesh around. Nobody needs to look at mine."

"Nobody's ever seen more than your ankle or wrist. That's the fascination."

"You have." I look around at the chattering students.

"Yes, but not much more," he says.

"I expect that'll change." Silence. Frowning, I look back at him. "Did you see something?"

He chuckles. "Not yet."

I flinch as he trails a gentle finger across my collarbone. "Rowan. We've established I don't like soft touch. It's irritating."

Darkened eyes meet mine. "I wish this had been a me and you date away from the dance like we planned."

"Well, needs must." I push at the tiara. "Another time."

One thing's certain, I intend reiterating to Holly that my preference for flayed skin and poisonous spiders remains, and next year I shall not attend. I blink. *Next year.* I have to make it to the end of this one yet; it's only spring.

"I need to talk to more people." I wander back over to where Mr. Hillside chats with Mrs. Lorcan and he regards me in surprise when I greet him. I sneakily sweep mental fingers through Mr. Hillside's mind, which is elsewhere—calculating how long until he can leave and no image of me or my outfit inside his thoughts.

"I apologize for missing class, Mr. Hillside. I shall rectify the situation."

"Not leaving us?" asks Mrs. Lorcan. "I thought you disliked Thornwood, Violet."

"What can I say? I'm learning many valuable lessons that will help me become a useful member of society." I flash my teeth. "I'm not going anywhere, Mrs. Lorcan."

Her laughter tinkles. "That almost sounded like a threat."

"Yeah, that's Violet," says Rowan. "You can never tell."

"How are your studies going, Rowan?" asks Mr. Hillside. "You've missed class recently too. I wouldn't like to see your grades slipping."

"I'm ten steps ahead of other students," he retorts, and I raise my brows at his impertinence.

"Well, I'm sure you won't want to miss the field trip next term." He reaches for a small parcel of pastry from a plate on the table and nibbles.

"A trip to a field?" I ask. "What field?"

Mrs. Lorcan's laugh rings in my ears again. "Not an *actual* field, silly girl." I bristle. "A short visit to a place of interest."

"Of interest to who? Because opinions vary on such matters," I say.

"If you come to class next week, you can join in the vote." He smiles. "Or abstain."

"Do you like any field in particular, Rowan?" I ask him. "Do we excavate said field?"

Quite rudely, Mr. Hillside now whispers to Mrs. Lorcan, and they bow their heads in conversation.

Fine. I walk away, and Grayson wanders over. "Anything?" he asks.

"Mrs. Lorcan didn't recognize the tiara," I complain after another tour of the hall, pissed at the number of bodies who knock into me. Some are perspiring from dancing and the colognes and pheromones are off the scale compared to Kai's party.

"Maybe there's only significance to whoever hid the items?" suggests Grayson. "We can leave if you want?"

I smile. "Your enthusiasm for the event matches mine, I see. I shall speak to other teachers." I point at the potions class teacher. "Mr. Woodside. I wonder if he's related to Mr. Hillside? I do find witch ancestral names rather predictable."

"You're making no sense," says Grayson.

I never warmed to the potions teacher or his sour face in the lessons I attended, but did notice some unwanted interest in him by a girl or two despite his rude manner. His soul-piercing eyes assisted him in keeping his class under control, but his seemingly attractive appearance interfered with several sets of hormones.

The teacher refuses to make eye contact with anybody and defines the word 'skulking'.

"Seems that few professors relish their attendance," I say and nod at him.

Mr. Woodside looks up briefly, meets my eyes, then—almost imperceptibly—frowns at my tiara.

A reaction. I stomp over. "Good evening."

"Is it?" He crosses his arms. "Congratulations on your detective work, by the way."

Grayson places a hand on Rowan's shoulder before whispering. I glare, unimpressed whenever they do this around me.

"My work isn't done," I say and watch the teacher for a reaction. "I believe there're greater things afoot."

He chuckles at me. "You always sound like you're a hundred years old."

"Do you like my tiara?" I ask and scrutinize him further.

"Not a style I would choose." He gives a tight smile. "You want to be careful wearing something like that."

"Why?" I ask, and a familiar buzz from discovering a clue runs through me.

"Because that looks extremely valuable. Your mother's?"

"No. Why?"

He shrugs. "Looks like an heirloom, that's all."

"You recognize it?" asks Rowan.

"No." He lifts his chin at me. "Hopefully I'll see you in class next week? Holly will appreciate your help. How is she after her fainting spell?"

"Such touching concern," I say.

"She's my student. It's my job. Enjoy your evening." Mr. Woodside dips his head and walks away.

I spin to Rowan. "I want you to tell me everything you know about Mr. Woodside."

"Violet." He sighs. "There's nothing sinister in what he said. Or in his mind, I looked."

"He noticed my tiara!" I protest.

"A lot of people noticed your tiara tonight. There's a prediction you'll stab someone with it by the end of the evening," says Grayson.

"Honestly," I mutter and focus on Mr. Woodside's walk to the exit.

"Violet…" says Rowan in a warning voice as I unfasten the purse. "Can you not start making notes?"

"I'm not." I pull out my phone. "I'd like to check for a message from Leif." *And make a note.* "If he isn't coming, I'm leaving."

"Yeah." Rowan nods towards the unmistakably large guy standing in the entrance, greeted by Ms. Lorcan the same way as everybody else. "About that."

I swivel around. Leif.

Chapter Forty

VIOLET

"IS that what you're whispering about?" I ask.

Without another thought, I rush across the space, then halt a hair's breadth from him. Has Leif grown? Or am I merely accustomed to Grayson and Rowan's smaller statures? The dark suit fits him better than his too-tight uniform and adds a mature air to him.

Leif opens his mouth to speak, and I place a hand on his chest, harder than intended, as he winces and stumbles backwards, bumping into a grumbling couple behind entering the hall. "Out," I say.

Leif's eyes glint. "Well, hello to you too, Violet."

"Why didn't you come back to the academy?" I demand and his walk continues backwards along the entrance hallway, my hand still on his chest. "I worried!"

"I wanted time out," he says. "I did not have a good few days back there."

"Neither did anybody else," I retort.

He scoffs, but Leif's amused. "Right. I call dibs on the worst."

"You should've come back to Thornwood. We should be together," I blurt. "All four of us."

Leif steadies himself on the wall and pauses, both of us in a corner close to the academy entrance. "You worried about me?" he asks quietly.

"Good grief. Of course, I did. Nobody would tell me where you were for a week. Even Dorian."

At the mention of his name, Leif's energy spikes with nervousness.

I slant my head. "Leif? Did my father do something to you?"

"No," he says softly and gazes at my face before touching a spike on the tiara. "I hardly recognized you when I walked in."

"Apparently a shared experience this evening." I straighten.

"Yeah, when I've sat at Mum's place picturing the next time I saw you, this wasn't what I imagined." He dips his fingers beneath the pendant, and my skin tingles as the rough tips brush me. "I'd all kinds of things I planned to say to you, but again, I didn't expect this weird welcome."

I take his hand away and untense my shoulders. "Right. Tell me everything that happened to you," I say. "I need to know what to fix."

He brushes one of the artful hair curls from my face, his eyes soft. "Thank you for believing in me. For helping, Violet."

"You're a nice guy, remember?" I smile. "You didn't deserve any of that."

"I missed you," he says quietly.

His scent with the subtle shifter earthiness adds to the realization just how much I missed Leif too and needed to see him tonight. Here's the guy I hugged when he asked; the one who taught me affection and comfort, and who left a strange void when he wasn't with us after everything settled down. Leif epitomizes larger than life in almost every way, and I've hated how everything that happened to him must've affected the gentlest of people I've ever met.

"Your absence unsettled me too. I—"

Leif's body suddenly engulfs mine, and I'm instantly squashed into an encompassing embrace to match a forceful kiss.

A large palm holds the back of my head, as if our lips meeting breathes life into him. There's no darkness edging him, no magical buzz, and his scent doesn't trigger desire for another's blood. He's Leif. Just Leif, joining with me in a strangely natural and a little disconcerting way.

His hands slip along my sides, and I startle as large palms close over my backside.

Good *grief*. I yank my head away and place a hand over one of his. "Well, that was exceptionally brave." I peel his fingers from my ass. "And you're lucky—if Rowan had tried that the first time he kissed me, I would've broken his fingers."

Leif barks a laugh, and I scowl. "Oh. You're serious." His hands disappear beneath his arms. "Sorry. I uh… Sorry. Shouldn't have done that without asking."

"No need for an apology. Your bones are intact, therefore, I'm no longer resistant to the idea of touch from a select number of individuals."

The energy between us that I noticed the first time we spoke alone on the lawn makes less sense than that caused by the bond with Rowan, or Grayson's blood, yet he affects me in the same way.

When I say we should all be together, I think of the strange synchronicity between Eloise and my fathers, at the emotional bond between them all that creates our family. The three men orbit around her, Eloise the gravity that holds them in place. I can't imagine my fathers always had the closeness they do—or that I'd cause the same situation with guys. But I am.

"I don't think we should stand here together. Not if my presence overwhelms you in such a way that you lose your mind and kiss me." He gawks as I hold out a hand, fingers spread to take hold of his. "Grayson and Rowan will be waiting."

Somewhat stupefied by my comment—and I expect the response to his unrequested mouth mashing, Leif allows me to take his hand, but as I walk away my arm pulls tight. "Wait. I need to talk to you," he says.

"I thought the kiss was in lieu of the talking?"

"No. About my time in custody. Something *did* happen that I haven't told anybody about." He darts a look around. "But I can't not tell you."

An uneasiness clutches at my chest. If someone hurt Leif... Or... "About the investigation? I'm aware that although some are now held accountable, we haven't found who's really behind all this, and I will continue to investigate. Do you have new information?"

Leif shakes his head and rests his back against the wall, shuffling downwards so we're face to face. He tugs me closer. "The night that Oz died. Died again. Properly, I mean."

"Did you see something? The story is his heart gave out. Constructs tend to return to the state they *should* be in eventually if their creator dies. Or perhaps this 'triggered memory' from the witches was too much and that killed him?" Leif visibly swallows. "The witches. They came for you?" I ask in hushed shock.

"Dorian came the night the real arrests happened."

"He wasn't permitted until two days later. How?"

Leif laughs. "He's Dorian Blackwood. The guy can get anywhere he wants, but only I saw him."

"Oh." Dorian never told me this. "What did he say?"

"He didn't speak, Violet. I'm unsure he *knows* that I saw him." Leif bites down hard on his bottom lip. "The detectives were considering allowing supernatural authorities to check both our minds for evidence."

And would discover the necromancy.

An odd feeling leadens my stomach. I told Dorian about the alleged spell in Oz's mind that would be triggered by Grant's death—Oz's unlife ended shortly afterwards.

"Are you telling me that Dorian did something to Oz?" I whisper.

"All I'm saying is, your father was in the cells that night and nobody had the opportunity to look into Oz's empty head the next day." He swallows. "Because he'd died."

No opportunity to detect necromancy or discover false memories. I catch a breath. Dorian chose to eliminate any possibility that I might be pulled into the investigation again. "Did you worry my father considered killing you too?"

"He had no reason to. I had the truth in my mind." But Leif's doubtful, his fear as evident as when Grayson met Dorian.

If necessary, Dorian would've killed anybody who might help a case against me. I've absolutely no doubt. Weeks ago, I would've shrugged this off. He's Dorian Blackwood. The shifter was dead anyway. Now? I can't. What'd already happened to Oz was horrendous, but he didn't deserve to lose his life again, alone and confused in that cell.

Nausea rises as the hallway momentarily lurches. I could've lost Leif that night. Permanently. If there'd been an iota of anything planted in his mind to place me at or near the scene, Leif would not be with me now. Nobody's safe from Dorian, whatever the person might mean to me.

"Dorian wouldn't kill you," I say with a false smile. "Ethan and Zeke are going to help you, remember?"

And I hug him, hard. Face pressed into his chest as his heart races against my cheek. My fingers grip his jacket. How can I protect these guys' lives and be part of them if I'm one of the threats?

I need to talk to Eloise about Dorian.

The tiara drags through my hair, strands yanking from my head, and I immediately raise a hand.

There's nothing there.

Pulling myself from Leif, I step away and spin around, darting a look in every direction. The hallway's busier than when we first moved to our corner, some students drifting in and out of the dance, as others crowd to wait for friends. We're close to the door. The thief must've left.

I'm through that door and out of the academy in moments, every sense raised in alert as I focus on my surroundings for footsteps. A handful of drunk students wander towards me, their stench and noise interfering with my scent detection, and I growl beneath my breath.

"Did you see who took the tiara?" I ask as Leif joins me.

"No. My focus was elsewhere." He grabs my arm as I prepare to charge into the dark. "No disappearing alone, Violet."

"But—" He arches a brow. And he's correct. I snarl in the likely direction of the thief. "Fine."

Leif half drags me inside and the music assaults me the closer I get to the door. As I shove my way through an annoying group blocking the route, I knock into Holly.

"Violet! You're supposed to be help—" She touches her curls. "Where did your tiara go?" I don't manage a response before she greets Leif with a squeal and enthusiastic hug.

Leif awkwardly hugs her back, looking at me over Holly's head. "Are you on the door and watching who comes and goes?" he asks her.

Holly inclines her head to where Mrs. Redfern stands, a middle-aged witch who teaches history and appears as thrilled by attending as I do. "Alcohol check. As if that'd work—most are having drinks before and after."

"After?"

"The Spring Ball doesn't stop when the music does!" she says, and I cringe. "But your tiara. Did you lose it?"

"Where are Grayson and Rowan? I'd like to show them Leif. They only glimpsed him before."

Leif chuckles. "Like I'm a rare specimen?"

"You are. Half-shifter." His smile slides away. "Oh. Still a problem?"

An ear-splitting whine from a guitar shoves me backwards, and I look in alarm at the stage. Are these guys students? Because the band's musical prowess is as lacking as the posturing male singer's vocal talents.

"Good grief," I mutter. "I am not setting foot in there again. Leif. Find Rowan and Grayson."

"Promise you won't run off." he says. Leif's only half teasing and I'm only half truthful when I agree not to.

Chapter Forty-One

ROWAN

WE SIT OUTSIDE, beneath the lights strung across the entrance below the banner. Well, I stand because that wall is bloody cold, but Violet barely budges an inch since she plonked herself there, still griping about the missing tiara. After her whirlwind tour of the dance where she examined every person she came across, we had to guide her away before she started lining up suspects to grill.

"Should we leave?" I ask. "We could have a couple of drinks somewhere? Celebrate Leif's return?"

"Alcoholic?" she asks.

"Of course," I say.

Leif grins. "Good plan."

"Hmm." Violet knocks the heels of her boots together. "I'd like to spend time together, but not if you're all inebriated."

"Either that or we stay here and watch everybody who comes and goes, in case they have the missing tiara," says Grayson cautiously. "All night."

"I'm sure someone stole the thing to annoy you, Violet," says Rowan. "We'll find the tiara again. They'll dump it somewhere."

"Perhaps. Perhaps not, but I will not be impressed if the tiara is now permanently missing." She stands. "I'd like to get out of this awful dress."

I'd like to get Violet out of that 'awful dress'. If Violet knew how many times I'd already imagined that tonight, she'd be pissed. Violet well knows that I don't dare objectify her, but I can't help the way my mind wanders when she's with me, let alone when she looks so bloody stunning and smells so amazing.

Fortunately, the small amount of telepathy that's happened between us hasn't accidentally included any of these thoughts. In fact, we avoid testing the telepathy theory—Violet states that the idea freaks her out too much, and I admit I'm not keen on anybody inside my mind.

But a telepathic link could prove useful if we're ever in a situation like the warehouse again. Let's face it, we'll need to practice the skill for that reason alone. Eventually.

I never believed Josef would kill me. The man has plans and wants to watch Dorian fall. To do that, he'd need to avoid placing himself as one of Violet's victims. But he took a risk, because I saw how Violet's whole demeanor switched when our bond reacted to my life in danger.

Personally, I never want to face an enraged Violet—the black pitted eyes, blood streaking from her nose, and a mouth filled with sharper teeth were bad enough, but I struggled hard to connect to the girl beneath, as her primal fury swirled as thickly as the shadows that grew around me.

She held back, which means I still haven't seen Violet in full-blown, Dorian-esque, psycho mode.

Grayson has.

Violet changed after that night; things didn't bounce off her the same as usual, and she disappeared back into herself. The last couple of weeks left me with a quieter girl, who barely rose to the occasion when I attempted to draw her into some verbal sparring. I would've let Violet win, but she's retreated back into her 'literal' world with no patience for nuances, instead shutting things down. I cautiously asked if my using shadows worried her and she bluntly asked if they'd left me again.

Truthfully, yes.

But the shadows are closer than they were.

Wherever Josef Petrescu went after tricking himself away from the scene, he took my secret with him. I've promised, again, not to use the shadows unless a last resort, but I now understand Violet's fear of something existing inside that she can't fully control. Violet has her dark part. I've encouraged mine.

Since the day I lost my shit with her after we left Leif at the station, something shifted. Did I get through to Violet about how her behavior affects others, or is she learning herself? Either way, Violet occasionally reminds herself to check if I'm okay with what she asks me to do. Usually after I go thin-lipped and give her a pointed look, but one step at a time, I guess.

Violet never stepped back from the new union that day, emotionally or physically, but neither have we moved much further on. But Violet expresses how she feels in her own way— who am I to complain that she prefers full-on, mind-melting, hard kisses to our lips hesitatingly meeting?

I want more of Violet. So much more. But the girl hated anybody touching her until a few weeks ago; I can't expect to push that aside and launch into the intimacy I'd normally chase.

Often, we sit in the library or one of our rooms, sometimes in silence, other times discussing Violet's weird thoughts on the world or theories about the situation around us, and the intimacy from that settles the soul she lights on fire at other times. I've something I never imagined—a part of Violet she's happy to share with me.

"There's a party—" begins Leif.

"Don't swear around Violet," I say with a chuckle.

"Party?" She looks at him. "You should go. Catch up with your other friends."

He blows air into his cheeks. "I can do that another time. Didn't you say we should all be together tonight?"

"Did she?" asks Grayson in surprise.

"That's a natural state of affairs," she says and adjusts the top of her dress upwards. "Despite our complexities."

Grayson looks away. Haven't they settled what happened between them at the warehouse?

"I shall inform Holly that we're leaving, then I'm changing my clothes. *Then* where do we go?" she asks.

"We could go into town?" I suggest.

"No, thanks. I've had my fill of the place and people," she shoots back.

"I've some booze in my room," says Leif with another grin.

"Go and find your alcohol, Leif. Then bring it to my room. I shall watch with amusement as you intoxicate yourselves. Rowan?"

"What?"

"I'm aware you all believe I'm about to start tiara hunting and possibly frightening people, so at least one of you should walk back inside the academy with me while I find Holly."

"Uh. Okay. Grayson?" I ask, as Leif already bounds towards Darwin House.

He scratches a cheek. "Yeah, I have a bottle in my room too."

"Well then," Violet says and stomps up the steps back into the academy.

"You sure you want us to come to Violet's?" Grayson asks me, as he watches her go. "I can tell Leif to stay away too."

I laugh at him. "The chances we'll do what you're imagining are extremely remote, Grayson."

He shrugs. "I don't know what you do when you're alone together."

"Nothing differently to you, I imagine."

"Has Violet torn your throat, taken your blood, and is now too scared to touch you?" he asks grimly.

"Oh." I chew my bottom lip. "Sorry. That sucks."

"Mmm."

Now I understand the weirdness between them—this isn't about the attack, but deeper. "I'll talk to Violet."

He scoffs. "Put in a good word for me? Nah. I'm fine."

I hold his gaze. No. He is not.

"Rowan!" calls Violet, not looking back

"Honestly, grab your drink and come straight over. Nothing will happen apart from her obsessing about the tiara." I smile wryly. "She'll probably give us research tasks and plan our next investigation."

Grayson's mouth tips into a half-smile. "Or sit you down to decipher a code."

"Yeah, so we definitely need a few drinks." He gestures towards the academy. "Be right back."

I catch Violet as she reaches the students who've taken refuge in the quieter hallway and take her hand as she pauses to scrutinize everybody's head. "We'll find the tiara."

"Oh, yes. *And* whoever told those witches to attack shifters and humans—and why they wanted to kill Kai." Her jaw sets hard. "This isn't over."

"Yes, Violet," I say with a smile. "You have told me that numerous times."

"Humph." She takes a deep breath, as if bracing herself to walk into a battle, not a dance, and walks inside. "Where is Holly?"

"Maybe she snuck off with Chase somewhere?" I suggest and nudge her. "A few couples will be up to no good now."

"I kissed Leif," she replies. "Or rather, he briefly kissed me, and I didn't react with violence."

"Um. Right?" Did I hear her correctly over the band's performance? I rub a brow, unsure what she expects me to say. "Weird time for this conversation."

"Does that bother you?"

My mouth parts in surprise. "Why would you and Leif bother me? Violet, my mother has several consorts. So does yours. Strong female witches always surround themselves with guys. Granted, they're normally all witches but what's normal, right?"

"Regardless, you may not like our decision to do such. We're bonded, Rowan."

"Oh, hell. Leif's my best friend and would treat you like a queen and probably fight to the death for you. The exact guy you should have in your life, if you want him."

She regards me with her big eyes. "It's rather a step to go

from not liking anybody to having two male companions that I hold affection for."

"And Grayson?"

"Can you see Holly anywhere?" she replies and takes a further step into the students writhing around to a familiar, upbeat song. Violet grimaces at the exuberance. "Why are the students all singing? Isn't that the band's poorly performed task for tonight?"

She's dodged that question for a reason and now makes her way towards the back of the main hall to the corridor with the bathrooms. "Talk to me about Grayson," I say as we emerge into the quiet again. "He's part of us—you said so earlier. I once thought you'd more than kissed him and tonight he told me you won't touch him."

Violet turns. "I've never kissed him, but his blood runs through me."

I blink. Something I'd never considered.

"You know that he cares about you?" I say cautiously.

"And I care deeply for him, which is why I can't risk what we might provoke in each other."

"You mean, like me and you?" I arch a brow. "If we submitted to the darker force we could create?"

"I've hurt Grayson once. That's enough."

I turn her face to me when she looks away. "But neither of you are happy about a distance. Sure, there are a lot of complications with the Petrescu thing. And the blood. But Grayson's the best person to help. He understands that side of you." I pause. "Or are you scared he'll hurt you?"

Violet splutters a laugh. "Please, Rowan. He tried once."

"Well, remember consorts isn't the sleazy idea some humans like to make out." I slant my head. "It isn't just a physical thing. We care about and protect each other."

"Precisely. That's strange enough for me. Therefore, I'm unlikely to throw myself into lust-fueled situations with multiple people." She pulls a face.

Yeah, considering the glacial pace of our romance, that's not a lie.

I never in a thousand years dreamed I'd stand in front of Violet and tell her she should open herself to Grayson Petrescu, or that I'd ever want her as anything but mine.

But one guy isn't going to fill everything in this girl's life—I can already see one vampire sized hole.

A panting girl with flushed cheeks stands partway along the hall and her shriek bounces through the quiet. She runs over when she sees us, almost tripping in her heels. Human. One of the girls Grayson insulted earlier? She's spilled something down the front of her teal dress, and her brown hair's no longer perfectly straight.

"You knew Sienna took your crown!" says the girl hoarsely. "What did you do to her?"

"I did not know, it's a tiara, and I haven't touched the girl." Violet looks down at Sienna's flustered friend. "What's wrong with her, and does she still have my tiara?"

"You know!" she blurts.

Violet's chest heaves. "No. I do not *know*. Unless you'd rather I read your mind."

"And what did you do to *her* mind?" The girl stupidly jabs at Violet's chest, and I close one eye, waiting for the bone to break when Violet catches hold.

"You're a little distressed… I don't know your name," she says evenly.

"Cassie."

"*Cassie.*" Violet releases her wrist. "I haven't touched anybody's mind, and I was unaware Sienna thieved the tiara."

"What's happened?" I finally interrupt.

"And don't say 'she knows'," warns Violet. "As I don't. Is the girl injured?"

Nobody needs vamp hearing to notice the scream from further along the hall, towards the bathrooms. Violet shoves past Cassie and darts towards the noise. Throwing Cassie a confused look, I follow.

"I can't get it off my head," shrieks a voice.

A group gathers around Sienna who's sitting on the floor, in the open bathroom doorway, pulling at the tiara lodged in her no longer sleek hair. Beside her, Mrs. Lorcan crouches and attempts to prise the thing away. Sienna squeals as if the headmistress is pulling her head off, and she violently shoves Mrs. Lorcan before curling her fingers around either side of the tiara.

Bleeding hands.

Violet's in front of Sienna in seconds, halting to stare. If Violet hadn't used mind magic before, she's definitely trying to find her way into Sienna's thoughts now. Another banshee wail comes from Sienna as she focuses panicked eyes on Violet.

"Make it stop! Get her out of my head," Sienna gasps, eyes glazed by tears.

"Is she possessed by a ghost?" asks a third girl, sitting on the floor beside Sienna and rubbing her back in comfort. Black streaks her face where kohl ran from teary eyes. "That's what I think!"

"Don't be ridiculous. There's no such thing," says Violet.

"There're vampires and witches! And shifters!" she shouts.

"Is the tiara really stuck?" Violet asks Mrs. Lorcan, ignoring her.

"Perhaps tangled in Sienna's hair?" the headmistress suggests.

"No! It's stuck." Sienna sobs and pulls again with bloodied fingers. The thing won't budge. This is insane. Someone must've messed with this human's mind.

"Why's she bleeding?" asks Violet.

"Show her," Cassie says to the blonde girl, attempting to comfort Sienna. Nodding, she stands, pale-faced and thin-lipped.

"What's happening?" asks a voice. Well, we found Holly, who dashes over, then pulls up short when she spots Sienna. Color drains from her cheeks. "Omigod!"

"Rowan!" calls Violet from the bathroom.

Holly's brow pinches. "What happened to your hands, Sienna?"

Girls bathrooms or not, I'm walking in after Violet. As I pass, I startle when Sienna's fingers snatch my ankle.

"Find her."

I look down. "Who? Violet?"

291

But Sienna's back to struggling with the tiara, sobbing and hyperventilating.

Several other girls stand in the bathroom, close to Violet. They're not touching up their lipstick in the brass framed mirrors over the square white sinks, but they *are* staring into one.

Words are daubed in red across one of them—and not in lipstick.

This isn't over until he is

"What the fuck?" I rasp out. "Did Sienna do that?"

Violet turns away, flicking her tongue against her teeth as she marches back out of the bathroom. "Where did Sienna go?"

"Mrs. Lorcan took her away to calm down. To the infirmary," says a shaking Holly. "I should go too."

"With the tiara?" Violet demands. "The girl is under somebody's mental influence. I need to see her."

"She's possessed by an evil spirit!" wails Cassie again. "Sienna told me her name's Madison."

But Violet's right. Ghosts don't exist—there's no spirit world where the dead are trapped. "She's hallucinating," I say.

"Madison," repeats Violet. "Well, I want to talk to this 'Madison', and she can tell me who 'he' is and why she's daubing her blood on mirrors."

There's entirely too much delight on Violet's face, and I nudge her. "Try to be more sensitive," I mutter.

She smiles at me. "I told you the tiara had secrets."

Violet and the guys' new investigations into both the tiara and the plot against the supernatural council (and the simmering romance) continue in

Thornwood Academy: Live To Tell

Printed in Great Britain
by Amazon